Once Upon a Greek Island

Willow River Press

Between the Lines Publishing
1769 Lexington Ave N, Ste 286
Roseville MN 55113
btwnthelines.com

First Published: January 2026

ISBN: (Paperback) 978-1-965059-71-5

ISBN: (Ebook) 978-1-965059-72-2

Once Upon a Greek Island

Gillian Barry

Part One

Chapter One

Kefalonia, Greece, June 1992

Oh, gosh, it's not supposed to be like this, thought Lisa as she walked out of the plane door and a wall of heat hit her. It was hot. Very hot. Treading carefully down the plane's steps, she followed a few other passengers towards the airport where they and the rest of the holidaymakers filed through unbelievably slow passport control with its bored-looking security staff, and on to baggage reclaim.

Lisa stood by the gondola where she thought would be a good place to retrieve her dark blue case with a pink identity bow on its handle. People milled around, and there was an air of quiet expectancy. The gondola didn't move. Keen to begin their holiday, a few started to get restless. Then, after what felt like an eternity, the gondola suddenly jerked alive. Then stopped. Then started again in creaky slow motion.

It seemed Lisa's idea of tying a pink ribbon round her case handle wasn't that innovative after all as there were at least three other dark blue cases with similar ribbons! Note to self, she thought as she patted her forehead with an already sweat-sodden tissue.

Lisa retrieved her case almost immediately. After checking its label with her name Lisa Barat, destination Helios Boutique Studios, Skala,

1

Kefalonia, clearly written on it, she looked round in a slight panic. Get a grip girl, she told herself as she walked out into the main area of the airport where she spotted a pretty girl waving a large sign saying 'Sunnyside Holidays'. With relief she walked over to the girl and got her name ticked off the list. Other passengers followed suit, and they all gathered in an uncomfortable, diverse group. Waving her clipboard again, the girl called for everyone to follow her to the coach with a 'Sunnyside Holidays' sign in its window.

Lisa was surprised to find herself at the front of the passenger crocodile. They all dutifully left their bags, cases, pushchairs and other items for the non-speaking driver to stow in the cavernous space under his coach before boarding.

Much to the annoyance of some passengers following on behind her, Lisa sat in the front seat so she could see where they were going – after all, this was her first time in Greece, and she was excited as well as nervous. She also wanted to watch the driver as she'd heard some could be very laissez-faire about driving, often smoking, talking, turning round and leaving just one hand on the steering wheel whilst negotiating steep, winding mountain roads! Oh god!

After much indecision about the best place to sit, everyone settled into their surprisingly comfortable seats, and an excited hum filled the air.

Then suddenly, the high-pitched voice of the pretty *Sunnyside Holidays* girl in her knee length dark blue skirt and white short sleeved blouse rang out. "Welcome to Kefalonia everyone," she trilled through bright red lips and startlingly white straight teeth. Sporting huge sunglasses on her dark smooth hair, and with microphone in hand, she continued, "I'm Sam your *Sunnyside Holidays* representative, always here and happy to help."

People shuffled slightly in their seats and avoided eye contact. So, having no response from her charges, Sam ploughed on. "Well, anyway, let's get this coach on the road!" She then said something to the driver, who lit a cigarette and drove off with one arm hanging out of the coach window. *Oh, goodness no, please don't do that*, thought Lisa, and then, as if he'd heard her, the driver withdrew his arm, closed the window and the very welcome aircon kicked in.

The journey from the airport to Lisa's destination at the end of the island took about an hour. During this time, the driver played Greek music at various volumes which clearly depended on which track was his favourite, whilst she watched in awe at the unfolding spectacular island scenery tumbling past the coach window. To one side, the dazzling dark blue Ionian Sea and pretty bays beckoned invitingly. To the other, an awesome boulder-covered mountain sprouted gnarled olive groves with unbelievably pretty, whitewashed villages clinging to the rock or perched perilously by the roadside. She didn't dare look down at the endless chasms on hairpin bends, and she didn't hear a word Sam said.

After dropping some passengers off at various points, the coach eventually navigated yet another steep, winding hill with more tantalising glimpses of the sparkling dark-ink blue and green Ionian Sea, and beautiful beaches before arriving at Lisa's own destination. She drew a breath. This was it. She was here at last. Don't panic. It'll be wonderful, she told herself.

"Skala, this is Skala," beamed Sam. Lisa and her four remaining fellow passengers gathered their things to begin disembarking. Lisa was first to step out into the brilliant sunshine. Squinting behind her Rae-Bans, she looked round. It was hot, very hot - even hotter than when she'd got off the plane! After easing the waist of her now too-tight pink crop pants and smoothing down her white t-shirt, she adjusted her sunglasses which had now begun to slip down her sweaty nose, before tucking damp strands of hair behind her ears. Her long, straight dark brown hair was in a ponytail, a change from either a messy bun or down and fastened back with clips. At forty-nine she felt she was getting a bit too old for clips, but neither was she ready for the obligatory short hair styles which so many maturing women seemed to adopt. Oh no, not for her! She'd promised her girls Bella, Scarlett and Tiffany-Mae that she'd grow old disgracefully and let her hair grow, so grow old disgracefully she would! Perhaps now was the time to begin.

Now looking round properly, Lisa could only stare at what she saw in front of her. Paradise, that's what it was. Paradise. There were pink and white flowering trees lining the pavements, and bright red geraniums shone in the sun everywhere.

Sam's voice rang out. "Hello everyone. Welcome to Skala. After you've got your luggage, I'll show you where each of you is staying. Please follow me."

Lisa retrieved her case from the coach driver and, after once more checking the label, pulled up its handle. Then, taking another deep breath, she dutifully followed behind Sam, a middle-aged couple and two giggling young girls up a hilly main road flanked by colourful flowers and palm trees. Set back from the road were a few old wooden village houses surrounded by beautiful gardens, several tavernas, two supermarkets, a bakery, a chemist and various small shops selling jewellery, clothes and tourist tat. They also passed a few modern apartment blocks, eventually arriving at the top of the hill at Helios Boutique Studios where brilliant purple and pink bougainvillea tumbled over the iron fence and climbed up the building's whitewashed walls. Lisa gasped and stared. She'd never seen anything like it, it was utterly gorgeous. Her adventure had begun.

Chapter Two

Lisa's first floor apartment had a twin bedroom with an aircon unit almost touching the ceiling. Aghast at how high up it was she softly said to herself, "Come on girl, okay so you're short but you can do this. Remember you can do anything. And anyway, there must be a remote controller somewhere!" She was determined to deal with anything and everything, and to embrace the change.

She poked around the kitchenette with its basic crockery and cooking facilities partitioned off from the living room by a small bamboo screen and then looked at the fully tiled bathroom with shower and toilet – oh, no shower curtain! After that she went out on to the balcony overlooking the main street. It had a limited view to the right of the sandy beach, and to the other side was the imposing mountain. As the studios were at the end of the main road the mountain felt quite close.

There were a small table and two chairs, and a large awning keeping the baking sun at bay. After she'd unpacked and changed into comfortable shorts and a strappy top, she sat on the balcony in the welcome shade whilst watching Skala's world go by. It was fascinating. If ever there was an idea for a story, here it was right in front of her!

Lisa heard some giggling coming from the apartment next to hers where her two young fellow travellers were staying. *This could be fun,* she thought. There'll probably be late night shenanigans and all that. She hoped they didn't keep her awake because she so needed to rest as well as to write. She'd seen the middle-aged couple shown to a convenient ground floor apartment: lucky them!

Then out of the corner of her eye, Lisa noticed a young, well-dressed Greek male strolling ramrod straight down the middle of the street, looking for all the world as if he owned it. Screwing up her nose, she thought what an arrogant sod!

It was a thought which one day she'd remember.

Then, for some unknown reason, Lisa suddenly felt homesick. Being a mother of three girls in their twenties meant that although they were grown up and living their own lives, she missed them when she wasn't near them. She hoped they were all okay. Daft bitch, as if they care about me! She thought. She shifted in her white plastic chair. Honestly, why plastic, it's so hot and sticky! She got a towel from the bathroom to sit on and resumed her observations of Skala life.

By now, it was five-thirty in the afternoon local time, which in Skala meant tourists were coming off the beach to go back to their accommodation to shower before setting off for dinner at a local taverna. *What a motley bunch,* thought Lisa as she watched all ages from young children to seniors slowly and hotly wind their way up the hill. *Still, we're all different and we are all on holiday!* She felt it would be interesting to get to know some people, to learn about their lives if they wanted to share them, and just to socialise. After all, it was a bit lonely being on her own, and even though she was getting used to her own company, somehow this aloneness felt more acute being amongst jolly families and couples enjoying their time together in such a beautiful place.

Lisa mentally pulled herself up. No time to dwell. It hadn't been her choice that she and husband Mark had parted, but she had to accept that's what he'd wanted so she just had to get on with living a very different, although often lonely, single life.

It was by pure chance that she'd discovered writing: a woman she'd got chatting to in the local Leisure Centre changing room told her she was thinking of writing her life story. Intrigued, Lisa wanted to know more but the woman wasn't forthcoming. However, it left Lisa thinking about all sorts of things. At grammar school she'd always been excellent at English, and she'd sometimes written poetry or the beginning of a short story – so why not try writing a book? After all, there was nothing to lose, and anyway who knows where it would lead.

As well as trying to get over the separation from Mark, she also really needed a break from her job as a Local Authority project manager. Being in charge and learning the new technology was making the job more challenging. Although she was well respected and brilliant at what she did, she was finding it exhausting and she could feel burn-out encroaching. So, one day she went online and booked her holiday to Greece which was somewhere she'd never been. She decided that as well as resting, she'd take a notepad and begin writing down ideas for a story. Madness. What was she thinking?! But she stuck with it, and so here she was with no idea about how and what to write!

It transpired that what happened next would become her book.

Chapter Three

After showering and changing into loose, orange cotton pants and a cream strappy top, Lisa decided to take a stroll down the main road, have a drink and find somewhere to eat. She came across a small bar named *Rebecca's* situated slightly back from the hilly main road next to a car hire business and, feeling nervous, went in.

She perched herself on a vacant high stool and looked around. The bar was set amongst beautiful gardens full of palm and olive trees and brilliantly coloured flowers, with soft Greek music playing in the background. Behind the bar, Lisa saw a tall, tanned and slim young woman dressed in tight white shorts and a white camisole top who she thought might possibly be Rebecca herself.

Spotting Lisa was on her own, the young woman strolled over. Smiling broadly, she said, "Hi, I'm Rebecca, welcome to my bar. My husband Yannis and I run it together. How can I help you?" As she spoke, her admirable head of dark blonde curls bounced, and her large, gold hoop earrings swung, making Lisa smile.

Lisa felt uncertain but relieved that Rebecca had kindly introduced herself. She felt butterflies in her stomach and coughed nervously before replying. "Hello, I'm Lisa. I'm staying up the hill at Helios Boutique Studios."

"Oh, that's Dimitri and Helen's place, it's lovely there and you'll be well looked after. What can I get you to drink?"

"Erm, I'll have a soda and lime please, with two pieces of ice."

Rebecca smiled again, "Is that all? You sure you don't want anything stronger?"

"No, that's fine thanks, I haven't had dinner yet. By the way, can you suggest somewhere to eat?"

"Well, take your pick!" laughed Rebecca. "But the best place is The Bay Taverna at the bottom of the hill. Ask for George, tell him Rebecca sent you and he'll look after you."

"Oh, thank you, that's really kind. What's the best thing to eat?"

Rebecca made Lisa's drink and then observed her with raised eyebrows. "Is this your first time in Greece?" She asked kindly. "If so, it can take a while to get to know all the different food, but most British people end up having favourites such as moussaka, souvlaki or pastitsio. Anyway, as this is your first time here, I suggest asking for moussaka with a Greek salad and see how you get on."

"Okay that sounds good. I won't ask what they are as it'll be good to find out for myself," she laughed, and then raising her glass said, "Cheers Rebecca and thanks!"

"No problem. Enjoy! Got to go as I can see some people have turned up. But don't forget I'm here if you need any help with anything. With that she moved away to serve two other customers.

Lisa twirled round on her stool to look at the street outside the bar. At the same time, a young male stepped into her vision. "Hello," he said in perfect English as he eyed Lisa's orange pants. "You are English?"

God, am I that obviously from England! Lisa thought. She looked sideways at the man before twirling her stool back to face the bar, hopefully sending him the message that she wasn't interested in picking up any strange men. It didn't work.

"Hello again," said the man as he moved to stand beside the empty stool next to her. "Please, let me introduce myself. I'm Christoph. And you are…?" he asked, leaving his question hanging in the air.

What a cheeky bugger, thought Lisa. Honestly, some men think they're every girl's gift. She twirled her stool back round again so he couldn't see her face but once again the man determinedly followed her.

Turning round yet again, and barely keeping the annoyance from her voice, Lisa said, "Look chum, you may think that you're wonderful, but I bloody don't so piss off to wherever you came from you slimeball."

Much to Lisa's annoyance, Christoph's reaction was to laugh. "I love a strong woman," he chuckled. "But I'm sorry for being a nuisance. Please forgive me and let me buy you a drink as an apology."

For the first time, Lisa looked properly at the annoyingly persistent male and realised it was the same man she'd seen walking down the road when she was sitting on her balcony. She took in his obviously Greek good looks, straight nose, square jaw, solid build, neatly swept back straight black hair and astonishing, clear green eyes. As he'd remained standing, she could see he wore loose-fitting black trousers and a crisp, white open-necked shirt with sleeves carefully folded back to reveal pleasingly neat hands and muscular arms lightly covered in black hair. She couldn't see his shoes without craning her neck, but she wasn't going to do that. He wasn't very tall, but his posture was upright and strong.

She instantly knew that he was different. And dangerous. Very dangerous.

Compelled to introduce herself, she nodded in agreement to the offer of a drink and said, "I'm Lisa. From England," adding with a smile because she couldn't help herself, "But then you know that."

"Yes," laughed Christoph. "It's the trousers. Only an English – or should I say British - woman would wear orange trousers. An Italian, French or Greek woman wouldn't be seen dead in them!"

Lisa swallowed a curt reply. She didn't want to appear ungracious on her first day in Skala!

Christoph ordered Lisa a white wine saying, "Please do try this, it's our lovely local wine Robola which is grown in the vineyard up near the old village." He ordered a lemonade for himself, and when Lisa questioned this, he told her he never drank alcohol.

"Old village?" asked Lisa curiously. "What do you mean?"

"Well, Skala is comparatively new. The village was originally up in the hills until the earthquake in August nineteen fifty-three destroyed it and many were killed, then after that it was rebuilt down here by the sea. The old village remains a memorial to the dead, but people can go to see the ruins so long as they respect them."

"Oh, how sad," Lisa said quietly. Then, after a pause she asked, "By the way, how come you speak such perfect English?"

"We learn English at school from the age of seven," replied Christoph. "So, speaking English comes naturally to us and definitely helps with the tourist trade." He smiled, showing perfect, but not perfectly white, teeth, then continued, "And we love football! Every tourist season we have regular football matches with us local men and boys playing against the Brits," adding mischievously, "We always win of course!"

Christoph took a sip of his lemonade. "Anyway, how would you like to take a walk around the village with me?"

Lisa immediately bristled. *Not on your Nellie*, she thought. But instead, she found herself saying, "Oh, yes, okay but only as long as we keep to the main roads."

Bowing his head, Christoph replied in a quiet, serious tone, "Yes, of course, I wouldn't have it any other way. So, please, do finish your wine and then I'll show you some of my village." He smiled his lovely smile, and continuing in his charmingly accented precise English said, "I assure you you'll be perfectly safe with me."

Lisa's stomach somersaulted and her heart started to pound. Oh, for goodness' sake, she chided herself crossly, you're a grown woman. It's only a walk round the village. Then she remembered she hadn't had any dinner. In fact, when *did* she last eat?!

"Christoph, can we stop and get some chips as I haven't had any dinner and I'm starving?"

"Chips? *Chips?*" replied Christoph with raised eyebrows. "No, not just chips, we will have a proper dinner, and I know exactly where we can go. But yes, we can also have chips!"

Lisa finished her wine which was gorgeous, then gently placing his left hand under her right elbow, Christoph guided her out of the bar into the pretty main road. His touch made her skin tingle, so she moved her arm away and shifted her bag on to her right shoulder to avoid him touching her again.

Chatting about the island, Kefalonian weather, food and drink, they wandered up the main road until Christoph took them into a small road on the right-hand side. "This is where we'll eat," he said, pointing to a small restaurant surrounded by vegetation and flowers. "This is my cousin Andreas's taverna, The Grapevine. Andreas makes delicious, traditional Greek dishes which some tourists don't want to eat."

Lisa was to discover that Christoph had many cousins in Skala, in fact nearly everyone, both male and female, would appear to be a cousin!

"It looks nice," she said politely. She'd decided to play it very cool, not distant, but just friendly.

Entering The Grapevine felt to Lisa like stepping into a different world. It was rustic, plain and a world away from the tourist-orientated so-called tavernas that she'd seen in the main road. It had a dark interior with a few, blue and white check cloth-covered tables and upright straw-seated chairs. Slightly wonky pictures of various places in Kefalonia adorned the walls, and a religious icon with a small oil lamp beneath hung beside the counter.

Christoph took them through to the garden where several small, white-clothed tables and rattan chairs were dotted amongst ancient olive trees, bird of paradise flowers, orange trees and bushes with pink and white flowers which Lisa remembered were called Oleander. Bright red geraniums tumbled everywhere. Nothing seemed to be looked after, and yet at the same time it was. It was simple yet stunning.

"Oh," managed Lisa. She couldn't think of anything else to say.

Christoph looked at her. "Are you okay?"

"Er, yes, yes, thank you. It's just that it's so….so…. lovely."

"Yes, it is. And thank you. Anyway, let's sit down, you choose."

Lisa spotted a table under an olive tree which surprisingly had a limited view out towards the sea; she hadn't realised the sea was that close. Pointing, she said she'd like to sit there if he agreed.

"Good choice," nodded Christoph. "Right, now this is how it works here. Andreas only makes two dishes a day, so we're limited as to what we can have. I'll go and ask him what's on the menu today." He then disappeared into the taverna, and Lisa could hear lots of chat in rapid Greek. Then, beaming broadly, Christoph reappeared.

"Today it's either moussaka or stifado which is a lamb stew. What do you fancy?"

Lisa took a breath and remembered Rebecca had suggested trying moussaka first. "Okay, moussaka please."

"Great. I'll have the stifado." At that moment Andreas appeared and introduced himself. Then turning to Christoph, he said something in Greek to which Christoph frowned, shook his head and fiercely muttered, "Ochi" - which Lisa knew meant 'no'. *Oh well, that's Greeks for you*, she thought.

Andreas noted their food choices and then produced a carafe of Robola. "Enjoy," he said to Lisa with a small smile. He then said something to Christoph before disappearing to prepare their food.

After a few minutes a waiter brought out a huge bowl of Greek salad and a basket of sliced, yellowy Greek bread with a dish of olive oil to dip the bread in.

"I hope you like it, Lisa. Andreas' wife Sophia makes the feta cheese from the milk they get from the goats they keep on their farm up the road."

Lisa thanked Christoph before taking a few large chunks of cucumber, some large slices of tomato and some of the feta cheese. She avoided the onion: breath and all that. Breath? Why was she so worried about breath? It wasn't as if she was going to get close to anyone!

Lisa thought she'd never tasted food like it. The warm tomato was sweet, soft and delicious, and the creamy but slightly tart feta cheese dusted with oregano melted in her mouth. Just pure heaven. Then she took a slice of the slightly yellow bread and dipped it into the olive oil. Oh, my goodness, it was amazing!

Christoph watched her with a smile playing round his lips. He'd never met anyone quite like Lisa - she wasn't the usual pretty, young British girl he was used to dating in the summer, there was something about her which he couldn't define. Yes, she was attractive, in fact her large, deep blue eyes with their long dark lashes mesmerised him, and she had a pleasing, fulsome yet trim, figure which he wouldn't mind seeing more of. But none of that was what intrigued him.

While Lisa enjoyed her salad, Christoph sat deep in thought with his elbows on the table and his fingers steepled.

After clearing his throat, he suddenly said, "Lisa, do tell me about yourself. That is, if you don't mind?"

Startled, Lisa paused in mid-chew and looked at Christoph with wide eyes. She finally swallowed hard before croaking, "What do you want to know? I'm the most boring person, ever, and I'm sure you wouldn't be even remotely interested in my little life."

"On the contrary, I find you very interesting. You're very much your own woman, and I find that refreshing because so many women seem to think they need to adhere to some sort of stereotype. I'm sure you know what I mean."

Lisa didn't know how to respond to this. A man understanding women, at least to some degree? Surely not! Lisa cleared her throat. Deciding there was no harm in supplying the basics, she began, "Well, I'm separated from my husband Mark – long story, don't ask – and I've three daughters in their twenties. I work as a project manager, a job I love but am taking some time out from. And I live in Sussex," she stopped and looked enquiringly at Christoph. "Is that what you want to know?" she asked, feeling she'd told him way too much anyway.

Christoph didn't reply at first but then said incredulously, "You've three daughters in their twenties? But I thought you're around my age, maybe a little older but not much!"

"Really?" laughed Lisa. "Well, thank you for the compliment. So just how old are you then?"

"I'm almost thirty," responded Christoph carefully.

"Oh, okay. Well, that's nice for you. I'm sure you must be wanting to get married soon and have a family – I know it's important to Greeks, especially Greek men, to at least have a son."

"Yes, that's the tradition and that's what my own family expects me to do, especially as I'm their only son. I do have a sister, Maria, who's married to Niko. They live in Athens with Niko's family, but they have no children. Anyway, I haven't found the right girl to marry yet, so my family are still waiting. But then it is a lifetime commitment so it's important to be certain."

"Yes indeed. I thought I'd found the right one, but unfortunately for me he had other ideas."

"Well, more fool him is all I can say because he's definitely lost out."

Just at that moment Andreas appeared with their food. Lisa drew a breath. Saved by the moussaka! The moussaka was served exactly right – in a large, just warm, firm wedge. It was delicious, and Lisa ate with gusto. She also drank quite a bit of the wine. As she finished her meal she started to feel a bit tired, and looking at her phone she realised it was getting near bedtime; after all she'd been up very early to get to the airport in good time, and the journey had been tiring as well as interesting and in parts thrilling – she would never forget the plane approaching Kefalonia airport, banking round so steeply that the wing tip seemed to be almost touching the beautiful clear sea. She'd felt she could reach out and touch the water - she could even see people standing in the sea and on the beach waving! Amazing!

"I'm going to my apartment now Christoph. But do let me pay for my meal. How much is it please?"

"Goodness me, no you're not paying, that's down to me. And anyway, being my friend Andreas probably won't charge me anything! I'll talk with him later."

"Well, thank you, that's very kind. And please do thank Andreas for the lovely meal, it was delicious." Gathering her bag, she stood up and together they left the taverna.

"Do you live near here Christoph?" asked Lisa as they walked towards the main road.

"Not far. Anyway, let me see you back to your apartment."

"No need to do that, thank you. I'll be fine. And anyway, I'll be going to the supermarket for some basics," Lisa said, extending her hand to shake Christoph's, but instead of shaking hers Christoph held it gently to his lips.

"It's been my absolute pleasure Lisa, and I look forward to seeing you again soon. Take good care. Bye."

"Bye, see you around. And thanks once again for a lovely meal," said Lisa, waving. She then made her way back, getting some basic supplies from the little supermarket near the studios.

Well, that was nice, she thought. Now I need to ring the girls to tell them everything's okay, also ring Fifi-Rose, my slightly outrageous, half-French friend who'd want to know all the details.

After that it'll be time for bed and maybe another adventure tomorrow.

Chapter Four

Lisa woke with a start, wondering for a moment where she was but then she remembered she was in Greece! She rolled out of bed, the one sheet which had been covering her falling to the floor. She could feel it was already getting hot when she threw open the door leading out on to the balcony which thankfully was still shady. Wearing her pale pink short and camisole top pyjamas, she stepped out and gazed in awe at the majestic mountain close by. As the sun slowly rose, the top of the mountain was gradually lit in a golden glow, and the sky became a magical blue shot with streaks of gentle pink and gold.

All Lisa could do was stare. It was like a painting unfolding in front of her eyes. She decided to have a cup of tea and went into the tiny kitchen area to put the kettle on. The night before, she'd bought tea bags, coffee, milk, cheddar cheese and peaches from the little supermarket. The large peaches looked delicious, so she decided to have one with her tea.

Setting her white mug on the table, Lisa sat facing the mountain. It was so quiet. She could hear birds chirping in a nearby tree and the occasional motorbike making its way up the mountain road but there were no other signs of life in the main street.

Lisa checked her phone which had adjusted to Greek time. It was only seven o'clock which meant that in the UK it was only five o'clock! Then she heard a noise coming from the beach and craning her neck she could just make out a vehicle going up and down, presumably cleaning the sand.

She suddenly noticed an elderly man dressed in baggy trousers and white vest setting up some tables and chairs in front of one of the tavernas. Then other locals began hosing the pavements outside shops and restaurants, and a couple of young female tourists dressed in modest wraps strolled past to finally sit at one of the restaurant tables, presumably to have breakfast before hitting the beach. It was all quite perfect.

The village slowly came to life as more tourists appeared, many with arms full of bags, sun umbrellas and a variety of other bulky items. Lisa finished her tea and peach and went to get the pen and large notepad she'd brought with her. She felt it was time to begin writing down her story ideas: if she was going to write a book then she had to begin somewhere! She opened the pad, and biting her bottom lip, thought, *well, here goes!*

After a few minutes nothing had come to mind, so she decided to consider exactly what she'd write about and jot that down in her notebook. Then, just as she was beginning to feel she'd never, ever think of anything, there was a loud beep from the road below and when she looked down, she saw a coach had arrived outside the studios, clearly to take some of the other residents somewhere. She realised that as it wasn't an airport transfer day it must be some sort of trip.

Now there's an idea, she thought. A trip! She vaguely remembered Sam the holiday rep talking about trips on the way to the resort but being absorbed by the island's scenery she hadn't paid any attention. She decided to investigate.

After showering Greek-style without a shower curtain and then walking carefully on the rather slippery floor tiles to the bedroom, Lisa dried herself and pulled on her new blue and white bikini, white shorts and strappy white vest. It was only nine thirty in the morning, but it was already very hot. Fanning herself, she wondered what the heat must be like later in the day.

Picking up her new mobile phone and her multi-coloured tote bag with various essentials in it including a bottle of water, she made her way, with blue flip-flops flapping, down the cool marble staircase and out into Skala's pretty, main road. Trying to keep to any shade she could, she eventually came across *Sunnyside Holidays* office, but no-one was there so she walked on to a shop which was advertising various trips.

Courage, she told herself as she nervously entered the shop. *Adventure is what you came for, and anyway, it might make a good story!*

"Hello, can I help you?" Asked the young woman behind the counter as she pushed large round sunglasses up into her short, bright red hair.

"Er, to be honest I'm not sure," stumbled Lisa. "I'm thinking of seeing a bit of the island so can you recommend a trip please?"

"Perfect," smiled the girl. "By the way I'm Honesty. Honesty by name, honesty by nature!" she laughed. "Totally corny but it is true!"

Immediately liking this young woman, Lisa joined in her laughter. "Well, that's fine by me! I'm Lisa and I'm staying at Helios Boutique Studios for a couple of weeks."

"Ah, yes. *Sunnyside Holidays.* That'll be Sam. Hasn't she told you about their trips?"

"Well, I think she may have done on the coach but to be honest I wasn't listening, I was too busy watching the scenery. It's so beautiful here," confessed Lisa.

"Ah, a Newbie. Yes, everyone's enthralled on their first visit. And most people return, not once but many times because there's something about the island which pulls you, and the awe never diminishes. Anyway, trips. How would like to go to the north of the island, to Aghia Efimia? It's a stunningly beautiful journey and you get a break on the way, lunch at a taverna by the sea in Aghia Efimia, and another break on the way back. What do you think?"

"Wow, that sounds ideal. How much is it?"

"Well, as you're with Sam's lot I'll give you a discount," offered Honesty, and then when Lisa nodded, she tapped something into her calculator. She showed Lisa the amount which Lisa immediately agreed with, and so Lisa's first trip was booked. She was on her way to discovering the beautiful island of Kefalonia!

Bidding Honesty goodbye, Lisa made her way down the road, then descended a few steps shaded by huge fir trees alongside a taverna playing Greek music. The steps lead to the seemingly endless sand and shingle beach, where she could see sun loungers and sunshades had already been set out in neat rows. A few tourists had bagged their favourite spots near the water's edge with their own sun umbrellas and towels.

She walked a little way along the beach as she didn't want to be 'on show' for all and sundry to see, eventually choosing a sun lounger at the end of the back row. After laying her red beach towel on the lounger and her tote bag on the sand, she took a long drink from her water bottle. Golly, it was hot! She then took off her shorts and top, donned her Ray-Ban sunglasses and floppy straw sunhat, and decided to investigate the sea.

Hesitantly walking across sand and then shingle, Lisa came to the water's edge. Looking down through water as clear as glass, she could see tiny silver fish swimming round her feet and ankles and shiny stones on the seabed. She gasped in awe. Gosh, it was like being in the Caribbean rather than in Greece!

Taking off her flip-flops and holding them in her hand, Lisa paddled further into the clear, sparkling sea until her knees were covered. The water was warm and soft as silk, and she felt very tempted to have a swim but then decided not to until after having some time on her sun lounger. Although she always smothered herself in high factor sun cream, she didn't sit in the sun these days, happy just to be feeling its warmth in the air.

Making herself comfortable, she intended to start reading the book she'd brought with her, but the next thing she knew she was waking up with the sun on her legs, having fallen asleep as soon as she lay down. Hoping she hadn't snored, she sat up and looked round. Lots more people had arrived and were either having fun on the beach or in the sea. *What a beautiful sight*, she thought.

Looking at her watch she saw that it was coffee time, so she donned her blue wrap, picked up her tote bag and set off for the nearby taverna. There weren't many people there and she was able to get a table overlooking the beach. When the young waiter strolled up, she ordered an iced coffee and made herself comfortable.

Lost in the view she wasn't aware of anything other than the Greek music playing softly in the background. Then suddenly she became aware that someone was standing beside her.

It was Christoph.

"Oh my god!" she blurted. "Where did you spring from?"

"Sorry Lisa, I didn't mean to startle you," Christoph said as he put out a hand to touch her arm.

"Well, you did." Lisa said as she drew her arm away.

"I apologise again. Please let me get you something to make up for my behaviour."

Lisa looked at him and wondered why she suddenly felt drawn to him. Yes, he was very attractive but there was something more to him which she couldn't put her finger on. "Okay, thanks. An iced coffee would be nice."

"Lovely,' replied Christoph with a smile and a twinkle in his eye as he waved to the hovering waiter to order two iced coffees.

Christoph sat down and looked at Lisa. He felt he wanted to know more about this beautiful and intriguing woman. "Is this the first time you've been to Kefalonia, Lisa?" he asked gently.

"Yes. And it's lovely, I especially like Skala and all the people here. There seems to be something very special about this village which I find very hard to describe."

"Yes, a lot of people, especially English people, say the same thing and a lot do return."

"I think maybe the mountain has something to do with it but then I'm a romantic at heart," Lisa laughed. She found it easy to talk with this enigmatic Greek man with the twinkly green eyes, he made her feel relaxed and comfortable.

"Yes, maybe. But Kefalonia does also have a lot of history and has known some tragic times although we Greeks are a tough lot and can survive anything."

Lisa looked at Christoph as he sipped his iced coffee and her stomach flipped. Batting away the feeling, she said, "Tell me about your family, Christoph. Do you have any brothers or sisters? I know that Greek families are often quite big. Sorry, maybe that's a bit too personal, please don't feel you've got to reply."

" No, that's okay. I've got a sister, Maria, who's married to Niko but they don't have any children. As I said, I'm the only son so there's a bit of pressure on me."

"Oh. Pressure? What sort of pressure Christoph?" Lisa asked quietly. She felt he was revealing a lot to her even though they hardly knew each other.

Christoph sighed. "In Greek families, the sons need to marry and have a son, however, as I said before, I've not yet met the right woman. Or maybe I have and just need to decide. By the way, do you have any siblings, Lisa?"

"No, I'm an only child," replied Lisa. Then, deciding to change the subject, she added, "Anyway, as you know, I'm here on holiday to relax and have a nice time. I booked for two weeks but it's so lovely here that I'm thinking of staying a bit longer, although having said that I do have three amazing adult daughters who I'm already starting to miss!"

Relieved that the intensity between them had eased, she laughed. She didn't like the feeling of discomfort his disclosure about having to marry gave her.

Christoph removed his dark glasses to look at Lisa, and as their eyes met, he felt a bolt of electricity fly between them. They both knew that something very profound was happening, but neither could speak for a few moments.

Christoph eventually broke the silence. "Well, anyway. I hope you enjoy your stay in Skala, Lisa. Remember that if there's anything you need, please ask your rep Sam, she's very good." Putting his dark glasses back on, he added, "And I've really enjoyed having coffee with you so I do hope we can do it again."

Lisa smiled and replied she'd also enjoyed having a coffee and agreed it would be nice to do it again. She held out her hand, but instead of shaking Lisa's hand Christoph kissed it. "It's been a pleasure," he murmured. Smothering the butterflies in her stomach this gesture caused, Lisa withdrew her hand quickly. "I'm off now, Christoph. Bye." Then with a hammering heart, she quickly turned round to leave. She decided a swim was in order so headed for the beach and the crystal-clear blue sea.

Entering the warm sea immediately soothed her, then dipping her shoulders beneath the water, she struck out in her usual breaststroke style. Oh, such bliss! Then she turned on her back to float, shut her eyes and let her mind empty.

She eventually returned to her lounger, dried herself off and took her book out of her tote bag. She'd chosen a book which would make light reading; she didn't want anything too thought-provoking! Lifting the back of her lounger into an upright position, she settled herself with the book resting on her bent knees. A gentle breeze carrying the lovely smell of oregano and pine wafted over her and she at last felt relaxed. This was the life!

She started reading the book which was basically a romantic 'girl meets boy, girl falls out with boy, but they get back together' story. Then suddenly a large pink beach ball landed in her lap, knocking the book out of her hands. Startled, she looked up causing her Ray-Bans to slip comically sideways.

A tall, handsome young man loped over full of apologies. "Oh, madame, please excuse. I am sorry. Mia fratello throw the ball wrong way," he said in heavily accented English. "I will take please, and make sure it doesn't happen again."

"Oh, that's okay, no harm done," smiled Lisa. "Here, take your ball and I hope you have a nice day," she said as she gave the young man the ball. How could she be cross – he was charming! And she just loved seeing the family enjoying themselves!

The large Italian family had arrived shortly before and had bagged four sun loungers with two umbrellas. They were very loud, demonstrative, loving, jokey and seemed to be having real fun.

What a lucky family, thought Lisa, *I wish I'd had that*. Being the only child of high-flying parents, she'd never felt truly loved; her mother, Patricia, was usually busy being a successful solicitor, and her father, Brian, busy being a successful neurosurgeon. Being a nurse specialising in neurology, her husband Mark had got on well with him. She'd often longed for a sister to play and share things with, so school and then work friends took on that role in her life.

Watching the family play, Lisa suddenly had a 'lightbulb moment': here was her story! An Italian family on holiday. Where did they come from? Why did they decide to come to Skala? Are there any clues? She'd noticed an older woman had been carefully sat in a sturdy beach chair under an umbrella by younger members of the family, and she guessed that would be the *Nonna*, the grandmother. Maybe this holiday was for her? She knew that many Italians had their holidays in August so there must be a reason why they'd come in June instead. She was desperate to find out!

For now, though, she'd concentrate on reading her book. But her mind kept wandering and wondering about the family. Completely lost in thought, she sat staring at the beautiful blue sea until suddenly the large pink beach ball appeared again as it hit the end of her lounger.

Once again, the young man loped over full of apologies.

"Oh, please don't worry," she said with a smile. "It's only soft so it hasn't done any harm." Then, seizing the moment, she added with a smile, "By the way, my name's Lisa. I just want to say how lovely it is to see a whole family enjoying themselves together, and, er, is that your *Nonna* sitting in the chair?"

Picking up the ball, the young man thanked her for her kind words, and bowing his head politely, introduced himself. "I am Angelo. Yes, that is my *Nonna*, Anna. It is her birthday tomorrow and she will be eighty-four years old. But we also come here for sadness."

"Oh, how nice, please say happy birthday to Anna for me," replied Lisa, continuing in a soft voice, "But I'm sorry to hear there's also sadness at this time."

Bowing his head again, Angelo nervously passed the ball from one hand to the other as he continued, "Thank you. Yes, the sadness is because her husband Davide Ricci, my *Nonno*, was a soldier on this island in the war, he died here. We think he was shot with many other soldiers by the Nazis in September nineteen forty-three. So, that is not a good month for *Nonna* because she still grieves for him too much, and she has bad heart, so we make sure she is near our doctor at that time. She is extra sad because Davide did not know his daughter, my mother Maria. When my mother married my father she became a Conti, so we have both Italian and Greek blood in us! Anyway, we come in June because of *Nonno*, also because it is usually not so hot for *Nonna*, although it seems hotter this year."

Shocked, Lisa couldn't think of anything to say. What a terribly sad story. She looked at Angelo whose deep brown eyes were full of tears. *Oh, bless him*, she thought.

A few silent moments passed. Then, suddenly smiling, Angelo invited Lisa to join them.

"Oh, thank you, that's very kind of you but I wouldn't want to intrude on your precious family time," replied a stunned Lisa.

"It is no problem, er, Lisa," grinned Angelo. "Italians are always happy to have people with them, that is our way. Come, please do join us if only for a short while."

Unable to resist, and with the potential writer inside her nudging, she thanked Angelo and asked him to give her a moment. After Angelo had moved away, Lisa stood up, tied her blue sarong round her body kimono-style, before picking up her bag and hesitantly walking over to join her new friend and his family.

Angelo introduced Lisa to his parents Maria and Luca, and to his two brothers Aldo and Enzo, and his three younger sisters Bianca, Isabella and Theresa. Then he introduced her to his *Nonna* Anna. "*Nonna*, this is Lisa. She is English."

A pair of sad, narrowed grey eyes silently scrutinised Lisa from head to toe. "Welcome child," Anna said quietly. "And thank you for being so kind about the beach ball."

Lisa looked at the older woman in whose lined face she could see a million stories and tears. "Thank you. And really the ball was not a problem," she said turning to look at the five children of various ages carefully watching them. "They are all beautiful er – bambinos? Is that correct?"

"Yes, they are our bambinos," replied Anna. "We love them just as much now they are growing as we did when they were born."

"Of course, and it's wonderful to have a such large family. You must be very proud of all of them."

Anna bowed her head but didn't reply. Lisa thought she looked tired so she decided she wouldn't stay long. But she had to be careful not to be disrespectful by leaving too early either. Tricky.

Luca, a tall, well-made man with greying dark hair, stepped forward to offer Lisa a drink. "I'm glad you've met my mother-in-law, Anna. Come, stay a while - we have lemonade. We also have Italian wine of course!" he said with a huge, welcoming smile. "We Italians do like our wine! And we also have food. Please, we would be most honoured if you'd kindly share this with us."

At that, a table and a hamper appeared from behind one of the sun loungers, and Maria and her daughters laid out various plates of delicious looking food, with, of course pizza, several plastic beakers plus a large bottle of white wine.

Gosh, thought Lisa, *they really know how to do things in style!* Her mind was racing. There was obviously a story here. She'd like to know more about Anna's life. Where was she born? How did she and Davide meet? And where does the family live now?

Putting her thoughts aside, Lisa politely took a slice of delicious, cold pizza and accepted a beaker of white wine to wash it down with. There was a lot of chat and laughter, and much joshing between all the children. Deeply moved, she watched as Luca kissed and hugged his son as well as his daughters, often playfully pretending to nudge them all. What a wonderful family.

Angelo came to sit beside Lisa on a bench which had also suddenly appeared. "Are you okay?" he asked.

"Oh, yes, thank you Angelo. I was just thinking what a lovely family you have."

"Yes, thank you. But we're not special, most Italian families are like ours. It is our way."

"Oh, okay. But if you don't mind me asking, where do you all live in Italy?"

"Ah. Well, we now live in Bologna in north Italy, but my parents come from different places."

Intrigued, Lisa asked, "Oh, where?"

Angelo paused before replying. "My grandmother, Anna, is half Italian and half Greek. She lived with her parents on this island in old Valsamata village, which is where her mother, Sophia, came from. My grandfather, Davide, lived with his parents in Monterosso as Mare which is a coastal village in north Italy. My grandparents met here in Skala. Not actually *here*," he said, emphasising the word. "They met in old Skala village." He paused, then added, "There's a rumour that old Skala village is haunted."

Lisa remembered Christoph telling her about old Skala. But haunted? Interesting! She decided not to ask any more questions. She also decided to investigate old Skala village as soon as she could.

A shiver suddenly went down Lisa's spine. Something didn't feel right. She couldn't put her finger on it, but it was there. And for some unknown reason she sensed it was to do with Christoph. But why?

Chapter Five

Lisa spent a pleasant couple of hours with the family before making her apologies and leaving them to enjoy themselves. It was now after one o'clock and getting even hotter. She'd overheard someone on the beach say the island was experiencing an early heatwave as it wasn't usually this hot in June.

She gathered up her things, and just as she was folding the back of her sun lounger down, a young Greek appeared wearing huge wrap-around dark glasses and a black money belt round his waist.

"You enjoy?" he asked. "You pay me for the day. It will be five hundred Drachma, please."

Taking out her purse, Lisa gave the man his money even though she thought it was a bit pricey. Oh, well, it was Skala in the tourist season and these people did have to make a living.

She made her way back to her apartment where she had a drink of water, lay down on her bed and fell asleep.

Waking two hours later, Lisa shot out of bed. The day was going fast! She splashed water over her face, picked up her bag and made her way back to the beach. It was still hot, and the sun had moved round on to her sun-lounger, so she moved it into the shade. She then took off her wrap and ran into the sea for a swim. Bliss!

She spent the rest of the day either swimming or reading then went back to her apartment to shower before making her way down to The Bay Taverna for dinner where she asked for George. George duly appeared and she told him Rebecca had sent her. He grinned showing two missing front teeth and lead her to a table overlooking the road so she could see what was going on. She ordered a Greek salad and stuffed tomatoes. Also, a small carafe of Robola wine.

As she was tucking into her lovely food, a voice out of the blue behind her said, "Hello, Lisa, how are you?"'

It was Christoph. *Bloody hell*, she thought, *is this man following me?* "How did you know I was here?" She asked him indignantly.

"Ah, well. I was just passing, that's all." What he didn't tell her was that a cousin had seen her and told him where she was. He had cousins everywhere in Skala.

Lisa looked at him squarely. "Do not creep up on me Christoph. I am on holiday and do not need your attention, so please go away," she said severely.

Christoph sighed. How could he tell this woman he genuinely liked her? He thought about her all the time even though he'd only just met her. It was driving him mad. He'd never felt like this before, and he'd known quite a few beautiful women.

"I'm going. I just wanted to say hello, that's all. Enjoy your meal." And with that he walked away.

Lisa finished her meal and walked up the main road stopping only to get some more water. When she got to her apartment, she set her alarm for 6 a.m. as she was going to Aghia Efimia the next day and wanted to ensure she was ready in good time. Then she undressed and lay on the bed.

The following morning, her alarm went off at exactly 6 a.m. She got up, had a breakfast of yoghurt and a peach and took a shower. By then it was time to go downstairs to wait for the coach.

When she stepped outside several people were already waiting, and others were walking up the hill to join them. Everyone introduced themselves and started chatting. After half an hour the coach arrived, and Sam got off to welcome them all aboard. How exciting!

Lisa again took the front seat so she could see where they were going. The coach stopped off at several other hotels and apartment blocks to pick up more tourists before winding its way up the side of Mount Aenos and heading north towards Aghia Efimia. The road wasn't very wide at times, and mostly full of hairpin bends causing Lisa to feel either terrified or thrilled. How did people cope with these roads, day in and day out?

Eventually, the coach stopped at a taverna for a comfort break and coffee. The view was utterly breathtaking. Everyone got out their cameras to take photos and then re-boarded the coach to continue to Aghia Efimia.

The journey became ever more breathtaking but eventually they arrived at the resort where Sam herded everyone into a taverna overlooking the beautiful bay to have lunch.

Lisa sat at a table next to an elderly couple who told her they'd been to Kefalonia many times, always returning to Skala because it was their favourite place.

"Oh, why is it your favourite?" She asked, looking from one to the other.

The couple looked at each other and smiled, then the woman said, "Well, we came here on our honeymoon. Second marriage for both of us wasn't it, love?" She said with a smile as she turned to look at her husband.

"Yep. And a happy one it is, too," replied the man. "By the way, I'm Tony and this is Annie," he said, holding out a hand to Lisa.

"Happy to meet you both," smiled Lisa shaking his hand. "I'm Lisa. This is my first visit to the island, but I've been told that I'll return because most people do!"

"Oh, yes, that's true," laughed Annie. "There's something very magical about this place, and about Skala in particular."

"Yes, so I hear. What is it do you think?"

Annie took a deep breath. "Well, it could be that it's not the original village and that the old village is haunted. But in a nice way," she added hastily. "I don't mean anything bad ever happens, it's just a feeling. Like as if someone's around but you can't see them."

Lisa's eyes widened. This was the second time she'd been told this, Angelo being the first to talk about it. "Really? Oh, crikey that's a bit…well, a bit…unusual," she said as she struggled to find the right words. "I've heard this before but it's an unusual story for a holiday resort, although I can see why such a thing might make a place feel special."

"The locals claim it's the old village that's haunted and that sometimes crying can be heard coming from up there," continued Annie. "We've driven up there and personally I have to say that there's certainly a sad atmosphere. No-one's allowed to build up there, but I expect that'll change, you know how it is. And the Greeks will want to cash in on what they have here, make the most of it. Tony and I think this is only the beginning of tourism in Skala, and in Kefalonia generally." Annie once again turned to Tony. "Don't we love?"

"Yes, definitely. Just the beginning. I bet in ten years' time we won't recognise the place. No more fisherman living in his hut on the beach, nor little café in the middle of the road or muddy lane and bulrushes by the beach. Like everything, it's bound to change."

Just at that point a waitress came over to ask what they'd all like to drink and eat. Lisa was intrigued by this couple's thoughts. There was certainly something to explore here, and she was determined to find out more. So, her next trip would be up the mountain to Old Skala.

Aghia Efimia was stunningly beautiful, and Lisa felt sad when the time came for them all to re-board their coach. The journey back down Mount Aenos was as gorgeous as going up it. Then suddenly there was a bang. Everyone was quiet for a moment and then started to talk at once. The coach shuddered to a halt as the driver said something in Greek.

Sam stood up. "Don't panic people. Spyros will sort things out. Stay calm," she said into her microphone. Lisa stood up and craned her neck to try to see what had happened, but Sam waved at her to sit down before she and the driver got out of the coach. Sam got off the coach by the rear safety door and quickly found a front wheel had hit a fallen rock, twisting the wheel out of shape. She had to think quickly. Fortunately, being on a flat stretch of road between two villages with the mountain on the descending side, everyone could safely disembark once there was room for them to do so. She shuddered at the thought of what could have happened if they'd been on the other side of the road where there was a steep drop beyond the barrier. Taking a deep breath to calm herself, she got out her new mobile phone to ring her manager for help but there was no signal, so she asked the driver if his phone had a signal, but he shook his head which meant she had no choice but to ask the passengers if any of them had one of the new mobile phones. Re-entering the coach, she went to the front, picked up the microphone with a smile and said, "Right, lovely people. Now, here's the thing. Nothing to panic about but I do need to phone my head office manager to tell them what's happened…"

A man standing up at the back of the coach shouted, "Well, what *has* happened? All I can see is the ruddy driver standing looking at the view and smoking a cigarette. It's not good enough. We need to get out of here."

"I completely understand, sir," Sam replied as she desperately tried to control her voice. "I promise you that as soon as I get someone out to help us, we can be on our way. Now, has anyone got a cell phone, you know, a mobile phone, which works please?"

The few passengers who had one of the new mobile phones frantically peered at their screens, but only one had a glimmer of a signal – Lisa.

"I've got a signal!" Lisa said in a loud voice. "It's coming and going but it's there!"

"Brilliant," sighed a relieved Sam, sensing Lisa wasn't the type to panic. "If you come outside with me then we'll see if we can phone my manager Crystal. First, though, I'd like the rest of you lovely people to please carefully follow me out of the coach by the rear safety door so you can be in the shade. Don't forget to bring your bags and water with you."

Amidst various murmurings and the occasional frightened shout asking what was going on, Lisa and all the passengers followed Sam out of the safety door. It was very hot outside, and the smell of pines and the sound of cicadas filled the air. Sam very carefully took her charges a few yards along the road to where it widened slightly and pine trees cast deep shadows, then after making sure they were all okay and had water, she went over to Lisa.

Looking at Lisa with a smile which didn't match the fear inside her, she asked Lisa if her phone was still working and was told yes, there was one bar. "Oh good, may I use your phone to call my head office please?"

"Yes, of course," Lisa said, handing her Nokia to Sam. At which point the signal disappeared. "Bugger, the signal's gone."

Just at that moment the coach made a groaning noise and to Lisa and Sam's horror tilted slightly sideways and forwards. *Oh god, this is a nightmare,* thought Lisa, her heart pounding. But no need to panic, she told herself as she held her phone high in the air. There was still no signal, so she told Sam she'd walk back up the road, and, if possible, climb slightly up the mountainside which at that point was just a gentle slope "Please be careful" whispered Sam, now sweating even more with anxiety.

Why did this have to happen on her shift? She was going away for a break in two days' time. With Christoph. He'd asked her ages ago when they were recovering from a particularly energetic couple of hours in her bed. She was used to their sort-of relationship being mainly sexual and not anything permanent. He was a good and considerate lover, but she didn't see him as a boyfriend as such even though she was probably in love with him. "Away? What do you mean 'away'?"

"Well, my pretty one, I thought it would be nice to get away from prying eyes and just relax on our own. Get to know each other. That sort of thing." What he hadn't told her was that his family was putting even more pressure on him to find a wife. He preferred non-Greek women, but Sam seemed to fit the bill: she was attractive and knew Greece and Greek ways so would adapt to living with his family. But whether his mother would accept her would be a different matter! Time would tell. He wasn't 'in love' with her but they made an attractive pair, and they got on well in bed. He knew she'd soon bear him a son which was the whole point of him getting married: the family name had to go on.

"Oh," Sam had said again. "Yes, of course that would be fabulous. Where had you in mind?"

"Athens. I have an uncle who owns a hotel there. Very discreet. Very opulent. Very nice. We could look at the sights, too. And maybe also visit my sister."

"Athens? Crikey, yes that would be amazing." Sam said before kissing him soundly on the lips – something he never normally liked to do. Which had always made her feel a bit uncomfortable. This time, he'd kissed her back, and it was delightful!

Returning to the present, she realised Christoph would be able to help if she couldn't get through to head office – such a relief, especially as Spyros the driver was useless and kept talking to her in Greek, most of which she didn't understand even though Christoph and her friend Rebecca were trying to teach her!

Lisa walked back along the mountain road and climbed up onto some rocks, still within shouting distance of Sam. "Sam, I've got a signal," she yelled. Sam immediately ran to join her.

Slightly puffed out, Sam climbed up the rocks to stand beside Lisa. "Thank god your phone's working, can I have it please?" Lisa nodded and handed Sam her phone, which thankfully still had a signal. Not getting a response from her head office, Sam rang Christoph's home phone, and after what seemed an age, he replied. With her heart pounding, Sam quickly explained what had happened. Christoph asked where the coach was and if anyone was hurt, and when Sam assured him everyone was safe, he said he'd tell Sam's manager and organise a rescue truck and another coach for the passengers. Sam gasped. Another coach? How will two coaches fit on this mountain road, and anyway, where will the other coach turn round? God, this was getting worse! But she couldn't let anyone see how worried she was. Her holiday guests were her priority, and she had to reassure them and make sure they were all okay. There were thirty-four adults and six children of various ages so it wouldn't be easy to keep everyone calm.

Sam and Lisa quickly walked back to the passengers who were either standing or sitting in the shade of the pine trees. A couple of the younger children were running around, their accompanying adults frantically trying to keep them still.

Sam cleared her throat. "Okay, folks, here's what's happening. Some of you may have noticed there's a tiny problem with a front wheel…"

"Bit more than 'tiny,' love," shouted the same man as before. "Stop patronising us and get on with what you're doing to help. Earn your money, ducky," he added rudely.

Sam ignored the sexist comment and continued. "My manager, Crystal, knows what's going on and another coach will arrive shortly to take everyone back to Skala. There'll also be a truck coming out to deal with the wheel. So, let's all stay calm until the coach arrives. Please make sure you've all got hats and sun cream on especially the children, and if you have a snack with you then I suggest you have it now while we're waiting. And please do drink water because it's very hot and we all need to keep hydrated."

"That's all well and good," said a red-faced, well-proportioned, woman in a bright yellow sundress sarcastically. "But what about if someone wants to go to the loo, especially the kids?"

"I'm afraid we'll just have to use what's available," Sam said with a sigh. "That means find a tree or a large rock. Sorry, but that's all we can do." She took a breath before firmly adding, "Also, we can't go on the coach for anything, not even the loo. Do you understand?"

The adults nodded, and a few muttered something under their breath. The children were oblivious and carried on skipping and jumping around, uttering the occasional "I'm bored, when are we going to get there?" No change there then! Sam thought.

An hour passed during which time Lisa chatted to a couple of other passengers, went for a short walk but soon returned because it was so hot. Sam also chatted with passengers, doing her best to keep them calm. The coach driver absented himself for a while, reappearing adjusting his trousers, and with yet another cigarette hanging from the corner of his mouth.

Lisa went to chat with a young mother with two children. At the same time, another creaking groan came from the coach as it again shifted slightly sideways and forward causing the front wheel to bend under the coach even more. *God, this is awful,* she thought as she clutched her tote bag to her chest for comfort whilst also sternly telling herself to stay calm.

Then suddenly, the dark shape of a young girl – the same one as before? - emerged from behind a pine tree and mouthed something, but Lisa couldn't hear her. She wanted to ask someone to help decipher what the girl was saying, but people were either lying down with their eyes closed or walking about. Then when Lisa looked back, she saw the girl had gone.

Those who had one of the new mobile phones tried to use them, but no-one could, and then suddenly a coach appeared round the bend in the road. A loud cheer went up, and some of the passengers clapped and laughed. The coach stopped and Sam went over to speak with the driver who told her in fractured English he'd go further up the mountain to where a small road branched off to a mountain village. This was also a popular sightseeing spot, and the road was wide enough for him to turn his vehicle round there. Within a few minutes of the coach setting off, a black Jeep roared up, screeching to a stop in a cloud of dust. Lisa and Sam screwed up their eyes to see who was driving, and much to their respective astonishment they saw it was Christoph.

Pushing his large sunglasses up into his immaculate hair, and striding towards the two women, Christoph announced there was a truck behind him which was going to look at the wheel and decide what to do. He suddenly stopped and looked from one woman to the other. Stunned to see both women together, he was unusually lost for words, and could only murmur, "Hello, Sam, my dear, how lovely to see you. Oh, and hello Lisa." He cleared his throat. "I didn't expect to see you, *both*, here. Together."

"Hello, Christoph," chorused Lisa and Sam at the same time, looking at each other in surprise. Then, turning back, Sam stared at Christoph with a frown. "Lisa's a holiday guest and I'm her representative so why should you be surprised we're here together?" She paused, then added, "But how do you know Lisa's name, Christoph? She's only been here five minutes!" She laughed but felt something wasn't quite right; she had that 'uncomfortable' gut feeling again.

Lisa didn't know what to think. Christoph seemed to know Sam very well, but then why wouldn't he know all the reps in Skala? It was a small place, so everyone knew everyone, and what was going on. But if there was more to know then it wasn't her business. On the other hand, if there *was* more going on then why was Christoph seemingly interested in *her*?

At the same time, Christoph's brain was working overtime. He was about to take one of these women to Athens and was also thinking of asking her to marry him, whilst he couldn't get the other woman out of his head. Tricky…

Chapter Six

There was an awkward pause. Then a large rescue truck suddenly arrived, and three men jumped out and went with Sam, Christoph and the coach driver to inspect the coach's wheel. There was a lot of rapid Greek and waving of arms, but eventually the rescue team of Yannis, Georgios and Michaelas, who, Sam discovered, were all Christoph's cousins, moved their truck to the front of the coach and then attached a heavy chain from the back of the truck to the front end of the coach, the plan being to pull the coach far enough away from the mountain side of the road for the driver to get in and guide it so that it could be straightened up and then towed down the mountain road to a garage in Skala.

Things became tense as the stranded holidaymakers nervously and haphazardly gathered to wait for the replacement coach to return whilst watching the rescue. Thankfully, no other traffic appeared but it was still very hot with no breeze, and everything felt pinned down by the heat.

Christoph desperately needed time to think about the sensitive predicament he found himself in with Sam and Lisa. He didn't want to hurt anyone but at the same time he didn't want to lose either woman which he knew was greedy, but he couldn't help himself. He finally decided to ask Sam to dinner that evening and tell her that he was very fond of her. Maybe they'd make love afterwards to sort of 'seal the deal'. And if the subject of Lisa came up then he'd just say he'd overheard George say her name when he was passing his taverna. Best to leave it at that.

Lisa and the rest of the holidaymakers cheered as the replacement coach drew up. Sam was relieved that at last her guests would be safely on their way back to Skala. She carefully helped everyone get on board and settled, then taking up the microphone and grinning encouragingly, trilled, "Okay, everyone, I hope that bit of excitement wasn't too much for you all!"

Several people laughed and a few said it all added to the holiday but that they'd be glad to get back to Skala. *So will I*, thought Sam. "Right," she said kindly. "Let's all now settle down and relax, then when we get back to the village, I'll buy you all a soft drink."

A cheer went up amidst the occasional jokey comment such as 'make mine a double,' and then everyone went quiet as the coach pulled away to begin the last bit of the journey down the mountain back to Skala.

Lisa sat back in her usual front seat. What an adventure! She decided she'd wouldn't like to do it again, so any future trips wouldn't involve a coach going up the mountain! She thought she might pluck up the courage to hire a car and drive to some of the other resorts, but to take the local bus to the main town, Argostoli, as that would be another adventure.

After less than an hour the coach pulled into Skala's main road, and Sam took her charges to *Rebecca's* for their promised soft drink. Then, after ensuring they were all okay, she made her way back to her office. What a day! As if the wheel disaster wasn't enough, Christoph needed to explain something. Being aware of his past reputation with the ladies, she was determined to ask him how he knew Lisa. She needed to get rid of that unsettling 'niggle.'

Relieved to be back in Skala, Lisa decided to take a stroll to look at the shops along the main road, before returning to her apartment and having dinner. A slightly more upmarket shop selling a few beach clothes and books caught her eye, so she went in to investigate. She saw several small books about Kefalonia, and one very interesting one, specifically about Old Skala which she thought might make good reading while she ate her dinner.

"You like?" Asked the male shop assistant. Lisa noticed his face was weathered and lined, also quite handsome! He continued, "It is a good book to read, very interesting. Do you know the legend?"

"Er, legend? What legend?" Asked Lisa.

"Ah, you are English. Yes, the legend. It is said that sometimes noises like cries are heard from the old village at night. They are from a young girl. Her name was Ariadne-Rose, and she died up there."

Rather taken aback, Lisa's eyebrows shot up. "A young girl? Why, how, did she die?"

"She died in the war. She had a friend, a lost Italian soldier who she hid in the, how you say, *kelari'*, you know under the floor," he said looking at Lisa enquiringly.

Ah, he means cellar, thought Lisa, and nodded her understanding. The man continued, "If she did not hide him, he would have been killed by the Nazis. Then one day she came home from working in the olive grove, she had to work hard because the men were fighting in the war. All the men had big courage to fight for this island, for their homes and families. The girl looked for the soldier but could not find him, and then she also disappeared. No-one found her either so she must have died." The man stopped, crossed himself and bowed his head. When he looked up Lisa saw he had tears in his eyes. "This was a very bad time. Nazis killed many Greeks and Italians. Ariadne-Rose looks and cries all the time for her soldier."

Deeply moved, Lisa didn't know what to say. This must be what Angelo, and Annie on the coach trip, had referred to. It may well be based on reality because such things did happen in the Greek islands in the war. She knew Italy was firstly an ally of the German regime and that consequently Greece then came under Italian administration. But when Mussolini surrendered to the allies, Italy and Germany became enemies. She'd also read, or heard, somewhere that subsequently many Italian soldiers on Kefalonia were massacred. Noises like cries may well just be the legend, or haunting, story, and not the reality because emotion can do strange things; even true stories can become 'enhanced' over time.

The man went on, "Then the earthquake came in August nineteen fifty-three and the old village was destroyed. Many people were killed including Ariadne's mother, Rose, and her grandmother, Ariadne. My family knew this family. The story is the two women went to the village laundry to wash the clothes, but the earthquake happened, and they just disappeared. Only three people in that family survived, an old man and a young woman and her little brother. Too many gone. Too many," finished the man as he looked sadly at the floor.

Full of emotion, Lisa couldn't speak. So much loss and sadness! She put out a hand to touch the man's arm in comfort, then after paying for the book she bid him a very respectful, '*Efharisto. Yasas*', and walked out into the warm, early evening sunlight. Not feeling hungry after all the day's excitement, she decided to go to her apartment and sit on her balcony to eat a small salad. And tomorrow she'd pluck up courage to hire a car and drive up to Old Skala village. She felt more than ever that it was something she really needed to do.

Chapter Seven

Christoph walked confidently down Skala's main street to Sam's office. He knew she had at least another hour more to work so he had plenty of time to ask her to dinner.

Sam looked up in surprise as Christoph opened her office door. "Hello, what are you doing here?" she asked in a cool voice, determined not to let any emotion show.

"Well, I know you've had a really difficult time today, so I've come to ask you out to dinner. Is that okay?" Christoph replied politely with a small smile.

Sam looked at him without speaking.

"Sam? Is that okay?" Christoph asked again. Honestly, some women! But he could wait. He remembered Theresa, the young Italian girl he'd met two years before when her family were on holiday in Skala. For the first, and probably last time, he'd thought he was in love, but the girl became possessive and very odd. And she'd lied to him. She'd caused Christoph and his family, and her own family, lots of trouble, so he was always wary now.

However, Lisa seemed to stir something similar in him, but he couldn't let that happen. Sam was by far the better marriage prospect because not only did she understand the Greek way she would also be a good wife and quickly bear him the son he must have - whereas, Lisa, lovely and desirable as she was, may not be able to do that.

Sam continued to look at him and could see her lack of response was irritating him although he was trying hard not to let it show. *That'll show the arrogant sod that I'm not that easily taken in*, she thought. Then after taking a slow, shallow breath, she finally said, "Well, yes, that would be nice. Say about 9 o'clock at The Grapevine?"

Surprised, Christoph asked, "You mean meet you there? But why don't I come to your apartment to collect you?"

"I've got things to do Christoph, so I'll meet you there. I've got stuff to get on with before I can leave here, and as I'm taking two days' leave…"

"Yes, yes, of course," breathed Christoph, now feeling really rattled. "I'm going. I'll see you at The Grapevine. I'll ask Andreas for a nice table. Take care."

Sam watched him walk out of her office. She didn't like treating him like that, but he had things to explain. She wasn't going to be anyone's pushover, not even his!

Lisa sat on her balcony with her home-made Greek salad and a glass of white wine and thought about the day. It had certainly been an adventure, but she knew she wouldn't have the courage to go on another coach tour which involved going up a mountain. She looked at the little book about Old Skala she'd bought and opened it at the first page with its illustration of Old Skala village as it was pre-earthquake. It looked so pretty! She read that 'Skala' means steps and denoted how the original village houses were built in stepping slopes on the mountainside.

She saw pictures of what's now left: the church ruins, a couple of old olive presses, some steps going nowhere, and further down, a structure which looked like it might have been the village washhouse. There was also an old, abandoned bus! Older pictures were of women in long dresses and headscarves, and men in traditional Greek baggy trousers and shirts.

The little book described the nineteen fifty-three earthquake and how Kefalonia is prone to these because it lies on a geological fault line. Life in Skala prior to the earthquake was very simple. Food and a meagre income came from olive trees and olive oil, sheep were kept for meat, milk and feta cheese, chickens kept for meat and eggs, and of course grapes were grown for wine and fruit. Corn, raisons, tomatoes, cucumbers and other vegetables were also grown and sold. There were hardly any cows. There were also hardly any cars except in the main town, Argostoli, and no tourism of any kind. To get around, most people kept a donkey as a mode of transport for themselves and whatever items they wanted to move. It was a hard life.

Lisa had always been interested in history and had gained a BA Hons First in the subject at the University of Kent where she was also lucky to be able to study for a term in Poitiers, France. She was fascinated to read that Kefalonia can be spelt several different ways, and that it's the only Greek island with a national park. She also read that the pine trees which grow on the island are unique, as are the wild horses and the goats with gold-coloured teeth! Reading on, Lisa learned that Argostoli was originally built by the Venetians and still has a bridge joining the town with the mainland so that people don't have to travel round Argostoli's lagoon each time they wish to go north from there.

She suddenly felt tired so closed the little book, drank her wine, took a shower and climbed into bed. Perhaps tomorrow would bring another adventure?

Meanwhile, Sam met Christoph in The Grapevine. He'd secured a table under a pine tree on the edge of the restaurant's garden which overlooked some countryside and the sea beyond. The sun had set, and the sky had turned to a brilliant scarlet shot with gold. Cicadas 'clicked' loudly, and Greek music wafted up from the restaurants and bars along the main street and beach.

"Hello, Christoph," said Sam cheerily as she reached their table. Christoph quickly stood up and pulled her chair out for her to sit down. She nodded and politely thanked him.

"Sam," began Christoph. "I'm so thrilled to see you. Are you okay after today's drama?"

"Yes, thanks, I'm fine. All in a day's work," replied Sam with a confidence she didn't feel. "But I guess that it's largely due to your three cousins kindly coming out with their truck that it all turned out so well in the end," she said with a laugh.

"Indeed. And it could have been a lot worse. Anyway, shall we order? Shall I go and see what's on offer tonight?"

Having been to The Grapevine several times before, Sam knew that there'd only be a choice of two dishes, so she waited until Christoph returned before choosing a simple chicken salad. After the day's drama she didn't really feel like eating anything at all, but she wanted answers from Christoph, so dinner was a good excuse to ask him.

They chatted about nothing in particular, and Christoph was polite and attentive. Then came the question he'd been hoping wouldn't be asked.

"Well, now Christoph," began Sam, looking intently into his green eyes. "How do you know Lisa's name?"

Christoph's heart beat a little faster. "Well, I happened to overhear George say her name when I was passing The Bay a couple of days ago. I guessed she had only recently arrived because George was explaining all the dishes to her. So, because she's new here, I was surprised to see her as one of your trip passengers." He stopped, mentally crossing his fingers in the hope that Sam would believe him. Then he continued, "Anyway, why do you ask? You know that I only have eyes for you, my lovely. I adore you. In fact, I think my feelings are perhaps deeper than that, but…" He stopped, leaving the rest hanging in the air for Sam to make of what she would.

Sam's eyes flew open. "Really? Deeper? You mean…" She couldn't say anything else because she thought it might sound as if she was asking for a commitment from him.

"Sam, let's leave it until we get to Athens, is that okay?" Christoph said gently. Sam nodded so he went on, "I'll pick you up the day after tomorrow at 9 o'clock so we can get to the airport in good time to catch the midday flight to the city. So, if that's alright with you can we now have a nice dinner?"

Much to Christoph's relief, Sam agreed, and the rest of the meal went well. He took her back to her apartment and made careful love to her so that she knew he really was the one for her - even though he knew in his heart that she wasn't.

Because the one who'd really stolen his heart was Lisa…

Chapter Eight

The following morning Lisa woke very early to the sound of a cockerel crowing nearby. She decided she wouldn't stay in bed but get up and go for a walk, maybe even a swim, before anyone else was up and about.

She pulled on a black one-piece swimsuit and old denim shorts, then packed water, suncream and beach towel into her tote bag and set off for the beach. Apart from the cockerel, it was wonderfully quiet and peaceful, with just the occasional local appearing to sweep the front of their shop. It felt like it was going to be yet another hot and sunny day.

As she reached the bottom of the steps, she looked out across Skala's vast beach at the sea which was as still as a millpond with not even a ripple on its surface. It looked like glass. The sun was just beginning to peek over the horizon, turning the sky a glorious soft peach, the light sprinkling the dark blue Ionian Sea with a million dancing diamonds. It was utterly breathtaking.

Lisa noticed that she was the only person around, and all she could hear were chirping birds. She walked straight ahead onto the soft sand, and then on to the shingle at the water's edge. Dropping her tote bag and slipping off her flip-flops and shorts, she walked slowly into the magical, silky sea until it was deep enough for her to swim, then, with her eyes closed, gently struck out towards the rising sun, feeling its emerging warmth on her face and shoulders. Then she let herself drift and float in the watery paradise.

She swam up and down for a while then got out, dried herself and lay down on her beach towel to sunbathe – something she'd only do when it wasn't too hot. Lying back with her hands clasped behind her head, she thought about the events of the day before, and of Sam's reaction to Christoph's surprise at seeing them both together. It didn't make sense, but she felt she wouldn't pursue it. Instead, she thought about Angelo, his family and his *Nonna* – what a story that was! This was what she'd been looking for, so she was determined she'd start making notes in preparation to begin writing.

Before that, she'd look for a car to hire to take up to Old Skala Village. Scary!

A few more people began to appear, bagging their chosen sunbed or beach space. The sun was also getting hotter, so she felt it was time for her to move on and so she quickly left the beach. When she came to the main village road, she remembered there was a car hire business next to *Rebecca's*, so she headed for it, arriving just as it was being opened.

"Kalimera," she said to the tall, young man who was just about to open the door.

"Kalimera," he replied with a smile. "Can I help you?"

"Well, yes. Or rather I hope so. I want to hire a small car for a few days, so what do you have and how much will it cost?"

"Ah, yes. This is good. You drive in Greece before?" The young man asked with raised eyebrows.

"Er, no. Er, not in Greece but I have driven in France, so I do have some experience of driving on the wrong side of the road."

The young man smiled, "Ah, yes you say, 'the wrong side' but here it is the right side!" He laughed. "Anyway, come in and we will talk."

Lisa followed him into his cool office and sat down.

"Now, what sort of car would you like?" He asked as he turned on his screen. "We have both automatic and manual transmission cars. Two doors or four doors. Hatchbacks, saloons, four by fours and Jeeps. Your choice."

"Oh," said Lisa in a small voice. "I'm used to an automatic four door car so one of those would be good."

"Okay. Well, I've got two. So, shall we go outside and look at them?"

"Yes," said Lisa trying hard to look braver than she felt. Then she saw a little yellow car glinting in the early sun. "Is that an auto, and what make is it?" She asked.

"Yes, it's an auto and it's a Fiat 500. Very reliable and easy to drive little car, not speedy but drives well."

"So long as it copes with these roads, that's all I want!" Lisa said with a laugh. "By the way, I plan to drive up to Skala Old Village."

The young man observed Lisa with half closed eyes. "The old village? I see. Well, the road's not very good in places but you'll be okay if you take it easy. We're hoping it's going to be levelled soon and then it will be fine." He stopped, still looking inquisitively at Lisa. He wasn't used to a woman saying she wanted to drive up there, it was usually a man. But, he thought, a hire is a hire, and it's nothing to do with him. He told Lisa how much it would cost for four days, and after she agreed with the car insurance and terms and conditions, she signed the Agreement and paid her money.

"I'll make sure the car's okay and then you can pick it up in an hour if that's convenient?"

With a fast-beating heart Lisa nodded and then made her way back to her apartment to change. She thought she was being very brave but then chided herself, she was going to have another adventure!

The little yellow car which, for some reason, she immediately named Bessie, drove like a dream round the village. It wasn't fast but it felt comfortable and quite nippy, which is all she wanted. After buying some more water and a lovely cheese pie from the bakery, and with the little book tucked into the car door, she set off up the hill towards Skala Old Village.

The road proved to be very uneven with some deep ruts, so she had to drive carefully, mentally crossing her fingers that she'd be okay every time she came to a tricky bit. But oh, the view! The higher she climbed the more spectacular the scenery became. It was so lush and green! She passed nothing on the way up and almost missed the correct road at one point when she came to a small crossroads. Because there weren't any signs, she had to rely on the map she'd been given, although it didn't seem to be the most detailed!

On reaching a sightseeing clearing surrounded by pine trees, Lisa decided it would be a good place to stop, have a drink and take some photos. She parked Bessie in the shade, got out, donned her sunglasses and straw sun hat and walked to the seat overlooking a vast valley dotted with little white houses, pine trees and olive groves. Goats and sheep wandered amongst the mountain rocks and olive groves, eating what meagre grass they could find. The only sounds were the soft shushing of the wind in the pine trees and the incessant 'clicking' of the cicadas. A heat haze shimmered over the beautiful blue and green water, smudging the horizon between sky and sea.

Lisa was suddenly startled by something moving out of the corner of her eye. She turned round to see who or what it was but there wasn't anyone or anything there. Odd, she thought. Must have been a trick of the light. She moved closer to the barrier and took some more photos, then as she turned round to return to her car, she glimpsed the dark shape of a girl running down an unmade track amongst the olive groves leading to…where? God, this is a bit spooky, she thought. But it must have been a local, probably someone looking for a lost sheep or whatever. Oh, well, time to drive on.

The road became steeper and much bendier until finally Lisa could see some tumbledown buildings in the near distance. She'd arrived at last! She parked Bessie under a pine tree and walked across ground covered in small rocks, pinecones and general debris. Looking around, she saw large aloe plants sticking up into the air, two lots of steps leading nowhere, one with a door hanging at an angle, two old, rusting olive presses and several old wells. The church had gone, just the bell tower remained, lying awkwardly on its side in the rubble. The cemetery had many broken elaborate headstones. Everywhere, pieces of wood were scattered amongst the rubble and ancient olive groves. There were also a couple of flat, clear areas with what looked like the ragged remains of tents on them - she'd read in her little book that some of the few earthquake survivors had been given tents to live in.

Then, shading her eyes, she saw something glinting in the sun. When she looked closer, she saw it was a fork, and next to it was a shattered white plate, a broken white cup, an enamel plate and mug, and a battered metal kettle and saucepan. A bit further on, she saw a distorted leather shoe sticking out of some rubble; it looked like a man's shoe. She was overcome with emotion: here were such deeply moving remnants of lives, of human beings, and of a village way of life long gone.

The air felt hot, oppressive and moody, as if something was about to happen. Feeling uncomfortable, Lisa walked further on up what had been the hilly village main street until she came across the four walls of a house which had fallen outwards, and a single stone wall of a house with a hole disappearing under it. Was this a cellar? Could this have been Ariadne-Rose's house and cellar where she'd hidden her lost Italian soldier?

A little way along, she came across a yet another half-demolished stone house with steps leading nowhere, and next to it a large, triple-arch fronted building with three, outside stone troughs. There was also a natural spring and water pump close by. Lisa realised this must have been the village washhouse.

Right next to that was a large dip in the ground, now overgrown with marjoram, thyme, oregano, sage and wild geraniums, their scent filling the warm air. Was this where the two women had disappeared? She wondered. A sudden shiver went down her spine at the thought. It felt like she was treading on people's graves. Time to move on.

Just at that moment she heard a scream and then a girl crying. She ran down the hill towards Bessie, looking round to see if she could find anyone. But there was no-one. There was also no noise other than the distant sound of running feet. Even the cicadas had gone eerily quiet. Getting quickly into her car, Lisa decided that this was most definitely a place she wouldn't want to visit again.

Sam's day was less dramatic. She did her usual daily visit to *Rebecca's* where she waited for her holiday guests to come by with any requests or complaints, and to book trips. It was still hot, so she'd decided to wear her summer dress uniform – not the most flattering item in the world, but being a pale blue, loose-fitting cotton dress, it was cooler than her white shirt and navy-blue skirt. She wore it with a dark blue belt lightly fastened round her slim waist, and her smooth dark hair was in a ponytail secured with a dark blue scrunchie.

Rebecca's friend Tracey poured Sam a soda with ice - which, after pushing her large sunglasses up into her hair, Sam sipped gratefully. In the three years she'd worked in Skala she'd never known it to be this hot in June. She hoped it would be an easy day with no more dramas, yesterday's coach drama was enough for one season! She'd arranged for her manager Crystal to cover her duties for two day and now had things to finalise and a case to pack to go to Athens with Christoph the next day. She'd chosen her clothes carefully: two non-creasing, chic semi-fitted summer dresses, one pale blue, the other cream, with low-heeled strappy sandals to match, and a variety of t-shirts and shorts. She'd bought a new red bikini which enhanced her lovely figure, and some black lacey underwear. And of course, she had all the other boring but necessary bits and bobs!

A couple came to book a trip to Lixouri, and to enquire about shopping in Argosoli. The two girls who were staying at Helios Boutique Studios booked an around-the-island trip, and a couple of other holidaymakers dropped by just to say hello and to have a chat. After that, Sam left to visit all the hotels and apartments which she was responsible for. Thankfully, there no problems to sort out, so she headed to The Bay for a light lunch.

As she was allowed two hours off, she then went to the beach for a swim and found a spot along the beach where tourists rarely went. She always took her swimming costume with her and was very adept at slipping it on under her large beach towel! The water was lovely and very cooling, so she struck out in a crawl and was soon treated to silver fishes swimming round her – and a turtle nearby! Turtles are common in Kefalonia and occasionally appear where they're not expected. The large, elegant creature was exquisite, but it very soon disappeared, and Sam swam back to the beach.

The rest of Sam's day was very quiet, ending with a drink in *Rebecca's* before going home to bed.

The following day Christoph got to Sam's apartment at exactly nine o'clock to take them by taxi to the airport for their midday flight to Athens. He was invariably early or exactly on time for everything. They arrived at the airport just before ten o'clock so went to a taverna beside the airport for coffee. They made an attractive couple: Sam was in a simple cream linen shift dress, accompanied by a black and gold Gucci shoulder bag and black strappy sandals. Her hand luggage was a small black case. Christoph looked very elegant in white trousers, black t-shirt and expensive loafers. His own hand luggage was also black. Sam knew their time together would be very special and was looking forward to making some precious memories with her handsome partner – it made her feel like they were a real couple.

Much to her delight, Christoph had booked first class seats, and so Sam's adventure began.

It was late afternoon when, coming out of one of Skala's supermarkets after buying some basic supplies, Lisa saw a coach draw up in Skala's main street. *More tourists*, she thought, looking away. Lost in thought and distracted by thinking how she might begin her story, she didn't see the tall, slim, fair-haired bearded man get off the coach and gaze around. Then something made her suddenly look up. She stood very still, a cold feeling running down her back. No, it couldn't be!

"Hello, Lisa. How are you?" Asked a familiar voice.

It was Mark. Her husband Mark…

Chapter Nine

Stunned, Lisa couldn't speak. What the hell was Mark doing here in Skala?

"Lisa, I know this is a bit of a surprise, but I wanted to see you." Mark said with a smile.

Wide-eyed, Lisa stared at her husband. "Surprised? You say *surprised*? I'm bloody shocked not just surprised. And anyway, how did you know I was here?"

"I saw your friend Di in Tesco who told me she thinks you're very brave to travel alone to Skala in Kefalonia, so she made it easy for me. Anyway, I miss you terribly so I thought it'd be good to come out so we can talk away from all the usual hassles, your job which seems to take everything out of you, as do the girls and all their stuff. You know."

Cheers Di, she thought. Then, oh yes, she knew, and she also knew what he wasn't saying was that he'd told her he wanted to 'find himself' but couldn't do that whilst being married. She also knew his nasty side, the frightening anger which no-one else saw so everyone thought what a lovely chap he was. And the moods, the deliberate ignoring of her when she said she wanted to talk about things, the spending of hours in the garage fiddling with his old car, never wanting to go on holiday, the lack of support of her work and its stressful impact on her. So much, too much. Years of it, during which she'd tried hard to make things right, to understand, make allowances for his own paint company managerial stresses. She'd encouraged him to see a doctor and, or, to have couple counselling, even separate counselling, but he wouldn't do anything. So, him saying he didn't want to be married anymore was the very last straw. Did that mean he wanted a divorce? And did she?

"Well," hissed Lisa. "How do you think coming here can make things right? Anyway, I'm on holiday, a deliberate holiday to get away from you and have some time for ME and me alone. To relax and enjoy myself," she said defensively.

"Time for YOU?" He queried. "What d'you mean, time for YOU? That's all you ever have!"

Feeling weary, Lisa replied, "Look, I'm busy right now so let's meet up later. I suggest the taverna at the bottom of the hill, it's called The Bay. I'll meet you there at seven thirty. I'm going now," she said without waiting for his reply. Mark started to say something, but she walked away. She wasn't interested in where he was staying or even if he could or couldn't get to The Bay. *God*, she thought, *this is a nightmare situation.* Feeling stressed, she bit her bottom lip and clutched her tote bag to her chest like a comfort blanket. She couldn't do this. But then she had no choice really, she had to find the courage to face Mark and tell him to go away. Forever.

Mark stood still for a moment. He hadn't expected such a bold reaction. What now? It was late afternoon so he couldn't go back to his hotel in Argostoli town and then get back in time for seven thirty. He decided it would be good to have a wander around Skala, look at the shops, restaurants and beach, see the place where his wife had run away to, maybe have a beer.

Lisa almost ran back to Helios Boutique Studios, arriving slightly out of breath to find the owners having a look round. "Hi, are you Lisa?"

Asked Helen with a warm smile. "I'm Helen and this is my husband Dimitri. We know Crystal's doing Sam's normal rep duties while she's away, so we've come to check everything's okay with the apartments as she can't fit everything into her busy schedule. Are you enjoying your *Sunnyside Holidays* break in Skala?"

"Oh, hello, Helen, Dimitri. Thank you, yes, I love staying here, the apartment is nice with good views, and it's always kept very clean. I really couldn't ask for better," Lisa replied. "And Sam is a great rep."

"Yes, Sam's a great girl. Anyway, we won't detain you anymore. Have a happy holiday. Bye!" smiled Helen, waving as she and Dimitri walked away.

Well, that was nice, thought Lisa as she climbed the steps to her apartment, deciding it would be good to relax on her balcony with a glass of Robola before mustering the courage to face Mark.

Lisa sank thankfully into her veranda chair with a glass of wine and a sigh of relief. This holiday was not turning out how she'd thought it would, but she was determined to ensure that things improved and that she'd spend the next day relaxing on the beach. Then she'd take the car into Argostoli, and during the next couple of days go to other nearby resorts such as Katelios and Lassi. There was plenty to see. She also pondered the idea of extending her stay but wondered how work would react to that request.

She eventually got ready to meet Mark, choosing to wear the most unflattering outfit she could think of – her orange pants! Christoph had clearly disliked them, so they were perfect to wear to meet her husband. She teamed them with a cream, sleeveless top which showed off her already-tanned arms, and a pair of flat sandals. She did consider wearing flip-flops but felt that was an unflattering step too far.

She set off for The Bay with a heavy heart. She really did not need this. Arriving dead on seven thirty she immediately saw Mark at a table overlooking the main street. Trust him to be so bloody obvious, she thought crossly. Anyway, onwards girl, you can do this, she told herself as she squared her shoulders.

Mark stood up to greet Lisa. "Lisa, hello love, hope you've had a good afternoon," he said with a smile. "I hope this table is alright?"

Lisa could barely muster a smile but said the table was fine even though it wasn't. She sat down opposite the man who'd ruined their marriage, looking at him properly probably for the first time in years. *Funny how you get used to people,* she thought. *I hadn't noticed how, erm, how ragged round the edges he was getting.* Sitting back, she surveyed his slight beard, dodgy teeth and greying and thinning untidy fair hair. Not a good look on someone over fifty. Or any time come to that.

Silence. Mark looked at Lisa, thinking how beautiful she was, especially now she had a slight tan. What a fool he'd been to say he didn't want to be married anymore! "Erm, shall we order?" He asked, mostly to fill the awful silence. He wasn't very hungry, but he had to eat something. Not that he knew what anything was because he'd never been to Greece before, didn't really like holidays. He was only interested in renovating his old car, so he selfishly and angrily ignored Lisa's pleas each summer for them to get away. Then it suddenly occurred to him that maybe he should have occasionally agreed to a holiday, he could have chosen where to go so it wouldn't have been too tricky. So long as it wasn't anywhere too long on a plane, or too hot.

Feeling pleased with what he thought was his generous thinking, he shuffled in his chair and said, "Well, this is a nice place, Lisa, I've had a look round. I suppose it's good for a short holiday, not for too long as it must get boring. I mean, what is there to do except go on that beach?"

Lisa looked at Mark incredulously. *What an ignorant, selfish sod,* she thought. And how amazing that a person can live with someone for a long time and not notice what they're really like. She suddenly realised she could never live with him again, not in a million years.

Then she found herself saying, "Well actually, I'm staying longer than my booked two weeks in this 'boring place' as you call it." *Bloody hell, where did that come from?* "I'm not sure for how long but I'm getting a job here." *Really? This was news to herself!*

Shocked, and with wide eyes, Mark said, "Job? What d'you mean 'job'? You've already got a job. You know, the one you're always stressed about. Anyway, what will they say if you don't go back for weeks?"

"It'll be more than weeks. I don't know how long I'll stay so don't ask. And anyway, I'm also writing a book."

"Book? Bloody hell, Lisa, have you completely lost your marbles? How can someone like you write a book? That's for, well, you know, 'other' people, especially famous ones, not the likes of us."

"Us? what d'you mean 'Us'? I'm as good as anybody so you can sod off with your ignorant, prejudiced views," she said in a too-loud, annoyed voice which made the couple at the next table look over inquisitively. Lowering her voice, she went on, "Anway, if you want to eat let's order because I've not got all night to sit here and discuss my life with you."

Mark looked at his wife. He no longer knew this woman, she seemed so different somehow. But he still desired her, probably more so now she was getting all puffed-up, silly cow. "Look, I'm sorry I offended you, Lisa," he said softly. "Yes, let's eat. But I just want to say that I am a tad upset that it seems you don't want to make a go of things. However, I still love you and want you back as my wife so I can wait for this…this…mid-life crisis, or whatever it is, to pass. Or maybe you're menopausal, love? Some women do go a bit dotty around that time," he said, looking and feeling hopeful.

"Crap. Let's eat and then I can go home," she said dismissively as she called the waiter over to order a Greek salad, not waiting for Mark to even choose what he wanted.

The waiter asked Mark for his choice. "Erm, I'll also have a Greek salad," he said because he didn't know what anything on the menu was. "And a bottle of white wine. Please."

"A carafe of Robola suit you, sir?" Asked the waiter who could clearly see what was going on.

"Yes, thanks. That'll be fine."

Lisa and Mark ate their respective salads and drank the whole carafe of wine in near silence until Mark asked Lisa if she'd like a coffee. "No thanks. Let me pay for my salad," she replied, getting out her purse.

"No, no, put your purse away," said Mark with a flourish of his hand. He paid the bill, and they both stood up. Mark offered to walk Lisa back to her apartment.

"No thanks, I can go on my own, I do this a lot," she laughed icily. "Anway, bye, have a good flight back," she said as she turned to go back up the hill. "Don't hang around, Mark. It won't make any difference." Then she walked briskly away.

Mark stood still, not sure what to do. Suddenly angry at being rejected, he started to follow Lisa up the hill. She walked very quickly so he had a job keeping her in sight. Then, just as they reached the smaller square, he managed to catch up with her, and as she turned round to see who it was behind her, he caught her right arm in a tight grip.

"Who the fuck do you think you are?" he sneered, showing his uneven teeth. "You can't walk away from me, you're my wife. It's your duty to be with me."

Lisa winced with the pain of his grip. "Let go of me, you bastard," she said through gritted teeth. "Let go of me. Now." Tears came but she wouldn't let him see how frightened she was.

But Mark wasn't listening, instead he forced her arm up her back until she felt it was going to break. Screaming with pain she yelled, "Stop it, stop it, you're really hurting me."

"You're never going to leave me, Lisa. Never. Do you hear? Never. You're mine and I'll kill you if necessary. Then you'll always be mine."

A terrified Lisa realised Mark had suddenly lost his mind. At the same time, Mark felt a heavy thud in his back, and a man's voice say menacingly in his ear, "Let her go, buddy."

It was Rebecca's husband, Yannis, who was then joined by Georgios and Michaelas. The three men surrounded Mark as he dropped to the floor. Having hit his head as he fell, he wouldn't be going anywhere for a while. If at all.

But of course, no-one had seen or heard a thing…

Mark was discovered slumped on the pavement by a passing local, an ambulance was called, and he was taken to Argostoli hospital.

Before the ambulance arrived, a shaking Lisa was surrounded by Cristoph's three cousins and gently supported to a nearby house, where yet another of Christoph's cousins, Thomas, lived. Thomas also ran the kiosk in the main street near where 'the incident' happened, but no-one asked Thomas if he saw anything.

Thomas's wife Daphne, a well-rounded, friendly woman of a certain age, sat Lisa in a comfortable armchair, gave her a brandy and inspected her arm where a large black bruise the shape of fingers was already appearing. Daphne tutted. "Bad man. Bad man," she said with lips drawn back over her teeth in anger. "You must not see this man again. He is dangerous. But he will not come here, my cousin Spyros is good policeman at the airport and has been told about bad Englishman," adding quietly, "the bad man would never get through the airport. Anyway, you stay in Skala now?"

"Stay? You mean live here?" Lisa whispered, still feeling dazed and fuzzy with pain and shock.

"Yes, you live here. But then maybe you can't? You have family and work?"

"Yes, I'll stay in Skala for a while, and I'll leave my job, I need a break from it anyway. My three adult daughters all work so can afford to come to see me. That is, if they want to," Lisa murmured. She suddenly felt very tired and within seconds dropped off to sleep. Daphne covered her with a multi-coloured crocheted blanket, tucking her arms in so she would feel safe and secure. She turned to the three men. "You know you must never talk about this. Ever," she said in rapid Greek. "This never happened. You understand?"

The men silently nodded in agreement. They all knew secrets, things which were never talked about; that's what Greek families do. They then all quietly left.

About an hour later, Lisa woke with a start wondering where on earth she was. Daphne rushed in from the kitchen where she'd been making bread. "You're awake. Good. I will make you some English tea and then you must eat. I have cheese pies," she said firmly. There was no arguing with Daphne!

Lisa ate a cheese pie and gratefully drank her tea. What had just happened? She felt confused and upset, and her right arm was killing her. Killing. Hadn't Mark said he'd kill her if he couldn't have her as his wife? Oh my God. "Daphne," she called out.

Daphne came running in from the kitchen again. "What's wrong?" She asked worriedly. "Do you feel ill?"

"No, I'm just thinking about what happened. What Mark said and did. Where is he?"

"Ah, now. You must not think about what happened. The bad man Mark fell over in the street and went to hospital. Too much drinking. After hospital he will be going back to the UK, so you don't have to worry about him now," Daphne said kindly.

Looking carefully at Daphne, Lisa knew this kind Greek woman wasn't telling her the whole story, but she also knew she would believe her. Because she had to. "Daphne, I need to go back to my apartment, I can't stay here, but thank you so much for helping me," she said as she went to stand up but then wobbled. *Damn*, she thought.

Daphne tucked some wispy strands of greying hair behind her ears and patted the bun at the nape of her neck. Smoothing down her small, spotless white apron, she looked at Lisa with piercing, all-seeing dark brown eyes. "Hmm. So, you think you're okay, do you? Well, you know you're not. You can stay here tonight. We have a bedroom at the back where you will be quiet and have a good sleep. Which is what you need. And you will have some dinner with us first. We have Greek meat pie. The meat is cooking now."

Lisa had already smelled a delicious aroma coming from the kitchen. Daphne always seemed to be in the kitchen cooking something! "Thank you, that's most kind," she said with a smile. *What lovely people these Skalians are*, she thought. So helpful, so welcoming. She knew this was the Greek way, the Xenia, always hospitable, and you shouldn't offend them by refusing to share food with them., so thank goodness the cheese pie was only a small pastry!

Although it was now very late, Lisa ate the delicious meat pie. She knew it was an 'ordinary' Greek dish but to her it was very special because it had been made with kindness and love. She slept well in the spotlessly clean, narrow bed, waking the next morning to the sun peeping through the wooden shutters of the bedroom's window. The house was single story, one of very few original wooden houses left from the village's early days. She thought it must be a bit cold in winter although she'd noticed a large fireplace in the sitting room with wood already piled beside it, and in the kitchen was a huge cooking range which she guessed would throw out lots of heat, a smaller gas cooker for summer cooking, a large sink, a washing machine, and an enormous, well-scrubbed wooden table with several unmatching chairs round it: clearly, the kitchen was the heart of this home!

After getting up and having a breakfast of yoghurt and a delicious, home-grown peach, Lisa thanked Daphne and Thomas for their kindness and help. She felt she could never repay them but also knew they would all be friends for life.

"You are most welcome, *canim*, you are like a daughter," replied Daphne as she held Lisa's hands in hers. "We lost our own daughter many years ago, she died of blood sickness, so maybe you come here in her place. We have no sons," she finished sadly.

Deeply moved, Lisa quietly said, "Well, I feel very honoured, thank you both. Perhaps I'm a little old to be your daughter but even so I do really appreciate you saying that as it means a lot. Now I must go." She lightly kissed Daphne on her brown, weathered cheek, and shook Thomas's hand warmly. Then she left the little house and made her way up the hill to her apartment. She felt it would take a little while to fully recover from what had happened.

But unbeknown to Lisa, things were about to change, and her life would never be the same again.

Chapter Ten

Lisa went in Bessie to Katelios, Lassi and Lourdas, and loved all three resorts. She got used to driving on the hilly and twisting Kefalonian roads but was still determined not to drive any distance up Mount Aenos. She also took the local bus into Argostoli where she had lunch in a taverna overlooking the lagoon. It was a busy town with a bus station in the middle of the main road, a harbour where little boats selling freshly caught fish and octopus bobbed in the clear water, and fish flashed like silver darts. Heaven.

She realised she really loved beautiful Kefalonia and wanted to see more of the island, so she decided to go to see Sam to ask about a trip to the blue lagoon which she'd heard a lot about.

Lisa found Sam in her office and the first thing she noticed was a sparkling diamond ring on the third finger of Sam's left hand. When she asked Sam about it, Sam told her that Christoph had proposed when they went to the Acropolis, and although she'd been shocked, she'd said yes!

Looking at Sam's pretty ring, Lisa smiled and told Sam she was happy for them both. Which she was. But then why did she feel a slight stab of envy? Maybe it was because of what happened with Mark. Why couldn't she have known such joy? Well, maybe she once did but had forgotten. Now she was on her own except for her three girls, who were due to come to Skala in a couple of weeks' time to see her which would be lovely. She wondered if they ever missed their father who they rarely saw. She decided it would be best for them not to know what he'd done to her a couple of weeks ago; what they didn't know wouldn't upset them.

"Have you arranged a date for the wedding yet?" She asked a beaming Sam.

"No," Sam replied, "We've got to have a huge engagement party first, then we can plan the wedding after that. Christoph said the wedding will be massive and will be in the church here in Skala. I can't wait!" She laughed excitedly. "I've met the family and they're all happy for us, even Christoph's mother!"

"That's good, and how wonderful!" Said Lisa. "I hope I get an invite!"

"Yes, of course you will. The whole village will be invited including you as you'll be here!"

Ah, so she's heard, thought Lisa. She decided to leave the turtle-trip for now and ask Sam if she knew of any jobs available in Skala.

"Yes," replied a surprised Sam. "As it happens, Sue and Trevor Robertson could do with some extra help. They run The Accommodation Shop next to The Bay, and their assistant, Jane, has just discovered she's pregnant so she's going back to England."

"Wow, that's brilliant!" Chuckled Lisa. "Thanks Sam, I'll go and see them straight away and let you know how I get on. Bye."

Lisa walked over the road to The Accommodation Shop where she found Sue Robertson busy on her phone. Sue waved at Lisa to take a seat by the window.

After a few minutes, Sue finished her call. "Hi, I'm Sue. How can I help you?"

"Hello, Sue, I'm Lisa and I'm not looking for somewhere to stay - well, not yet anyway - but I am looking for a job, and Sam told me your assistant's leaving, is that right?" Lisa asked with her fingers mentally crossed.

Sue's eyebrows shot up. "Really? Have you any experience of working in accommodation? Or of selling? Of people?"

"Well, I'm a project manager in the UK and am used to working with people of all kinds, from all backgrounds and at all industry levels, so I guess you could say I'm a 'people-person," replied Lisa.

"Perfect," beamed Sue. "You'll fit in just fine. When can you start?"

Taken aback by the sudden offer of a job, Lisa manged to stutter, "Erm, tomorrow?"

Laughing, Sue said, "I was thinking more of next Monday as Jane leaves on Sunday, and you could also have her apartment if you wanted it. Would that be okay for you?"

"Yes, thank you, that would be great," replied a relieved Lisa. Her holiday accommodation would finish in four days' time so that fitted in perfectly. Also, hopefully by then her bruises would have gone.

"Good. So, let me show you what we do here." Sue got up and invited Lisa to join her at her other desk where she opened her computer and clicked on to the pages showing what accommodation was available. She explained that she and her husband Trevor privately owned a couple of small apartment blocks and a hotel, but the majority of Skala's accommodation was owned by other people with most of it let to holiday companies, and that in addition to the apartments and hotel, she and Trevor also owned a jewellery shop in Argostoli.

Sue told Lisa she could have the ground floor apartment in one of her small, two-storey blocks facing the sea which Jane had rented. She also arranged with Makis who owned the car hire, for Lisa to keep

Bessie at a very reduced fee; Sue and Trevor paid her a small car allowance in addition to her wages.

Lisa thought her duties at The Accommodation Shop would be easy – she was moving on with a new job and a new chapter in her life! She emailed her notice to her very astonished employer, and asked her eldest daughter, Bella, to supervise the renting of her cottage, furnished, on a long-term lease. She decided she'd think another time about what she'd do for money once the holiday season was over, although the rent from her cottage would help.

Things were moving so fast! Feeling buoyant, Lisa bid Sue goodbye and went back to her apartment. She could hardly believe she had a new job, and with such a nice boss, too! Lisa had immediately warmed to Sue who was clearly very much a family person as well as having a good business head on her; she'd told Lisa about her two children, Chloe and Richard, and her husband Trevor, who also sounded a nice person. They all lived in a large house in one of the side roads off Skala's main street. What with the family and various other people coming and going, it sounded wonderfully chaotic to Lisa.

Lisa felt her new job called for some sort of celebration, so after changing she went down to *Rebecca's* where she ordered a large Robola and ice and then settled herself down at a table in front of the bar overlooking the street. It had been a good day, and she was able to ignore the flashbacks of what Mark did to her. For now. It wasn't that easy in the night, though, when there was nothing to distract her brain from remembering - which meant she was often up and sitting on her balcony in the early hours of the morning, waiting for dawn to break.

During these times, Lisa made lots of notes for her story which she thought she'd base on Anna, Angelo's *Nonna*, and her husband Davide's, experiences. But, of course, they'd both have different names, her characters would be fictional. She'd think of a few twists and turns to ensure the story was interesting, and there might even be a haunting. She knew she'd need to do lots of research as it was important to ensure any historical facts were correct. But then a while ago, she had considered writing a story about a woman of a certain age going abroad and falling in love with a younger man, although it all went pear-shaped when she told him to find someone younger and she returned home. She'd thought her heroine might return years later to find he was now married with children even though he'd never stopped loving her! For some reason, it made her think of Christoph, and then she chided herself for being so daft. Hmm, she thought, maybe she could combine both story lines?

Whichever story line, or lines, she chose to write, Lisa didn't expect her book to be published, and anyway she had no idea of how to go about that process. Writing was just something she wanted to try to do, and for all she knew, she'd give up after a while, she'd just have to see how she got on.

Lisa closed her eyes and thought about which story would be best. Suddenly, a voice interrupted her thoughts. "Hello, Lisa, how are you?" Startled, Lisa opened her eyes to see Yannis smiling at her.

"Oh, hi, Yannis. I'm fine thanks. How are you?" She said as she sat up a bit straighter.

"I'm well, thank you. Thomas and Daphne told me they'd looked after you after the…er…the…" stumbled Yannis.

"You mean Mark?" Supplied Lisa gently.

"Yes, Mark. Anyway, I hope your arm is a lot better now. We all care about you. I hear you'll be staying with us, which is good news, and I also hear you've got a job with Sue and Trevor?"

Crikey, news really does spread fast here, Lisa thought in astonishment. She realised that with so many of the locals being related, there'd never be any hope of keeping anything secret!

"Yes, that's right. I'm taking over the apartment their assistant Jane had so I'll only be moments away from work. I expect you already know that Makis has let me keep my car?" She said looking at Yannis quizzically with a wry smile.

"Yes, he told me. By the way, it's great news about Christoph and Sam, isn't it?"

"Fabulous! I've never been to a Greek wedding, but I know they're always huge!"

"Yes, they are. Anyway, I need to go and sort a few things out in the bar now, so goodbye," Yannis said politely.

Watching Yannis walk away, Lisa thought how lucky Rebecca was to have such a caring husband, likewise Helen with her husband Dimitri. And soon Sam will have Christoph!

Sam and Christoph's engagement party four weeks later was phenomenal. The whole village was decorated with fairy lights, and almost every Greek woman cooked something. In the main square near the beach, people danced to the band playing a mixture of traditional Greek music and modern tunes. Often the young local men would spontaneously break into a traditional Greek dance with lots of 'Opa!' as they immersed themselves in the music.

The church in the small square was lit up with powerful spotlights, its bells set to toll at midnight when the fireworks went off. There was generally lots of clapping, laughing and shouting, and the holidaymakers who were lucky to be in Skala were invited to join in the celebration.

Sam and Christoph were treated like Greek royalty. Sam had to show all of Christoph's family the gold and diamond ring which Christoph had bought in a jewellery shop in the Plaka when they were in Athens, its large central diamond surrounded by many small diamonds twinkling brightly in the fairy lights as she held out her hand for its inspection.

Although very happy, Sam also felt slightly apprehensive. If this was the engagement party, what on earth would their wedding be like? Christoph had already warned her that there'd be at least two hundred or more guests at the wedding which seemed a huge amount of people to Sam. And that was without Sam's family being there! Unfortunately, her parents had been less than enthusiastic when she'd told them about her engagement.

"What d'you mean, you're marrying a *Greek*?" Her mother, Andrea, had shouted. "What's wrong with a nice English boy, like Alex?" Alex was Sam's ex who she'd not seen for two years. Her mother had never forgiven her for the break-up, as she'd adored Alex.

"Mum, Christoph and I love each other so that's all there is to it," replied Sam tersely. "You and Dad are of course invited to the wedding, also Auntie Mabel and Uncle Tom." Reluctant to argue with her mother, she'd then changed the subject and hung up.

What Sam didn't tell Andrea was that Christoph's family had already decided that the wedding would take place in late October when all the holiday guests had gone home. As mother of the bride Andrea would undoubtedly not be happy with Christoph's family arranging everything, so she decided to ring her the next day to let her know she should start looking for her and Dad's outfits. Also, to ask her if she'd like to contact Christoph's mother, Thalia, so they could share wedding plans.

Christoph's father, Vasilis Papadakis, was a lovely man who Sam had instantly warmed to. However, his mother was a different kettle of fish; even though she'd seemed pleased at first, she now clearly didn't approve of her only son's choice of wife, so Sam felt she wouldn't take to her own mother, either. Sam knew that after she and Christoph were married, they'd be expected to live with his parents, and that she'd mostly have to do what Thalia told her to do. Well, she'd see about that!

Lisa joined in the celebrations with gusto - this was her first proper Greek party, and she was determined to enjoy it. She sang, ate, drank and danced with anyone who would dance with her until she felt she couldn't dance anymore. Then finally, at midnight, the church bells rang, beautiful fireworks lit the sky to lots of cheers and clapping, and her heart was filled with happiness at being able to be part of such a wonderful celebration.

Little did she know just how dramatically things would soon change.

Chapter Eleven

Lisa woke the following day with a slightly fuzzy head, but she also felt relaxed and happy. What a fun evening it had been! Yawning, she stretched her arms above her head and decided she needed coffee. She got out of bed and threw open the double doors leading onto the balcony. She knew she'd miss the view of the mountain she had from there, but then she would have a view of the sea when she moved down to her new apartment in a few days' time.

She took her coffee to the small table and sat facing down Skala's main street where the night before loads of happy people had wandered up and down. Surprised to see it looking completely pristine, she looked at her watch and saw it was gone ten o'clock, realising that she'd had a lie-in for a change. She considered what she'd do for the rest of the day. She had thought of driving into Lourdas but decided it wasn't a good idea because she might still have a fair amount of alcohol in her veins! The beach was the place to be, best to spend a nice relaxing day doing nothing except making major decisions like when to reapply sun cream, turn over, move the sunbed, drink water, swim or go for lunch. It was a hard life!

After showering, she gathered up all her usual things and headed off down to the beach. As usual, she decided to go to a less busy part, walking in the shade of the tamarisk trees and bullrushes which grew along one side of the uneven beach track. Beyond vegetation to her right, was the tumble-down shack the old fisherman lived in, a couple of small, modest tavernas and a two-storey apartment block. The beach and sea were to her left.

Even though it was still relatively early, it was already getting hot. Sunbed owners had laid out their beds and umbrellas in neat rows on the newly cleaned sand. There weren't yet many holiday guests around, some liked to breakfast where they were staying or in one of the tavernas in the main street before going to the beach. But she saw there were a couple of people in the sparkling, azure sea - which was exactly what she wanted to do, maybe before settling down on her sunbed.

Seeing a family of Italians arrive reminded her of Angelo and his family; she'd seen them at Sam and Christoph's party and had joined them for a while; they were such lovely people and had welcomed her like an old friend. They'd told her that they were going home in a few days and would like to meet up with her before they left, so Lisa had given Angelo her cell phone number so he could ring her from a phone box in the square. She knew she'd miss them all even though she hadn't seen them very much. Angelo had told her at the party that as well as going to Skala Old Village, they'd visited other resorts around the island. "It is such a beautiful place," he'd said thoughtfully. "It makes it worse somehow to remember what happened here in the war and how my grandfather must have died."

"Oh, Angleo, yes, it's so sad." Lisa had murmured as she'd gently placed her hand on his arm in a gesture of comfort. "By the way, how is your *Nonna*? Is she okay?"

"Yes, she's fine, thank you. Except..." He'd paused, looking worried.

"Except?"

"Well, except she did say she had some chest pain so we were a bit worried and thought we might have to call *il medico* - sorry, doctor – but she told us not to. And then thankfully the pains went away."

"Oh, that's good," Lisa had said with a sigh. "But if there's anything I can do just let me know. Anyway, let's meet up for dinner in two days' time, on Monday, at The Bay Taverna, say seven o'clock? Is that okay?"

Laughing, Angelo had replied, "That is very early! We Italians do not usually eat until about nine o'clock or later!"

"Oh, okay, Let's say nine o'clock then," Lisa had chuckled. "Sorry, that was me being very English!"

Just at that moment her soon-to-be employer, Susan, had walked past and invited Lisa to join her and her family for a drink which Lisa was very happy to do. Life was good!

Coming to the end of the beach track, Lisa stepped onto the warm sand and made her way to the last row of the sunbeds before the beach became a 'natural' area. Here, people were allowed to discard beach wear if they were so inclined, and huge rocks stood proudly amongst the sea which seemed to be even more stunningly crystal clear.

She laid down her towel and hid her tote bag under the sunbed before removing her sunglasses and light blue beach sarong which covered her matching bikini. Feeling the warm sun on her body was blissful, and as she entered the water it felt like warm silk wrapping itself round her legs. Sinking down gratefully she struck out in a breaststroke towards one of the nearest rocks. She spent twenty minutes swimming and floating on her back before returning to her sunbed to relax. This was the life!

A few more people arrived but everyone respected each other's space so there wasn't any problem. Lisa could hear children laughing as they played in the sand or squealed as they tried to negotiate the pebbles at the water's edge before having a paddle or tentative swim with whoever was looking after them.

She knew she wouldn't be able to enjoy this for much longer because she started work in four days' time. But then she *was* living in Kefalonia, one of the most beautiful Greek islands. How lucky was she?! Occasionally, she wondered what had happened to Mark although her eldest girl, Bella, had told her that once when she'd gone on the off chance to see her father in his rented house, he wasn't there. Like her two sisters, Bella wasn't close to her father anymore, but nonetheless this news upset her, and she didn't know what to do.

When Bella told her sisters, they all agreed it would be a good idea to take some long-overdue leave from their respective jobs and go to see their Mum. Bella was a paediatric nurse, Scarlett a PA in a local law firm and Tiffany-Mae was cabin crew with Flyjet. Each woman worked hard and knew their employers would understand that the leave was required for compassionate reasons: a mother in crisis and a missing father.

They felt Lisa should know about Mark, and anyway she was being a bit weird, so they also wanted to check she was alright. Tiffany-Mae and Scarlett were single, but Bella was married so wanted to discuss their plan with her lovely husband, Alan. The girls guessed Alan would be okay about it - but tough cookie if he wasn't, they were going anyway!

"Do you think Mum's lost it?" asked Tiffany-Mae when the three of them were having a Costa coffee. "I mean, do you know of anyone else's mother who's just gone off to live on a Greek island?"

Both Bella and Scarlett frowned. "Hardly 'just gone off', Tiff," said the ever-pragmatic Scarlett. "I mean, we knew she was going to Kefalonia for a holiday to try and get over Dad leaving."

"Yes, but to stay on? I mean, who does that?"

"Shirley Valentine did!" Laughed Bella. As the oldest she often had a down-to-earth view on things. She was also a natural carer. She'd only been two when Scarlett was born and although only a toddler, she'd seemed to Lisa to want to care for her little sister. Tiffany-Mae on the other hand didn't give a hoot about anyone. As the youngest, she'd got away with all sorts, and subsequently had a very independent way about her, she was a free spirit. She also always spoke her mind. Her parents had chosen her hyphenated name after neither could decide which of their favourite names to choose for their pretty baby girl; the resulting 'Tiffany-Mae' seemed to fit her individual personality perfectly! Unlike her dark-haired, deep blue-eyed, petite, curvy sisters who took after their mother, she was taller, slim, blonde and bright blue-eyed rather like their father, making her different in every way to her siblings!

"Whatever. I think it's a load of bollocks, if you ask me," guffawed Tiffany-Mae, adding, "Dad leaving I mean. What woman tolerates her husband saying he wants to 'find himself'? So, all power to Ma's elbow. She's doing what she wants after having been married to Dad for donkey's years and raising us three brats virtually single-handedly because Dad was always working and tired. Then she got a job herself, so her workload became even bigger. I don't care if she is doing a 'Shirley', she's brave enough to do what a lot of people, both women and men, would like to do if they could. It doesn't mean she thinks she's in a film or has gone a bit potty. She isn't bloody talking to a wall or ordering chips and egg!"

"What d'you mean?" Bristled peacemaker Bella, totally ignoring what her sister had said about their mother. "Dad wasn't that bad."

"No, he wasn't to us, but I heard him being horrible to Mum when he thought no-one could hear, saying unkind things to her in a nasty voice. And then pretending he was 'Mr Nice Guy' when other people, including us, were around. Didn't wash with me, though."

Scarlett bit her bottom lip. "Is that true, Tiff?" She asked worriedly. "Do you think he was, well, you know, even worse towards Mum?" Scarlett liked to ensure she had her facts right, with all her ducks neatly in a row so to speak. She needed to know the truth.

"No, but I think he liked to be in charge and throw his weight around. You know he was quite selfish, and he's proved it by telling Mum he wanted to find himself and couldn't do that in a relationship. I mean! Talk about hurtful. Poor Mum. Anyway, let's not dwell on Dad, let's focus on how Mum is."

Bella rang Lisa to tell her they were coming to see her in two weeks' time. They'd managed to get a last-minute cancellation and were going to stay in a small hotel near Lisa's new flat for a week. Lisa was surprised but also pleased that her daughters were supporting her in this way and went to Sue's house to tell her they were coming. It was Saturday evening so she was busy getting ready to do a shift in the Accommodation Shop; in two days it would be Lisa doing the same!

"That's brilliant, Lisa," beamed Sue. "But I'm afraid I can't give you any time off as you'll only have been working in the shop a little while!"

"That's okay, thank you Sue, the girls are only here for a week, and we'll meet up every afternoon when the shop's closed and then in the evenings, so we'll have time together."

"That'll be nice. I'm looking forward to meeting them, they sound lovely daughters."

"Yes, they are," agreed Lisa, adding thoughtfully, "I just hope they aren't coming to try to make me return to the UK."

"Well, I'm sure you'll put them right about that," laughed Sue. "Anyway, come to the shop tomorrow so we can make sure you're okay with everything before you start on Monday.

Bye for now."

Lisa left to go and get ready to meet Angelo and his family for a meal before they flew back to the UK on Sunday. Arriving at The Bay just before nine o'clock she saw the family were already there. There was lots of chat and laughter, and they all enjoyed themselves, even Nonna seemed very chirpy and chatty!

When Lisa was talking to Luca, she saw Christoph walk past. Smiling, he came over and Lisa introduced him to Angelo and his family. They were all very friendly except for Theresa who just scowled and didn't say anything. "Theresa, say hello," scolded Luca.

"I don't need to. He knows who I am," Theresa said coldly. The whole family and Lisa looked from Theresa to Christoph and back again. No-one knew what to say. Then Christoph spoke.

"Yes, I met Theresa once when she was here a couple of years ago," he said, bowing slightly in the girl's direction. "I hope you're well, Theresa?"

"Well, as if you care, you bastard," Theresa spat.

Everyone went quiet. Nonna Anna leaned forward, and Lisa coughed. *Awkward.* Clearly something had gone on between these two, but she didn't want any part of it. She felt a flicker in her stomach. God, was she *jealous?* Theresa was definitely stunning, but then so was Sam in her own way, and she hadn't felt jealous of her and Christoph getting engaged. *This is ridiculous*, she thought. *Get a grip girl.* She had to say something.

"Look, can you please just leave Christoph?" She hissed. Then, turning to Angelo and his family, continued, "I do apologise for that interruption. But anyway, I'm going now but it's been truly wonderful to meet you all and I hope we meet again soon. I'll pay my bill on the way out."

"No, it's us who should apologise," said Luca as he stood up. "And I'll pay the bill, so please don't worry about that." He held out his hand which Lisa took and shook warmly.

"Safe flight everyone," she said feeling very sad. "Bye."

Lisa walked as fast as she could away from the taverna and back to her new apartment. She felt furious. How dare Christoph ruin her last evening with her lovely friends? She turned the corner to the beach road and saw Christoph just ahead of her, but she ignored him and continued to her apartment. She was in no mood to talk to anyone right now, especially him.

The next Monday, Lisa started work in The Accommodation Shop. It wasn't very busy, but Sue had told her that was normal for a Monday, it should pick up in a few days, and over the next couple of weeks as the season progressed. It was now early July and hotter, so Lisa was grateful for the shop's aircon although she did find it a bit difficult at times being inside working when she could be outside enjoying the sun!

She felt happy to be working and felt a sense of satisfaction at being able to help travellers from many different countries around the world find a place to stay. Susan had warned her that by the end of July most accommodation would be gone so she'd need to use contacts in nearby resorts. Unfortunately, this often didn't go down well with some people who really wanted to stay in Skala so all her diplomacy skills would be required to keep people calm, which can be especially tricky when dealing with those travellers with limited English!

Lisa loved her job but was relieved that she could now look forward to a short break when her three daughters came to visit her. She knew that they'd have a lot of fun together and wondered if the island would capture their hearts as it had hers.

Chapter Twelve

Bella, Scarlett and Tiffany-Mae arrived in Skala late on a Thursday afternoon and were taken to their small hotel a few yards away from Lisa's apartment. Bella rang Lisa to say they'd arrived safely and would meet up with her as soon as they'd finished unpacking and freshened up.

Lisa was over the moon to see her daughters, and there were lots of hugs and kisses, plus a few tears. The girls hadn't seen Lisa for weeks, and they'd missed her, and she'd missed them, too.

They all decided to go to for a drink, and Lisa suggested *Rebecca's*. It was a good choice and they all enjoyed themselves, the three girls loved the ambience of the bar. They then went for a bite to eat in The Bay. George came over and introduced himself with a toothy smile.

"Such beautiful ladies!" He beamed. "Just like their Mama!"

The three women laughed and thought he was charming, if a little 'gappy' in the dental department! Then after taking their orders, George left, and a young waiter arrived with a basket of bread and a carafe of Robola.

Looking at her watch, Lisa said, "I've got to go back to work in half an hour, but we can meet up this evening if that's what you'd like to do."

"That'd be fabulous, Mum," said Bella. "We'll come round to your apartment. What time?"

''Well, my shift finishes at eight-thirty, so I'll see you just after then."

The three girls agreed, and Lisa went back to work feeling very happy.

This was repeated many times over the week. When the three girls weren't seeing Lisa, they went to the beach or to one of the tavernas. None of them was inclined to go sightseeing, it was all about relaxing and ensuring Lisa was okay. Which they discovered she was. And when Scarlett started talking about Mark, Lisa didn't bat an eyelid to hear of what might allegedly have happened to her husband.

"Well, he's a grown man and can look after himself," she responded primly. "After all, he wanted to 'find himself' so he can do just that. Anyway, end of conversation about Dad now please girls."

Her three daughters nodded agreement, and with a small laugh, Tiffany-Mae added, "Okay Mum, we've got the message and will shut up!"

It was important to Lisa that she didn't spoil her daughter's memories of their father, who'd clearly lost the plot, in fact, he'd probably started to lose it a few years before. What would she achieve anyway? Her girls might even resent *her* for telling them, and she wouldn't risk that. And despite everything, she didn't wish Mark ill. It wasn't as if he'd always been tricky, they'd had some lovely times when they were first married and when their babies came along. But it seemed that he couldn't cope with his work stress and then hitting middle age. She hoped he'd be okay but that was as far as any feelings for him went now. She hoped he got some help and decided it was best for everyone to leave it there.

Changing the subject, she told the girls about Sam and Christoph's fabulous engagement party. The girls thought it sounded wonderful and were pleased that Lisa was fitting in so well with the locals.

Lisa had also decided it was best not to mention the fact that Christoph had made some inappropriate advances towards her - after all, if they knew that, what sort of mother would they think she was?!

All too soon it was time for Bella, Scarlett and Tiffany-Mae to leave Skala. Lisa felt very sad but was glad to learn her dear daughters had already planned to return next year for two weeks. "Wonderful!" She beamed. "I can't wait! But we'll see each other before than as I hope to be back in the UK for Christmas, so let's arrange it when you're all home, okay?"

The girls readily agreed and raised their glasses to their Mum who'd turned out to be far stronger and focussed than any of them had ever imagined! Cool Mum!

Lisa took a couple of hours off to go to the airport with them, waving goodbye with tears streaming down her face as their plane took off into the bright blue sky. Her babies were leaving her and going home. She then realised that this would test her more than anything would. Would she stay? Or would the pull of her family prove to be too strong?

As Susan had predicted, Lisa got much busier at work, often having several travellers walk into the shop at the same time. She occasionally saw Sam and the others whom she'd got to know and felt that she was beginning to fit in just a little to the tight-knit Skala community. Then one Wednesday, just after she'd bid some happy travellers goodbye, her door flew wide open letting out the cool air-con air, and in strode Christoph. Lisa's heart flipped. Looking at him sternly, she demanded, "What are you doing here? I'm busy."

Christoph stopped and stood ramrod straight and still. "What is this I hear about your husband hurting you?" He shouted. "You didn't tell me."

"Why would I tell you?" Asked a shocked Lisa. "There's no reason I should tell you anything. And anyway, it was dealt with and finished ages ago."

"I know. But..."

"But what?"

"I'm upset. For you. I care. About you. Deeply. You must know that."

Silence filled the shop. Lisa held her breath and bit her bottom lip. This couldn't be happening. Finally, with a dry mouth, she managed to respond. "Care? Deeply? What d'you mean Christoph? You're engaged to Sam, so this is very inappropriate. Go away."

"I can't. I love you," Christoph said quietly. "My heart broke when I heard you'd been hurt. I can't help loving you. I fell in love with you the minute I saw you," he finished, looking at her with tears in his eyes. Unbelievably, this strong, opinionated, proud Greek man in front of her was almost crying.

"But you also had a 'thing' with the Italian girl, Theresa," Lisa whispered.

Shaking his head, Christoph said, "It wasn't a 'thing'. It was lust on her part. It was two years ago and was finished almost as soon as it began. She was, is, angry about it. You must believe me, Lisa. She caused her family and my family much misery by trying to accuse me of all sorts but thankfully no-one believed her. Then one day she ran away up into old Skala village and was gone a whole day and night. Her poor family were beside themselves with worry. But the police searched and found her hiding in the old laundry and brought her back. By then she was almost insane with hunger and thirst. She could have died in the heat, so she had to go to hospital to be checked. They all went back to the UK shortly after that. They didn't come to Skala last year, but because of their *Nonna* they came this year."

Lisa looked at Christoph in horror. No wonder she'd felt that Christoph was somehow involved with Angelo's family! Had she sensed Theresa's misery when she was at the laundry ruins in Old Skala? Had it been a sort-of 'memory ghost' of her running away down that path that she'd seen, and not the legendary Ariadne-Rose ghost? Frozen to her chair, Lisa took a breath, swallowed and smoothed strands of her now-damp hair back over her ears. She felt slightly faint, but Christoph looked like he wanted to say more, so she silently nodded to him to continue.

"Lisa, Sam is someone I'm fond of but don't love. I asked her to marry me because I think she could have a son for me. My family are insisting that because of my age I must now marry and have a son to carry on the family name." He stopped and looked pleadingly at Lisa. "I have to do this," he ended miserably.

Lisa suddenly felt angry. "You mean, you think I can't have any more children? Is that what this is all about Christoph? You think I'm past it, so you don't want me?" *The question is, do I want him?* She shook her head to try to clear her thoughts. "Anyway, how do you know about this? Who told you?" She demanded hoarsely.

"Daphne's cousin Spyros the policeman told Yannis who told Rebecca who then told Sam who told me," Christoph replied. "I'm sorry, that happens sometimes when people care about someone. Like we all care about you."

Stunned, Lisa didn't know what to say. Yes, she was angry but how could she stay angry when all these people clearly cared about her enough to quietly tell each other what had happened?

Christoph interrupted her thoughts. "I understand you're angry," he said as he made to move towards her.

Standing up, Lisa held her hand up to stop him. "Don't. Don't even think about it. I'm at work so you must leave but I will talk with you later. Meet me in the main square at eight thirty. Now, please leave. Bye." She needed to get back into work mode pronto.

Distraught, Christoph nodded agreement and left, quietly shutting the door behind him. Lisa couldn't believe what had just happened. It was unreal. What was she supposed to do? What would she say to Christoph? How could she stay in Skala now?

Lisa was busy for the rest of the day, and it passed quickly. She took her mid-afternoon break in a small taverna at the end of the main part of the beach. Only locals and a few tourists went there so she knew it would be quiet, and she could think without being disturbed.

She ordered an iced coffee and sat at one of the taverna's little tables on the beach. She wasn't hungry. How would she handle this latest drama? Her life seemed to be full of them lately. Did she really have feelings for Christoph? Even if she did, she was forty-nine and he was only thirty-something. He'd never actually said how old he was but had hinted at thirty or so. And he'd mentioned his family saying, 'at his age', so she knew he must be about thirty or so. Whatever, it was a large age gap between them. Lisa knew that Sam must be aware of how Christoph had taken the news about Mark and her; how would she react? Would there be even more trouble to have to cope with? Suddenly, living in Skala didn't feel as good as it did. She'd only been there five minutes so how could she have fallen in love with someone? Ridiculous.

She asked herself if she'd miss Christoph if he wasn't around, and the answer was yes, she would. Even though she found him annoying. She remembered when she'd first seen him walking down Skala's main street and had thought what an arrogant sod he was! And all those cousins! Life was never dull with them getting into all sorts, things which no-one ever asked about or commented on. They just got on with things, kept quiet and looked after each other, their families and their friends. Lisa sometimes felt there was a whiff of something deeper going on, but no-one ever referred to it. Best not to ask questions.

So, did she love Christoph? She remembered his touch and how she'd wanted him to touch her again but had smothered the thought. However, that was lust, not love. She thought about Christoph as a person. He was proud but also very kind, and very much a respectful, family person. He also seemed to understand women to a degree. She realised she thought about him a lot and recently had come to look for him when she was in the village, and when she did see him, her heart lifted. She'd answered her own question.

Lisa left the taverna to walk barefoot along the edge of the sea with the sand between her toes. The sun warmed her body and her shoulders dropped. She sighed. This could be her life for ever. With the man she loved. Would the age gap be a problem? Then the thought suddenly struck her that, bizarrely, here she was beginning to live the life of her initial story's protagonist: an older woman going abroad and falling for a younger man! Bloody hell, how unreal was that! Well then, she'd better start writing and think about the ending. Maybe she'd bring Ariadne-Rose's ghost and the Italians' sad story into her book somewhere along the way, too.

Lisa closed the shop at eight-twenty and left to go to the main square to meet Christoph at eight-thirty. They had to be discreet, so she decided she'd say hello and then quietly tell him she'd meet him outside the last small hotel on the Poros coast road, suggesting he go first with her slowly following. They could then sit on the wall just beyond the hotel. Hardly anyone ever went this far unless they were going to Poros.

She saw him before he saw her. Seeing him, her heart leapt and beat faster. Standing by the biggest fountain looking at the ground, she thought he looked unusually unsure of himself as water sprays twinkled and glinted in the red-gold setting sun behind him. He was wearing a neat black shirt with cuffs turned back over his lower forearm, and immaculate black trousers. Large sunglasses hid his green eyes.

Lisa still had her work clothes on. She always dressed smartly to work in the shop and had chosen a short-sleeved, boat-necked, long handkerchief-hem pale pink dress with a delicate pattern of small darker pink roses all over it. She always wore comfortable open leather sandals to work because it was hot when she left the shop, and she knew her ankles would swell. Today, her sandals were red, matching her red tote bag. She also wore her Ray-Bans because her eyes felt sore.

Sensing her presence, Christoph looked up. "Lisa, you came," he breathed. "I thought that maybe you wouldn't."

"Why wouldn't I when I said I would?" She queried with a small smile, feeling touched that he cared so much. "Look, we need to be discreet so let's move on to the last small hotel on the Poros road. Is that okay?"

Christoph nodded.

"Right, well you go first, and I'll follow slowly. Now go." She watched him walk quickly away, knowing that in the next hour or so, huge decisions might be made.

Would these mean she'd stay in Skala, or would she have to go back to the UK?

Chapter Thirteen

Christoph was sitting on the wall at the edge of the small hotel's front garden. He stood up when Lisa arrived and held out his hand. "Lisa, I'm really glad we could meet. There's so much I want, need, to say."

"I know. Me too."

"Well, you start. Please."

"Okay. Well, firstly I'm deeply upset that Sam must realise that you care for me when she's expecting to be married to you in two months' time. Whatever must the poor girl be feeling like Christoph? Have you asked her?"

"No, I haven't because I just left when I heard about you. We were about to have lunch at The Grapevine, I'd asked Andreas to save us a nice table." Christoph's face was drawn with sorrow. "I don't know what to do now."

"What you have to do is two things," replied Lisa. "Firstly, you need to decide if you love me enough to leave Sam, and all that will mean because it will be huge, and you know that. Secondly, you need to talk with Sam and probably also her family and your family. That will take great courage on your part because it will upset many people.

Finally, you haven't asked me how I feel. You've been selfish Christoph. Also, thoughtless and impetuous.

"I know. I've thought of all that too, Lisa. I'm sorry I've caused so much upset. But I love you and I hope you love me although I doubt you do. How can you?"

Lisa didn't reply at first. Then, biting her bottom lip said, "Well, I've done a lot of thinking since you barged into the shop. I've also weighed everything up and decided that yes, I do love you, but nothing can ever come of it. For a start, I'm older than you and probably can't give you the son you and your family are so desperate to have. Then, how would Skala see us? They would all hate us. We'd have to leave Skala and find somewhere else to live. Or I'll have to go back to the UK. I can't decide which. It's all too complicated," she finished, suddenly feeling drained.

Christoph started to say something but stopped as they both heard the church bells tolling and lots of noise coming from the village. "*Thee⁻ mou'*," he breathed. "Fire! There's a fire!"

"What d'you mean 'fire' Christoph? Tell me, what's wrong?"

"The mountain will be on fire, that's why the church bells are ringing. I need to go. Now. I am needed to help put out the fire. If it gets to the village, everyone will be in danger because we only have the sea. All men help to put out fires, so I need to go. Bye Lisa," he shouted as he started to run.

Lisa couldn't do anything except stare at Christoph's rapidly disappearing back. There'd be no answer now for some while to their predicament. Neither did she have an answer to the question of what he did for a job. He always seemed to have enough money, but she had no idea where it came from, and she'd intended to ask him about this.

Every man, young and old helped to fight the fire which was raging on the side of Mount Aenos. Plumes of black smoke and huge flames rose into the sky turning it dark red, as the fire continued its destructive way down the hillside to a forest just beyond the village. The men beat the flames with anything they could find. They all became black with choking smoke, and a village elder collapsed and was carried back to the village where he was looked after by the women.

Two fire engines arrived and began unravelling their hoses which sucked water from the village's vast water tanks. The water was then sprayed onto the forest trees to try to stop the fire spreading. It was a heavy, arduous, fiercely hot and dangerous job.

Further up out of the village near the burning forest, two village men shouted as the first old wooden village house caught light. Christoph was not far from the house, but even so the heat was intolerable. He could barely breathe, but he had to keep going. He knew an old man lived in the house although he'd not been seen for a while. He had to make sure the house was empty.

Covering his mouth and nose with a small scarf one of the women had given him as he'd run through the village, Christoph made his way to the house, and pushing open the old wooden front door called out, "Yassas! Yassas!" The smoke was choking, and he felt faint from lack of oxygen. Suddenly, there was a loud bang and a creak, and a wall fell in, part of it hitting Christoph on the head knocking him out as the floor collapsed beneath him.

No-one realised Christoph was missing. The fire raged for hours until finally it was brought under control by water scooped from the sea by slings suspended under many small aircraft. Skala had been saved. But where was Christoph?

Chapter Fourteen

Christoph came round in total darkness lying on his back. He couldn't move his head or his legs without excruciating pain. His confused mind scrabbled to make sense of his situation but couldn't. Then he remembered Lisa. He had to get to Lisa. But why? He tried again to move his legs, but they felt heavy and hurt. He tried to move his head and although that also hurt, he managed to lift it up and look around. To his right was a blurry chink of light of some kind. Daylight? Fire? No! Not fire!

Christoph suddenly remembered what he'd been doing. Yes, he'd been helping put out a mountain wildfire before it reached the village. He then realised he must be in a *kelari*, a cellar. The floor which should have been above him was now lying in dangerously broken wooden pieces all around him. With a huge effort he managed to turn over on to his front and use his arms to pull his body along the floor towards the light which he realised was coming from a narrow tunnel. His legs wouldn't work, and his head felt as if it didn't belong to him. His mouth was so dry he could hardly swallow so he tried to keep his mouth closed but it was difficult because the air was heavy with smoke and dust. He felt he couldn't breathe.

Determined to escape, he slowly managed to get to the narrow tunnel and began to pull himself along it. After a long time of slowly dragging himself along the tunnel floor littered with stones and small rocks, Christoph's arms and hands were torn and bleeding. Finally, he reached the end of the tunnel, pushed open a broken mesh grill, and gulped in the air which, although colder, wasn't much fresher. He realised it was dark outside, and the light he'd seen was moonlight. But not bright moonlight, it was grey and misty with smoke from the fire.

Where was he? He knew he'd tried to help put out the fire but not where he'd gone.

With his legs suddenly starting to tingle, he was able to wiggle his toes a little. He only had one shoe on, having lost the other one somewhere along the way. He pulled himself out of the tunnel and up into a kneeling position even though his right ankle felt as if it was being torn in two. He could just about make out the burnt remains of the wooden house he'd come from, and charred grass, scrub and trees. Then he realised he was on the edge of a steep mountain slope.

Christoph shook his head to try to clear his mind. He knew he might be concussed but had to make himself think. He remembered that in past times the cellar and tunnel would have been constructed not only to predominantly store wine and perishables, but also for safety in times of danger. He foggily realised he'd been lucky to have the wooden floor of the house collapse into the cellar, for without that and the tunnel, he'd have died, and no-one would know where he was. But where was he? Feeling confused, he crawled a few yards through the vegetation to investigate for clues. Then he passed out.

Skala was full of people noisily wandering around checking houses and people. Holiday guests were counted and then taken by Sam and other reps to the safety of the main square where they watched in awe as the flames spread, turning the sky dark red and orange. Small planes with buckets slung under them constantly flew down to scoop up the sea which was then deposited on to the flames. No-one had ever seen anything like it.

Lisa went to Rebecca's for a drink and some company but didn't stay long; she was too worried about Christoph to be sociable. She then went to see Daphne and Thomas and found them sitting outside the kiosk so they could watch what was going on.

"Are you okay, Lisa?" Asked Daphne kindly.

"No, not really, thank you Daphne. I'm worried about Christoph. He's gone with the men to help put out the fire."

With narrowed eyes, Daphne shrewdly observed Lisa. "Ah. I see," she said, then, taking a breath, quietly continued. "You love him, don't you?"

Taken aback, Lisa couldn't reply for a moment. "I er…er… I don't know. But I do care about him, I know that."

"More than care, my dear. Anyway, enough of that for now. Have you eaten? I'll get some food." Daphne said without waiting for Lisa to reply. She beckoned to Thomas to follow her, and they disappeared, returning fifteen minutes later with a small table, cutlery, water, a Greek salad and moussaka. "We were going to have this for our dinner, you must join us." There was no arguing with Daphne the feeder!

Lisa murmured her thanks and to be polite ate a little although she wasn't at all hungry. They sat in near silence as people wandered, shouted, cried, ran or just stood still to watch the inferno and the water planes dipping and diving as they dropped water scooped from the sea on to the flames. The tavernas gave out free drinks and food, everyone was welcome no matter who they were, villagers and holidaymakers alike.

"You must be getting cold in your pretty dress Lisa. I'll get you a coat, and you'll stay here tonight in the back bedroom where you were before," Daphne suddenly firmly announced.

"Oh, thank you," said a surprised Lisa. "That's really most kind, I'd like that. I don't want to go back to my apartment because it's too far away from here. Anyway, I wouldn't sleep."

People milled around, and not long after Daphne, Thomas and Lisa had settled down outside the kiosk to watch and wait. Sam walked past, glaring at Lisa with hatred, making her flinch, Lisa couldn't bear it and decided she'd have to leave Skala soon – but not until she knew Christoph was safe and well.

The hours ticked by with most adults, except the most senior residents, and some older children, staying up to watch and wait. Then, suddenly, at three o'clock in the morning, there was loud cheering at the top of the street, and the brave men of Skala slowly appeared out of the smoke. Women and men ran to hug and thank the exhausted, blackened men who couldn't speak because their mouths and throats were scorched by the heat.

Like many of the women, Lisa cried with relief as she ran from one man to another. She recognised most of them but was shocked to see some were barely teenagers. They were so brave, and apart from some burns and scrapes, thankfully no-one had been seriously hurt. But there was no sign of Christoph.

Chapter Fifteen

Lisa, Daphne and Thomas eventually went to bed, but Lisa only slept fitfully from exhaustion. She was up again at seven o'clock, made herself a coffee, splashed some water on her face and crept out of the house so as not to disturb her kind friends.

Making her way down the main street to her apartment, she saw Sue and Trevor going to the supermarket.

"Sue, have you seen Christoph?" She asked breathlessly. "When the men returned, I couldn't see him, and no-one could tell me anything. I know he went to help with the fire, but no-one seems to know exactly where he went. I'm so worried," she said as tears threatened.

"No, I don't know where he is either, Lisa," said Trevor looking at Sue as she shook her head. "I volunteered to help but the men told me it was their job to fight the fire. A matter of Greek male pride, I guess," he finished with a small smile. "Proud lot, the Greeks."

"Yes, I know. But I need to find Christoph. Anyway, thanks. I'll be in the shop once I've freshened up."

"No, you won't," scolded Sue. "You need to rest. Only the tavernas are open and I doubt if any holiday makers are even awake yet. And there won't be any travellers because of the fire. I heard another fire near

Argostoli also had to be put out which means no-one will be going anywhere for a couple of days."

Lisa thanked her employers and returned to her apartment where she showered, had a coffee, changed into a white t-shirt and black jeans, and then lay on her bed. She slept for a short while and then woke up thinking of Christoph.

Grabbing her tote bag, and with her heart racing with anxiety, Lisa ran from her apartment and back to the main street to try to find out where Christoph might be. She noticed the sun was periodically shaded by thick smoke from the cinders and charred vegetation, briefly turning the early day into unreal night.

She first went to ask Rebecca if she knew anything about Christoph, but she didn't although she assured Lisa that she'd ask Yannis when he woke up.

Lisa rushed from one taverna to another asking over and over if anyone had seen Christoph, but the answer was always 'no.' Then she saw the old fisherman who lived in the beach house walking up the steps from the beach. Would he know? She approached the man hesitantly. "Excuse me. Sir. Er, sorry, do you speak English?"

The old man surveyed Lisa with small, screwed up black eyes and sniffed. "Who's asking?"

"Oh, you do speak English. Sorry, my name's Lisa. I'm looking for someone and wondered if you could help me."

"Why?"

"Why? Oh, yes, why. He went to help put the fire, but no-one's seen him return or even knows where he went."

Impressed, the man grunted, "*Entaxei.*"

Lisa looked expectantly at the man, waiting for more information. He looked down and then up at Lisa, continuing in perfect English. "Yes, I saw him. He went with some of the village men up the Argostoli road. There are two old wooden houses up there. They may have gone together to check on the people living in them, but that's all I know."

Lisa's heart soared. Someone knew. "Oh, thank, thank you. Thank you so much," she breathed. She fleetingly considered shaking the man's hand but stopped herself when she noticed his dirty black nails. "I'll go there. *Efharisto poli. Yassas.*"

Lisa ran back to the main street where she considered what to do. She needed help. Thomas. Thomas would be the one. Even though he'd stayed up to watch and wait with her and Daphne, hopefully he'd not be too tired. She ran up the road, then approaching Thomas and Daphne's house, she stopped, took a breath and knocked on the old wooden door.

Thomas appeared almost immediately. "Lisa! Are you okay? Can I help you?" He asked kindly.

Without waiting for any formalities, Lisa told Thomas why she was there and asked him to help her. He immediately agreed and then went to tell Daphne who emerged wiping her hands on her white apron - as usual, she'd been cooking. "Take care you two. You're very special to me," she said softly. Then she disappeared, returning a few minutes later with two bottles of water and two packages. "Take this water. You'll need to drink. And eat. These are cheese pies. I've always got cheese pies," she smiled. "Now go. Go find Christoph. *Gifses.*"

Lisa and Thomas waved goodbye and set off up the main street. The air was still thick with smoke, so Lisa put the rolled-up kimono which was always in her tote bag over her mouth and nose; it was way too big, but it had to do. Thomas was wearing a red scarf round his neck which he removed and tied over his own mouth and nose.

Lisa and Thomas eventually came to the final big bend in the mountain road before it straightened out on its way to Argostoli. They could see the devastation the fire had caused. Everything was charred, and a few buildings just beyond the village were burnt to the ground. The fire had been perilously close to Skala village. The smoky air made them cough and their eyes water. Walking on, they saw a path leading off to the right, and the remains of what looked like a house. Was there another one beyond it?

Lisa had told Thomas that the beach fisherman said this is where Christoph may have gone with some of the village men to check out a couple of old houses and their occupants. Perhaps these were the houses?

"Well, we'll only find out if we go looking. Are you ready?" Said Thomas quietly. He thought Lisa was very brave. And she obviously had feelings for Christoph because if she hadn't, she wouldn't be doing such a risky thing.

"Yes, I'm ready. Let's go."

The two picked their way carefully between rocks of all sizes and charred vegetation, dodging blackened hanging tree branches as they went. Lisa had put her trainers on, and Thomas always wore boots whatever the weather, so their feet were well protected. They walked for about fifteen minutes until the remains of the first building appeared. There wasn't much left, just a few charred timbers. A wash tub and a falling down metal table stood forlornly amongst the rubble. They looked at each other and nodded, then carefully picked their way forward into the rubbish. There was nothing left except a mud floor.

Thomas's heart sank but he wouldn't, couldn't give up. "Okay. Let's see if there's another house."

Lisa nodded. Even if she'd wanted to talk, she couldn't because of the smoke and the emotion she was feeling; tears threatened whenever she visualised Christoph hurt somewhere and unable to get help. Or worse.

They walked together down the small, winding path littered with debris until they came across the burnt remains of another building perched on the side of the mountain. Smoke rose from the cinders and a couple of nearby trees, and the air was stifling.

Thomas turned to Lisa and told her he knew some of the old Skala houses had cellars. Some even have had a small tunnel for safety because Kefalonia had been invaded so many times, and some older people were still afraid of that. Maybe there was someone in the tunnel, possibly hurt or dead? He decided not to share this thought that with Lisa, she was distressed enough.

With a sinking heart, Lisa felt she couldn't look any more and turned away. "It's no good, Thomas. He's not here," she said miserably. "He must be lost somewhere. We need to go back to the village."

"No, we can't give up," Thomas said earnestly. "You stay here, and I'll look for a cellar," adding hopefully, "you never know. Anyway, I'll shout if I find anything."

Lisa nodded and sat on a large rock. She watched as Thomas poked around in the charred timbers - then disappeared out of view. Her heart stopped. God, what now? "Thomas. Are you okay?" she shouted. Then in a muffled voice, Thomas replied he was. All she could do now was wait.

Thomas trod carefully past part of a fallen stone wall. Unusual to have a stone wall in a wooden house but then the people who'd built these houses were always a bit different. They'd obviously used local materials, rock being one.

Then he saw a glint of dim light in the chasm where the floor had been. Ah, he thought, the *kellari*. It was a long way down so what would he do? Looking round, he saw some nearby rocks with an almost flat surface on one side. Would he be able to build some sort of rough steps with them?

"I'm okay Lisa, I've found a cellar so I'm going to take a look," he shouted. "Don't worry if I'm gone for a while, I will be back." He knew he'd have to take great care lifting and placing rocks to create steps because of his back.

Lisa shouted okay and moved to a different rock to wait for Thomas to return. *Bless you, Thomas, you're so brave and kind and I'm being such a wus,* she thought as she screwed up the remains of a sodden tissue in her hands. She so wanted to go with him to find Christoph but knew she couldn't.

Thomas threw down the first rock and then the next one which missed the first, landing on the cellar floor. So, he tried with another rock which also missed. He needed more rocks and looking round spotted four others just a few yards away. The next rock stayed in place on top of the first one, leaving a slim 'ledge' on one side. Then it was much easier to do the same with the next three. Finally, it was finished, and despite his bad back, he'd made a rough stone staircase even though there wasn't much ledge on each stone to step onto.

Feeling proud of his achievement, he carefully lowered himself down from the edge of the remains of the floor on to the first rock ledge, and then down the next four. After the last rock, he stepped with much relief onto the mud cellar floor which was littered with wood and other debris. Ahead was the dim light he'd seen. Oh, no! It was a narrow tunnel, would he fit in it? The only way to find out was to try. Squeezing himself into the narrow entrance he was pleased to see the tunnel widened out a little so he could crawl along the tunnel floor more easily. After what seemed an age, Thomas eventually reached the end, pushed past the broken mesh grill and crawled out onto the side of the mountain.

Stopping to take a breath and wiping his bloodied hands, elbows and knees with his scarf, he stood up and looked around. Visibility was poor, but he could see a rough, narrow mountain road going off to the left. It was the old Poros road which everyone used when the village was still situated on the side of the mountain. No cars in those days, only donkeys which knew the road well.

Peering through the occasionally thinning smoke, he thought he could make out some sort of shape in the vegetation at the side of the narrow mountain path and decided to investigate. He knew Lisa would be worriedly waiting, but he had to look - he'd never forgive himself if he didn't. It might be an injured animal, or a brave village man.

It might even be Christoph.

Chapter Sixteen

Sam had tried to come to terms with what she'd witnessed. Christoph had completely lost it when he'd heard Lisa's husband had hurt her. She'd stared in disbelief at the man she was marrying. No longer the suave Greek, he was beside himself, all control gone.

"What are you doing?" she demanded as Christoph made to rush out of her house. She pulled him back by his right arm. "Stop. You can't help her. And anyway, why would you want to, she's a nothing, just a holiday guest who thinks she can stay here and become a local. Like so many middle-aged women do when they come here, stupid cows," she spat. "But she'll soon be going home when she discovers the reality of living here isn't all roses round the door."

Christoph looked at Sam with wide eyes. "Stupid, eh? She's not stupid, she's one of the smartest women I've ever known," he said through gritted teeth.

"Oh, yeah? Well, of course you've known a few of them in your time haven't you, Christoph?" Sam said bitchily. *God,* she thought, *I'm losing him to that…that…older woman.*

Ignoring Sam, Christoph walked out, slamming the front door behind him. All he knew was that he had to get to the woman he really loved. But he'd have to go back to Sam and make it up with her because he was expected to marry her and have a son, just like his father and past generations of family men had done before.

After seeing Lisa, Christoph returned, but neither he nor Sam mentioned what had happened. They made a real effort to be civil to each other, and Sam went back to work.

Christoph went to The Bay for a coffee to try to clear his head. What a day! Then evening came, and Sam got home from work early so she and Christoph could have some time together, but Christoph told her he had to go out again to meet Michaelas about something, although he wouldn't be long. After eating a small amount of the meal Sam had made, he showered, changed his clothes and left at ten minutes past eight.

Sam anxiously twisted her shiny engagement ring round and round her finger. What if Christoph didn't want her after all? And if he did, could she forgive him for rushing off to see Lisa? Would she be able to move on? Would they *both* be able to move on?

She decided to check what Christoph was up to. Looking at her watch she knew Lisa would soon leave work so she might see her as well. Hurrying from her rented house in a small side road not far from the main square, she arrived at the bottom of the main street where she stood in the shadow of a palm tree to partially hide herself from view. She needed to be able to see the Accommodation Shop as well as the main street and square but didn't want to be seen in her uniform as that would easily identify her.

After five minutes, she saw Christoph in the main square near the big fountain. But why was he there? He was supposed to be meeting up with Michaelas, so what had happened? Then she realised he must have seen Michaelis quickly and was on his way home because he'd said he wouldn't be long. But wouldn't it be great if he and Lisa had seen each other and had had a row! Although highly unlikely, the idea lifted her spirits, and she found herself smiling. She now didn't care if she saw Lisa or not. But had she waited just five more minutes, she would have…

Sam felt there was still hope that everything would be okay between her and Christoph. She couldn't – wouldn't - lose her lovely fiancée to an older woman. And she couldn't lose the status of being married to a Greek man. Not many English women got to do that. Yes, the men would willingly have sex, it was all part of the 'holiday thing,' with the men making the most of the 'honey pot.' *Yuk*, she thought. Sadly, some females got pregnant but didn't return to claim their child's Greek paternity because they knew they'd risk losing that child, especially if it was a boy.

Sam knew that if she and Christoph had a boy child, she'd be revered big time, and any thoughts of Lisa would be banished from his mind. So, she'd make sure that happened. Very soon. No more Pill for her. She'd show that cow Lisa she couldn't have her man. She decided she'd turn on the charm as soon as Christoph got back, and to stay charming. Also, more importantly, to stay desirable to make sure she got pregnant very quickly – unless, thanks to a - deliberate? - 'slip-up' in Athens, she wasn't already! If that had happened, Christoph would obviously ask 'how?' So, she'd tell him she didn't know, suggesting maybe it was when she'd recently had a tummy upset causing the pill not to work. *Good idea*, she thought happily. At least then she'd not have to carry out the vague idea she had which would ensure Lisa had a car 'accident.' After all, it wasn't unknown for people unused to driving on the twisting, steep and often scary mountain roads, to have an accident. Even though it would be very tragic, it would look perfectly 'normal.' And it would be the end of Lisa.

She suddenly realised she needed to get back to the house before Christoph did. Then this evening she'd start the 'staying together' process by wearing her new, flimsy, pale cream underwear which she knew enhanced her slim, tanned body to perfection. How exciting!

Running all the way, Sam arrived home in double-quick time. Opening the front door, she called out, "Christoph?" Silence. Good. She bounded upstairs to the bedroom where she tore off her uniform and threw it in the wardrobe. Then she put on her new underwear: sexy, oh yes, very sexy, she could hardly wait. Sitting in front of her dressing table, she fussed with her long, dark hair, and made sure her make-up was perfect. Not long now, she breathed.

Half an hour passed but still no Christoph. God, where was that man? He could be so bloody annoying! Feeling cross, with all desire gone, she put on her white silk wrap and went downstairs. It was beginning to get dark, and she could hear Skala getting ready for the evening. As she poured herself a glass of wine, she thought she could hear church bells. Church bells? That was unusual at this time of the evening, but then maybe it was a practice session.

The church bells continued, and Sam could also hear screaming and shouting outside. What the hell was going on? After quickly changing back into her uniform in case she was needed by her holiday guests, she rushed out into the main street to find absolute chaos with people running all over the place, some shouting "Fire, fire!" *Oh, no,* she thought worriedly. She knew there'd been wildfires near Skala before so this could be one now. The island was famous for its forests and fires spread quickly when the forest trees and ground were tinder dry like they were now.

As Sam hurried past the bakery, she bumped into Rebecca. "Oh, Becca, what's going on? Is it a fire? And have you seen Christoph at all?"

"Yes, it's a fire and all the village men including Yannis have gone to try to put it out," said Rebecca. She hated being called Becca. "And no, I've not seen Christoph," she added crisply. "Sorry, but I've got to dash as I'm needed in the bar. Bye."

Completely oblivious to Christoph's life-threatening situation, Sam walked up the main street. So many people! She passed the supermarket and then saw Lisa sitting outside the kiosk with Daphne and Thomas. Trust that bloody woman to be in the thick of it! As she walked past, she stared hatefully at Lisa and saw her flinch. Good, she's got the message, she thought with bitchy satisfaction. Then she realised that because there was a fire, she needed to make sure her holiday guests had all made it to the safety of the muster point in the main square. Right now, her guests were her priority.

But where was Christoph? She wondered, starting to feel worried. Clutching her clip board with its list of her guests and their accommodation, she hurried to the square. No time to ask around any further about Christoph, she'd have to continue making sure her guests were safe. But then maybe he'd just appear, and everything would be alright. Yes, that's what he'd do, she consoled herself. It'd be okay.

Rubbing his back, Thomas limped to the vegetation where he thought he'd seen a shape of some sort. He couldn't be long because Lisa would be so worried. Then it struck him that to get back to her, he'd have to return through the tunnel and haul himself up off the last of the crude stone steps onto the edge of the floor of the burnt-out house.

It wouldn't be easy for a man of his advancing years, and with a bad back. Thomas wasn't sure how old he was because his parents were very vague about his actual birthday, and they'd never celebrated it. He thought he was about eighty-ish as his mother had told him he'd arrived at the start of World War One. Then when he met Daphne, she'd decided his birthday should be on July 28th and she'd make a cake! Because of Thomas's parents' vagueness, Daphne always secretly wondered if his father wasn't his birth father; she knew it happened and was usually hushed up so never spoken about. Some people only discovered their true parentage when they were older, most often when they needed their birth certificate for something, although back when Thomas was born many children weren't even registered, especially in remote areas of Greece where many people weren't very well educated. Thomas came from farming stock, his parents had lived and worked in a mountain village and had received very little formal education, just like their parents before them. Their priorities had been to look after their animals and land, to survive, not to trek into a town to register a birth. Or even a death.

After his parents died, Thomas moved to what was then the mountain village of Skala. Then after the earthquake he and Daphne moved to the 'new' Skala village by the sea; they felt very lucky to have survived the earthquake when so many they'd known hadn't. Here, Daphne cooked and cleaned for one of the first hotels, and Thomas had his own small goat and sheep farm, selling the feta cheese to Skala's grocery shop which later became Skala's first supermarket. The feta cheese was kept in a large round tub on the supermarket's counter, and villagers would indicate how much they wanted. He also sold his goat and lamb meat, rabbits and chickens to the village butcher. He made a very good living and was well respected in Skala.

Daphne had been born in Argostoli in nineteen twenty-seven, so was a mere sixty-five. Her parents lived in a house near the lagoon, and her father had been the port manager looking after the fishermen and their boats, and any other boats which arrived in the port. Her mother had been a cook in one of the fishing Captain's houses in Argostoli, so

Daphne grew up cooking. Her birthday was September 3rd and she always made sure Thomas remembered it!

Thomas and Daphne had met one day when Thomas came to the harbour to buy some squid, and Daphne was sitting by the lagoon watching the sea and the boats. He was immediately taken by her dark-haired beauty and boldly sat beside her to ask if she was having a nice day. Daphne was then twenty-five and thought Thomas was very handsome with his elegant moustache and sparkling dark brown eyes! They married a year later in Argostoli's Greek Orthodox church, Agios Eleftheris.

Thomas walked slowly through the burnt scrub, carefully picking his way between rocks and debris. Then, peering into the gloom, he realised that the shape he'd seen was a man lying on his front. Taking a deep breath, he bent down and touched the man's arm. *"Eisai kala?"* he asked quietly. The man didn't respond, so Thomas knelt and rolled the man over very carefully. It was Christoph.

"Christoph! Christoph! Please wake up!" He cried as he gently shook Christoph's arm. Christoph moaned. Thomas tried again. "Christoph, you must wake up my friend. I need to get you to safety and have someone look at you. Please wake up."

Christoph moaned again and then opened his eyes slightly. "Thank god!" Breathed Thomas with relief. "Can you talk, Christoph?" No answer.

Thomas sat back on his heels. What could he do? How could he drag Christoph when he's so obviously hurt, and moving him could cause even more damage? But Thomas knew that he'd need to get help soon or Christoph might not survive. Looking around he thought that being on a steep slope might be useful if he could only get Christoph to wake up more. Thinking carefully, he realised that the only way to help

Christoph would be to drag him as far as possible, even though he didn't want to do that and there was a real danger of injuring Christoph further. He knew it would take every ounce of his strength and probably hurt his back, and maybe also hurt Christoph's, but he really had no choice.

Christoph murmured something and Thomas bent down to hear him. "Tell me again, Christoph," he said into his ear. "I'm listening."

With a huge effort and through burnt, cracked lips Christoph whispered. "Help me, Thomas. Please."

"I will," promised Thomas. "I will. But first I've got to tell Lisa I've found you and ask her to get help. I'll need to leave you for a short while, but I'll be back, I promise. Then I'll get you away from danger and as near to the main road and help as I can." He stopped, then went on, "Christoph, listen carefully - if you can hear and understand what I've said, then blink your eyes or raise your right hand." Thomas waited patiently until eventually Christoph raised his right hand just enough for Thomas to see.

"Right. I'm on my way. I promise I'll be back as soon as I can. Bye for now my friend." Returning to the tunnel, Thomas crawled as fast as he could, praying he'd have enough energy to call out to Lisa and then make the journey back again to help Christoph. After reaching the end of the tunnel he swallowed hard and took a breath. "Lisa! Lisa, can you hear me?" He shouted. He waited for several moments but there was silence. Then Lisa suddenly appeared at the edge of the collapsed floor. "Thomas, where have you been?" She cried. "I've been so worried."

"Don't worry, Lisa. I've found Christoph but he's badly injured so you must hurry back to the village and get help. He's on the side of the mountain just beyond this house." Then without waiting for Lisa to reply, continued. "Go quickly now. Time is short. Go my child and may God be with you. I must go back to Christoph now. I will try to drag him away from danger and as near to the road as I can. I will wait there for help." Then he disappeared back into the tunnel.

Lisa started to shake and cry but then gathered herself and began to tread carefully amongst the burnt scrub and rocks along the narrow, dark, partly hidden path leading to the main road. After what felt like ages, she eventually reached the road and began to run to the village. It was dark and she couldn't see very much, but the blurry moon gave enough light to enable her to keep to the road she now knew so well. Running like the wind, she soon came to the top of the hill down to Skala's main street. With shaking legs, she stopped and bent down with her hands on her knees to get her breath back. Then she ran as fast as she could into the village to tell Daphne what had happened.

Knocking hard on the front door, she shouted, "Daphne! Daphne!" Daphne quickly opened the door to find a breathless Lisa with tears streaming down her dirty face.

"Thomas has found Christoph! But he's badly injured so we must urgently get help," Lisa gasped. "Thomas said he's on the side of the mountain near those old houses on a partly hidden path. He's going to try to drag Christoph as far as he can towards the main road. It won't be easy for the rescuers to find them, so they'll need to look very carefully." Lisa finished, suddenly feeling utterly drained.

"*Entaxei*," breathed Daphne, relieved that both men were still alive. After ushering Lisa indoors and ordering her to sit down, she immediately rang Michaelis to tell him what had happened and asked him to tell Yannis and the other men that they urgently needed to rescue Thomas and Christoph. She thought Michaelis's truck would be very helpful. Everyone would be needed to rescue the men.

Thomas reached Christoph as quickly as his body and the small, smoke-filled tunnel would allow. It seemed endless and even worse than before, and he had to stop a couple of times to ease his breathing.

He eventually reached the open iron grill and crawled, gasping for air, out into the night. After taking a moment to recover, he went to find Christoph and pulled him up into a semi-seating position. Taking off his dirty shirt, he wrapped it as best he could round Christoph's lower spine to provide a bit of cushioning while he was being dragged.

Christoph moaned but Thomas ignored him. After crossing himself three times, he very slowly began to drag Christoph, centimetre by centimetre, metre by metre, onto a small path through the burnt scrub and away from fire danger, stopping every metre or so to rest his back and chest, and to ease Christoph's pain a little. As he dragged Christoph, he unashamedly cried for his friend and for himself, his tears forming rivulets down his blackened face.

The rocky path was narrow and partly hidden and he felt the journey would take forever, but he couldn't give up. He would never give up. They were going home to Skala.

Chapter Seventeen

The news about Christoph and Thomas spread quickly through the village. Those men who weren't too exhausted from fighting the fire offered to help and soon there was a group of eleven, including the doctor with his medical bag and his nurse. Michaelis took his truck, and other vehicles were also acquired. Ropes, blankets and water were gathered up, and with Michaelis and Yannis leading the way in the truck, the group quickly set off for the Argostoli road.

They soon saw the devastation the fire had caused and how close it had come to the village. Driving up the hill out of the village and then slowly along the main road with the vehicles' headlights on, every man also shone a torch from side to side for any sign of Thomas and Christoph; no-one knew how far Thomas might have been able to drag Christoph, nor if he and Thomas would be okay.

When someone thought they saw something, they stopped and got out of their vehicles to look but quickly moved on when they found nothing. No-one spoke; they all knew there was every chance that Christoph might not have survived, and they also didn't know if Thomas had been injured. These were things that no-one wanted to think, let alone speak of.

Coming to a halt, the men agreed to split into two groups to search the scrub on foot. Michaelis and Yannis took Georgios, the doctor and his nurse and another man, Spyros, to search the scrub on the right-hand side of the road. The remaining five took the left-hand side.

Michaelis rubbed his eyes; the strain was severe on everyone. He and Yannis strode ahead of the others but kept within shouting distance. Eventually, they came across the first of the burnt-out old houses and all five approached with care, very wary of the danger that could be lurking. Nothing. Michaelis felt the urge to walk beyond the house, and, using binoculars, spotted the remains of the second burnt house in the distance.

"Yannis," he called. "There's another house. Let's all go to look."

"Okay," shouted back Yannis. Then turning to the others, he motioned for them to follow.

Approaching with great care, the men and the doctor and his nurse searched the burnt house but found nothing except an empty shell where once there had been walls and a floor. They gathered to discuss what to do next.

"Let's keep together and use the binoculars to see if we can find anything. Anything at all," Yannis said desperately. "We can't give up. Come, follow Michaelis and me."

Michaelis used his binoculars to scan the terrain but to no avail. The doctor thought they were wasting their time and that they should return to the village, but Yannis said no and shouted to the other group to follow his group. Half an hour passed during which time they realised they were nowhere near the main Argostoli road. Then suddenly, Michaelis thought he saw something in the vegetation a little way ahead. The men formed a tight group as they picked their way through the rocks and debris and along a very remote, narrow goats' path which only the animals and their shepherds used.

"Look!" cried Yannis, pointing ahead to a shape by a large bush which had escaped being burnt. "There's something there! Maybe it's an animal. Or a man. Let's go and find out. Follow me."

Within a few minutes the group found the shape. They stopped and silently stared. For there, with Christoph's head gently cradled in his hands, was Thomas lying on his right side with his eyes closed. It was obvious to everyone that he'd lost his way, ending up on the side of the mountain a long way from the Argostoli road. It was a miracle that he and Christoph had been found, for if they hadn't been they wouldn't have survived. That is, if they were alive now.

The doctor and his nurse quickly checked the two men's pulses and heartbeats. Placing his stethoscope back round his neck, the doctor proclaimed them both unconscious, Christoph's pulse and heartbeat were very faint, his right ankle was probably broken, and he might have head and spine injuries. He said he was in a critical state. Thomas's pulse and heartbeat were rapid, and his breathing wasn't good. Both men needed urgent hospital treatment.

The two groups and the doctor decided that the village was nearer than the hospital, and anyway to transport Christoph to hospital without an ambulance could be fatal. Even if someone got to the village to call ambulances for help, the crews could waste precious time getting to them through the rough terrain, so they decided to transport the two injured men back to Skala where they'd call for two ambulances.

The rescuers rapidly made two rough beds out of blankets in the back of Michaelis's open truck, keeping two back to carry Christoph and Thomas in. The doctor and nurse would stay in the back with the two men throughout the journey.

Yannis, Michaelis, Georgios and Spyros very gently removed Christoph's head from Thomas's hands and then slowly lifted Christoph onto a blanket, taking a corner each to carry him to the truck.

Taking great care as they trod slowly over burnt scrub, small rocks and stones, they eventually reached the truck where the doctor and nurse were waiting. "Careful! Careful!" The doctor said firmly. "This man could have spine and head injuries so we must take great care not to jar him."

After gently easing Christoph onto the makeshift bed, the men returned to help Thomas. The doctor quickly examined Christoph and found that thankfully he was no worse than before.

Next came Thomas. As with Christoph, every move the men made was considered and gentle. It was a long way in the semi-dark but eventually he, too, was lifted onto a makeshift bed in the back of the truck and re-examined by the doctor. Both men were then covered with blankets.

The search teams returned to their respective vehicles and set off to Skala as fast as they could without jarring Christoph and Thomas. As they approached the top of Skala's main road, they beeped their horns to announce their arrival. Villagers ran out, and when they saw Christoph and Thomas, many cried with both relief and sadness. Yannis shouted to them to get more blankets for the injured men and yelled to Daphne to phone for two urgent ambulances. Daphne nodded and rushed indoors to make the call.

Having driven at mega-speed, the ambulances arrived within twenty minutes. The crews quickly jumped out, and after noting the men's names and possible injuries, put them on drips before gently lifting them onto spine boards and into their vehicles. Then they drove off to the hospital at speed. Time was of the essence. Would Christoph and Thomas survive?

Daphne and Lisa were both deeply worried about Christoph and Thomas, and Yannis said he'd take them to the hospital after he'd seen

Rebecca. Lisa cleaned herself up as best she could and then waited with Daphne for Yannis to return. Although, like Daphne, she was desperately tired, she was anxious to know how both Christoph and Thomas were. Yannis arrived with his car and took the two women to Argostoli hospital where, after explaining why they were there, they were shown into a side room near the emergency area. After a few minutes a tall, thin, young doctor in a white coat and a stethoscope round his neck, appeared.

"I am Doctor Akesos," announced the doctor in Greek. "Are you relatives of Kirios Christoph Papadakis and Kirios Thomas Samaras?" He asked, looking from one woman to the other.

"I am Kiria Samaras," replied Daphne anxiously. "Is he awake? And can you please speak in English?"

The doctor didn't reply but looked at Lisa and asked her in English, "And you are?"

"I'm Lisa Barat, a friend of Kirios Christoph Papadakis." Lisa replied nervously, adding, "his parents don't yet know he has come to hospital." She stopped, looking hopefully at the doctor. "Is that okay?"

The doctor didn't respond for a few moments. "Hmmm. Usually, we only allow relatives to have details of a patient." He paused, then added. "But, because Kirios Papadakis is so unwell, we will make an exception. Wait here." The doctor then disappeared before either woman could ask him anything else.

After a few minutes a nurse in a white, dark-belted uniform arrived. "Come with me," she said to Lisa and Daphne. "But you must not talk. And you must remember that both men are unconscious."

Lisa and Daphne followed the nurse down a short corridor. Stopping in front of double doors, she beckoned to the two women to follow her, then pushed the doors open into a stark white, brightly lit room.

Immediately inside the ward were dark blue fabric screens on wheels which the nurse pushed slightly to one side to reveal four occupied beds, each with various beeping machines beside them. "Those two there are your people," said the nurse pointing to the two beds on the right-hand side. "The first one is Kirios Papadakis, the next is Kirios Samaras."

Both Lisa and Daphne gasped when they saw Christoph and Thomas lying very still with closed eyes and oxygen masks partly covering their faces. They were also attached to drips and blood pressure machines. The nurse cleared her throat and quietly said. "This is our Intensive Care Ward. Kirios Papadakis will be going to theatre soon because he needs an urgent operation on his right ankle. He also has a wound on his head which requires investigation under anaesthetic. He is in a very poor state, so he is being monitored very carefully. Kirios Samaras is also being closely monitored because his breathing is not good although he does seem to be gradually waking up. He doesn't need surgery, but he may have a head injury, so we are keeping a careful eye on him, too."

Lisa felt the room sway. Putting an arm round Lisa's shoulder, the nurse asked her if she'd like some water. Lisa gulped. "Yes please. It's just a shock to see them," she whispered. "They both look so, so…*ill.*"

"Yes, well, they are," replied the nurse in a low, brisk tone, whilst wondering what on earth this woman expected the two men to look like. "And might I say they're both lucky to be alive, especially Kirios Papadakis who has many cuts and burns to his body, face and hands." She then looked at Daphne who was very quiet, and kindly whispered. "Are you alright Kiria Samaras? Can I get you anything?"

Daphne dragged her eyes away from her beloved Thomas and took a breath. "No. Thank you," she whispered in return.

Pointing, the nurse said, "There's a chair by each of their beds, and you can stay until Kirios Papadakis goes to theatre but then you must both leave." Then turning to Lisa, she continued, "The doctor will contact you when Kirios Papadakis is back in the ward after surgery. So, can I have your telephone number please?" Just then the doctor quietly returned.

Lisa duly gave her number to the nurse who wrote it down in Christoph's medical notes. "And he lives in Skala? Is that correct?" asked the nurse as she continued to write in Christoph's notes.

"Yes," confirmed Lisa. Then she suddenly realised she hadn't told Sam where Christoph was. "Er, he does have a fiancée, but I don't have her number. Anyway, she'll be the one to contact, not me. Er, sorry," she stuttered, then added. "She's a holiday rep and may be with her holiday guests. I'll tell her where Kirios Papadakis is when I get back."

The nurse stopped writing, and with pen poised looked curiously at Lisa. Also intrigued, the doctor stared at Lisa with slightly raised eyebrows. Now here was a potentially tricky situation, he mused. This woman clearly cares for the younger man, but he's engaged to be married to someone else! Perhaps it's a menage a trois. Human beings, especially his own countrymen and women, never failed to surprise him!

Putting that thought from his mind, and coughing politely to cover a wry smile, the doctor quietly asked. "Lisa, are you able to give us the name of the woman he's engaged to?"

"Er, yes, It's Sam. Samantha. But I can't remember her last name. Sorry," Lisa replied as she worriedly bit her bottom lip. Jeez, why hadn't she thought to tell Sam about Christoph before he went to hospital? *She already hates me, and this will only make matters worse because she'll think I deliberately didn't tell her just to spite her.* Could things get any worse?

Chapter Eighteen

Despite having sustained a complex ankle facture, Christoph's operation went well, and his deep head wound was cleaned and stitched. His burns were treated by a specialist, and the cuts to his arms, hands and face were also cleaned and dressed. Two days later, he slowly began to wake up but was kept on oxygen. Once awake, he couldn't at first remember anything that had had happened, but then very slowly he began to put the pieces together.

Thomas had woken up the day before Christoph. His burns and cuts were also cleaned and dressed, but because his breathing was still very laboured, he was also kept on oxygen. Christoph improved enough for both men to be moved to a general ward and finally allowed visitors. Daphne couldn't wait to visit Thomas and almost ran down the ward to see him. Then, with their arms tightly around each other, they both sobbed with relief that Thomas had survived, and they were together again.

Lisa had asked Rebecca to tell Sam what had happened to Christoph because she couldn't face doing it herself. Sam was firstly very angry that Lisa knew about Christoph before she did and hadn't told her, and then very frightened for Christoph. And herself. As soon as she knew, she telephoned the hospital to explain who she was and to

124

ask for visiting times and regular updates on Christoph's progress. Then she waited impatiently for the day when she was allowed to see him. Finally, that day arrived.

Walking down the long, stark ward to where a nurse had told her Christoph's bed was, Sam felt nervous and slightly sick. So many ill men! What would Christoph look like? Would he also look ill? Would she be able to cope? She wasn't good with illness at the best of times, not even when it was herself. And if a holiday guest ever got ill, she couldn't wait to 'offload' them onto the local medic!

When she saw Christoph mid-way down the ward on the left-hand side, her heart began to pound with anxiety. He was propped up on several white pillows and had a cage over his legs under the bedding. His eyes were closed, and his usually handsome face was thin, drawn and still darkened by fire smoke, his lips still blackened and cracked. He had a long dressing on the left side of his face and a bandage round his head, covering his usually lustrous hair.

Christoph's heavily bandaged arms and hands lay unmoving on the white sheet neatly folded over the top of a pale green bed cover, and what she assumed was a blood pressure machine stood sentry-like beside the bed as if waiting for action.

Feeling very sick, she swallowed as she reached Christoph's bed. Christoph. The man she loved and was going to marry. But this wasn't her handsome man, this was someone else. "Christoph?" She murmured. "It's Sam." Watching him carefully, she waited for him to respond. Nothing. "Christoph, it's Sam. Please open your eyes," she said in a slightly louder voice. Her slim, black skirt and pretty, pink blouse suddenly felt too tight, and she felt she couldn't breathe. With her left hand, she nervously smoothed her already smooth dark, tightly pony-tailed hair and cleared her throat.

Christoph's lips moved but no sound came out. Pulling up the hard hospital chair to sit beside him, Sam thought it was all totally unbearable. She needed to go.

She sat for ages closely watching Christoph for any sign of speech, then just as she stood up to leave, Christoph croaked, "Sam. Sam. Where's Lisa, Sam?"

Sam froze. Lisa?! What the fuck did he want Lisa for? Sitting back down with a bump she said, "She's not here Christoph. It's only me." Adding bitterly, "Sorry to disappoint."

Christoph opened his eyes to form narrow slits just wide enough to be able to see Sam. "You must thank Thomas and Lisa for saving me," he croaked before closing his eyes again and taking a crackly gasp of breath.

Sam sighed. Well, she thought, obviously she'd thank Thomas, but she most certainly wouldn't thank that middle-aged bitch Lisa. "'Yes, of course I will darling," she lied. "I'll leave you to sleep now but I'll come back soon." She bent to quickly kiss his dark cheek which felt dry and alien. "Bye for now. Love you." Hoisting the gold-chained, black imitation Lois Vuitton bag which she'd been nervously clutching to her body, back on to her right shoulder, she then walked quickly out of the ward without even saying hello to Thomas who was in the very next bed and had seen and heard everything.

Over the following weeks, life in Skala returned to normal for everyone. Lisa frequently wondered how Christoph was getting on, but because she couldn't visit him had to rely on Daphne for updates of his progress although she only gave Lisa minimal information. It was late autumn and there were very few customers, so Sue closed the Accommodation shop and offered Lisa a temporary position in the Argostoli jewellery shop which she and Trevor also owned. Lisa told

Sue it could only be until Christmas because she planned to go back to the UK to see her daughters then. Lisa knew this would mean she'd have to make another huge decision: to return to Skala in the New Year or to stay in the UK.

After three weeks, Michaelis brought Thomas home in his comfortable car to a hero's welcome. Always a quiet man, Thomas found all the balloons, bunting and cheering rather overwhelming but was deeply moved by everyone's love and gratitude. The traumatic rescue had taken its toll, and he was much frailer and thinner and didn't sleep or eat well. His chest was a bit better, but his breathing still wasn't good, and his back was often stiff and painful.

After five weeks, and with a plaster cast still on his foot, Christoph came home in Yannis' car, stopping first at the church to give thanks for his survival. Wanting to avoid all the villagers Yannis had told him were waiting in the main square to welcome him home, he asked Yannis to take him straight home to his large house tucked away out of sight amidst an olive grove on his land at the edge of the village. Despite his appearance and demeanour, Christoph wasn't a particularly sociable man, and it was rare to receive an invitation to visit him at his home - it was very much his private space.

Sam had visited Christoph twice a week, choosing days when his parents and friends didn't go. She'd been thankful his mother, Thalia, had done his washing and got him anything he'd needed. Each time she'd visited, she'd dressed smartly, usually in black because she didn't want her nicer clothes 'contaminated' by being in a hospital. Much as she tried, she couldn't feel thrilled about Christoph going home; at some point they'd have to talk about their proposed wedding which, to the annoyance of Thalia, had been indefinitely put on hold.

Sam had told Christoph she wouldn't be there when he arrived home from hospital because she had to attend a *Sunnyside Holidays* conference in Athens. In truth, this was an avoidance tactic. Christoph had changed from being a handsome, upright, strong and robust lover into a thin, scarred and less attractive man that she felt she no longer knew or fancied. Angrily twiddling her diamond engagement ring, she asked herself two things: Did she still want to marry Christoph? If not, what was she going to do? What a mess her life was now.

Lisa enjoyed working in the Argostoli jewellery shop which was uninspiringly named *The Treasure Chest*. To dampen the longing to see Christoph, she started work early and always left late. Even if it was dark when she finished work, she'd go to the harbour before driving Bessie back to Skala just to spin out the time.

It was early December and Christmas was approaching fast. The shop became very busy with gift-seekers of all ages, mostly Greeks, but occasionally someone from another country. Lisa became very adept at finding just the right gift, and her reputation as a first-class salesperson quickly spread throughout Argostoli, and beyond. Sue and Trevor were delighted and hoped Lisa would decide to return quickly from the UK so she could continue to boost their jewellery business.

The usual Christmas decorations went up all around the town, and a huge Christmas tree which had been felled in the nearby forest was erected in the main square and lit with numerous fairy lights. The whole town looked totally magical, making Lisa's heart lift for the first time in several months. Things were beginning to improve at last.

Then, one Thursday just as she was about to close the shop for lunch, the shop door clicked open. Looking up from the tray of rings she was tidying, she couldn't believe her eyes. Standing in front of her and swathed in a voluminous black winter coat was Sam.

Lisa's heart leapt with fear. "Sam! What are you doing here?" She managed to blurt.

Sam observed the woman who'd caused her so much aggravation. She looked…well, she mused, she looked *younger*. How dare she look so good at her age?!

Ignoring Lisa's question, Sam dipped into her large black bag and took out a small red box which she thumped down on the counter. "I'd like this appraised please," she said briskly.

Lisa stared. It couldn't be! Stunned, she managed to reply, "Erm, okay, although I'll have to ask the jeweller to do that. But do you mind if I look at it first?"

"No. Not at all. Help yourself."

Opening the little red box, Lisa immediately recognised the engagement ring Christoph had bought for Sam in Athens. Without any words it literally spoke volumes.

With downcast eyes, neither woman uttered a word until Sam suddenly looked up and hissed. "Happy now bitch? He's all yours. And fucking good luck to you, he's a fucking useless wreck." And with that Sam slammed a piece of paper down. "This is my number. Ring me when you've got the fucking price," she swore angrily, her unbuttoned coat falling wide open as she turned. Then she turned back again and stared at Lisa with challenging, cold, hard eyes. Lisa couldn't help noticing she was pregnant, which was Sam's intention. Without another word, Sam then left. She didn't want anything to do with anyone from Skala.

Pregnant. Sam was pregnant but clearly no longer with Christoph. Did he know? Had Sam told him? If she hadn't, what would happen to the baby? How far along was she? Lisa guessed Sam might be about five or so months. Which meant the baby might be born around April or May next year.

A million questions filled Lisa's mind. But this was none of her business, it was between Sam and Christoph and nothing to do with her. She quickly locked the shop, rushed to where Bessie was parked and drove to her favourite taverna overlooking the lagoon where, on the other side of the water, the island's mountain soared majestically up into the sky. She needed to escape. Drinking a much-needed coffee she decided she'd go back to the UK tomorrow. To hell with Skala, she'd had enough.

When she got back to her apartment, she immediately booked herself on the next day's first domestic flight to Athens where she'd then get the nine o'clock morning Olympic Airways flight to Heathrow. She'd leave Bessie at Kefalonia airport, and then, no matter what it cost, take a taxi from Heathrow back to Sussex.

Then she rang Sue, but it went through to answer phone, so she left a message saying she was very sorry to be leaving so suddenly. She also thanked Sue for kindly helping her and asked if she'd say thanks to Daphne and Thomas as well for all their loving help and care. By then she was sobbing so hard she couldn't speak and put the phone down.

Lisa threw as much as she could into her one suitcase. No time to even think about taking any more, she just had to leave with what she could pack. Quickly checking her passport and money she was then done.

She spent a restless night, eventually getting up at five o'clock for a quick coffee before showering, and dressing in jeans, jumper and dark blue padded jacket. She looked round the apartment she'd called home for so many months. What a lot had happened. And how she'd miss this magical island and the lovely people of Skala. This was her spiritual home and always would be, for this was where she could be her true self, not a wife, mother, project manager or anything else. Just her, Lisa Barat. But it seemed at a cost.

Pulling the apartment door closed behind her, Lisa felt more tears slip down her face. She didn't want to leave, but she couldn't take any more stress and trauma and needed time to heal. Maybe one day she'd return, who knew, and with that thought she climbed into Bessie and drove off up the hill and out of Skala.

A month later, reclusive Sam suffered a distressing late miscarriage resulting in a stillbirth. The baby was a perfect, tiny, little boy, the son Christoph had always been told he should have. Sam named their son Jason. After registering the stillbirth with the authorities and making sure it was just her name on the birth certificate, she leased a tiny burial plot and paid undertakers to make a small marble headstone reading: 'Baby Jason. December 29 1992 - December 29 1992'. She also arranged a date and time for her baby to be taken in a tiny white coffin from Argostoli hospital to the town's newest cemetery overlooking the Ionian Sea. She didn't want any service for her baby, or to attend his funeral because she was still unwell after his birth.

Sam stayed for a few weeks with a *Sunnyside Holidays* rep who owned a flat in Argostoli, claiming she'd had a 'big operation' and needed to rest. Then she resigned from her job and returned to the UK to recuperate on her Uncle's Teddy and Auntie Gwen's farm in Hampshire where she was lovingly looked after. She'd always been close to Teddy and her Mum's sister Gwen, and their two children, Cathleen and Roland. Sam told Teddy and Gwen about Jason, but she didn't tell her parents, claiming instead that she'd gone to Teddy and Gwen's farm to recover from a major operation.

During the following months, Sam slowly came to terms with the tragic loss of her baby, and of Christoph. She became less angry, with no more unpleasant thoughts about Lisa, and gradually returned to being a warm and friendly young woman working hard on the farm looking after the sheep and chickens. She was once again healthy and happy, and it showed in the glow in her cheeks and smiley demeanour.

Christoph never knew he'd fathered a son. After being discharged from hospital, he spent the next few months in his wealthy Uncle Tony's Athenian hotel recovering back to full health except for scarring on his face, body, legs, arms and hands. Once again, he stood proudly upright and strong - but he was also different. Thinner, greying at his temples, and no longer arrogant, he became caring and careful, always keen to help others. And always aware that he was very lucky to be alive.

In March 1993 brave Thomas passed away and was buried with full ceremony in Skala's cemetery. His headstone memorial included the words 'Hero of Skala.' The whole village attended his funeral. Daphne and Christoph were beside themselves with grief. Christoph would never forget that he owed his very life to dear Thomas, and poor Daphne felt totally lost. But she found some solace in village friends, in cooking and making lots of cheese pies.

Then in late March, the old fisherman was found dead in his shack on the beach and was buried in unmarked ground on the edge of Skala cemetery because no-one knew his name.

In April, Skala's wealthiest elders gathered to debate the future of their village. They agreed Skala was now a popular place for tourists to visit, and there was no question that tourism made money. So, they also agreed to build three more hotels, plus several new apartment blocks, and to engage another big tour operator to take up the extra rooms.

Eventually, Daphne worked as chief cook in the biggest new hotel, Hotel Anabella, which was located by the sea. Three tavernas upgraded their premises, but The Bay and The Grapevine were determined to remain traditional.

Lisa deliberately didn't keep in contact with anyone in Skala so didn't know about the changes. The only person she did keep in contact with was her friend Janey who lived in the village of Ratzakli. Lisa had met her when she'd gone to the tiny village taverna where Janey worked. Janey had left the UK three years before; she'd holidayed in Ratzakli, loved it and never went home. She earned money working in bars and restaurants, and cleaning holiday properties. But Janey wasn't very forthcoming about anything much because she didn't want to be seen as a gossip. People had gossiped about her, usually inaccurately, so she was very cautious.

Suddenly, everything in and around Skala was changing. But would it be for the better?

Part Two

Chapter Nineteen

England and Kefalonia 1993-2001

Christmas 1992 was full of joy for Lisa. She loved being back in the UK with her daughters who'd taken her to a plush hotel in the Sussex countryside which they'd booked as a surprise Christmas present for her. The four women stayed at the hotel from Christmas Eve until the day after Boxing Day, enjoying the Christmas ambience and hotel facilities such as the spa and swimming pool, as well as the wonderful food and drink! Lisa hadn't had time to buy presents for her girls, but they didn't care, they were just happy to have their Mum home, which they told Lisa was their very best Christmas present ever. On Christmas morning, just as it started to snow, Father Christmas arrived with presents for hotel guests of all ages. It was a truly magical day and a wonderful, happy Christmas to remember.

They all gathered again, this time with Bella's husband, Alan, for a New Year's Eve party at a local pub, clinking glasses and wishing each other a happy new year as the clock striking twelve heralded in 1993. Lisa got drunk and had a terrific hangover the following day, but she didn't care! She spent the day with her two single girls, Scarlett and Tiffany-Mae, at Tiffany-Mae's lovely first-floor flat overlooking the sea at Seaford. After lunch, they all went for a brisk, bracing walk along the seafront before returning to the flat for afternoon tea.

Lisa stayed the next two nights with Tiffany-Mae before returning to her Iden cottage. It was time to get a job. She didn't want to be a project manager again so needed to consider what her skill set was now. She remembered how much she'd enjoyed working in Sue and Trevor's Argostoli jewellery shop. Oh, Argostoli. Kefalonia. Skala. Many happy memories came flooding back to her, and she felt a deep longing to return. Should she? Could she? She decided that it wouldn't do any harm to look at Kefalonia holiday prices in the local travel agent shop where she'd booked her first holiday to the island. After all, she had nothing better to do, and as it was a Monday the shop might be open.

Looking at the clock she saw it was approaching nine-thirty, so she rang the travel agent and was told they were open but were closing at one o'clock. She hurriedly picked up her bag and car keys and sped off to Rye in her little red Honda Civic before she changed her mind.

The travel agent assistant, Jenny, was curious because she'd only arranged one holiday to Kefalonia before. Getting a brochure from the rack on the shop wall, she flicked through to the Greek section where it explained that Kefalonia was also confusingly known as Cephallonia, Cephalonia and Kefallinia. Then she saw there were holidays which Lisa might be interested in, noting one in the Hotel Anabella, which was a new hotel located near the beach in a village called Skala in the south of the island. So, turning the brochure around, she showed it to Lisa, saying, "Look, I think this might suit you. What do you think?"

Lisa's heart leapt with both excitement and nerves, and before she knew what she was doing, she asked Jenny to check availability and flight times for two weeks in the Hotel Anabella from June 20th to July 3rd flying from Gatwick. But could she go? What if she wasn't welcome? What about Christoph? And Sam? Supposing things went wrong, and she got stressed again? Feeling confused and a bit shaky, she quickly thanked Jenny and told her she'd ring her if she decided to book the holiday, then, gathering up her things, she rushed out of the shop and returned to the car park with her heart racing.

When she got home, she went to the fridge for milk to make a cup of tea and spotted the bottle of her favourite wine which had been a Christmas present from her friend, Fifi-Rose, a woman she'd known since primary school and had grown up with. They'd shared everything: school and college life, boyfriend and marriage traumas, having children, and finally working together in their local building society where Lisa was project manager and Fifi-Rose a much-valued colleague as well as a dear friend. Fifi-Rose had been horrified to hear of everything Lisa had gone through in Skala and hoped her dear friend would never go back.

When younger, the two women had spent many happy times being totally outrageous; Fifi-Rose even had a butterfly tattooed on her bum cheek! Now, she always wore long, colourful dangly earrings and bright clothes to match her bright personality, unusual name and short, thick, spiky pink hair. Despite having had three children, who she rarely saw because they were scattered all over the globe, she had the figure of a teenager but was never conscious of it. She just did her 'thing.' She was once married to her children's father, but they'd amicably separated when their youngest went to The Sorbonne to study for an arts degree.

Fifi-Rose was a lot like her half-French mother, Francine, who'd been an 'arty' single mum, no mention of a dad, and still living in the Montmartre district of Paris selling her art, even though she was now well into her seventies. Fifi-Rose was an absolute breath of fresh air and Lisa adored her and didn't know what she'd do without her.

But now, the second half of Fifi-Rose's name, Rose, reminded her of Ariadne-Rose, the girl in Skala who'd hidden an Italian soldier. In a cellar. Oh. Cellar. Fire. Christoph.

The mind can play tricks. Suddenly, Lisa was back in Skala, secretly looking out for Christoph. In her mind's eye, she clearly saw him confidently striding down Skala's main street and smiled to herself at the memory. She also remembered him telling her he loved her, and their last meeting when she was going to say goodbye to him but didn't because he left to fight the fire. And then he was injured.

If she went to Skala this year, would she see him? And if she did, how would he be? If Sam was still in Skala, how would she react to seeing her? Would she have the baby, and if so, would it be a girl or a boy? So many questions, which did nothing to quell the overpowering longing to return to her spiritual home. But then, she thought a break like this could also be just what she needed to continue with her writing.

After a welcome cup of strong tea, Lisa rang the travel agent shop and told Jenny she would like to book the holiday and would nip back to pay a deposit and buy travel insurance, which she did an hour later just before the shop closed. The remaining cost of the holiday would be due six weeks before she went, so she'd have to get a shift on and find a job!

Lisa remembered the local paper she'd bought last week which still advertised a few job vacancies. Scanning the jobs page, she couldn't see anything suitable. Maybe she'd have to go to the job centre if they were still around. She decided to re-read the job adverts. And there, right at the bottom of the page, was a small ad which she'd missed before. It read:

FULL TIME TEMPORARY ASSISTANT WANTED FOR SMALL JEWELLERS IN RYE HIGH STREET.

SEND CV WITH CONTACT DETAILS TO JAMES AT THINGAMABOB HIGH STREET RYE.

Lisa loved the name '*Thingamabob*,' it was quirky and fun. She hoped the same would be said of 'James'! Typing as quickly as she could, Lisa cobbled a CV together, emphasising her experience of working in the Argostoli jewellery shop. After printing it, she found an envelope and, happy days, a first-class stamp, then she took it to the post box as fast as she could to catch the four o'clock post. All she could do now was wait.

Lisa didn't have long to wait. Two days later, her telephone rang at eight thirty in the morning. She'd only just woken up, and scrambled out of bed with her long, dark, tangled hair hanging over her face, and her pyjama trousers falling down round her ankles. Pulling up the trousers and clutching the waistband with her left hand, she hopped to grab the phone before it stopped ringing.

"Hallo?" She said breathlessly into the receiver.

"Am I speaking with Lisa Barat?" A deep male voice asked.

"Er, yes. Who's calling?" Said Lisa as she tried to blow her thick hair off her face without making a noise.

"Hi. I'm James. From *Thingamabob*. You sent me your CV for the job."

Crikey, thought Lisa, that's quick. Is he desperate? Maybe he's not good to work with. Or for. Or whatever. Instead, she said, "Hallo, James. I'm Lisa. Oh, but you know that," she cringed, squeezing her eyes shut. Stupid or what?! "Thank you for ringing me. How can I help?"

"Actually, Lisa, it's how can I help *you*. Get a job, that is if you still want the job. In the jewellers. In Rye," replied James awkwardly.

Bloody hell, thought Lisa, *he's about as articulate as I am.* "Oh, yes please, I'd like the job. That is, if that's what you're saying," she added quickly, while at the same time thinking it was the oddest job offer that she'd ever had in her whole life.

"Good. Good. Er, when can you come to the shop? Today? Is that okay? If you're not busy? Say about two thirty? There won't be any customers in the shop because we always close at one o'clock on a Wednesday."

"Super. Fine. Yes, thank you, I'll be there," breathed slightly shocked Lisa as she let go of her pyjama bottoms. *Good job he can't see me*, she thought. She knew she was about to giggle so swallowed hard. Then she continued, "Anyway, bye for now. See you later."

"Goodbye Lisa, see you soon," said James.

Lisa stared at the gently buzzing receiver in her hand. What had just happened? Was that *for real?!* There she was with hair like a birds' nest over her face, wearing scruffy sleep pants and pyjama bottoms round her ankles and she'd just been offered a job! On the phone! She couldn't help laughing at the absurdity of it all. She just had to tell Fifi-Rose who she knew would totally crack up!

Lisa spent the rest of the morning shopping and ironing, then left her Iden cottage which was idyllically situated only three miles north of Rye, at one forty-five to get to the town by two thirty. She was leaving plenty of time because although she knew where to park, she didn't know where the jewellery shop was so needed to look for it. Also, she hated being late for anything; she'd been born six weeks early and had liked to be early for everything all her life! One of the things about Mark which had driven her spare had been his inability to be on time. Being so incompatible, she should have known they'd be doomed. But then he did also turn into a nasty individual. Shuddering at unwelcome memories, she reminded herself there was no point in pondering the past, it was now time to look forward to a new and better life-chapter.

Lisa parked her Honda Civic in the Cinque Ports car park, paid, and then turned left round the corner into Market Road, and left again into the High Street. She didn't see *Thingmabob* at first. She looked down one side of the High Street, but it was nowhere to be seen, so she crossed over the road to look carefully for the shop there. Still nothing, so she returned to where she started. Then, on her second recce, she saw the jewellery shop with its ancient bow window and crooked door squashed between a shop named Herald and Heart and a bespoke Milliners. It was so cute!

Taking a quick look in the shop's window, she saw all sorts of unusual new and second-hand jewellery, and bits and bobs. It was fascinating. As she pushed open the wonky door, a tinkling bell announced her entrance. Standing in the middle of the shop surrounded by glass cabinets full of sparkly stuff, she waited for James to appear.

"Hello!" Said James as he hurried in from his workshop at the back. "Lisa, I assume?"

Lisa stared silently at James. "Sorry, yes, I'm Lisa," she eventually managed to say whilst telling herself to stop staring.

James was very handsome. Tall and slim with thick, swept back salt and pepper hair touching his collar, he had strong features with just a touch of grey beard. His eyes were the most gorgeous clear blue she'd ever seen on anyone, let alone a man. He wore a pale blue, long sleeved shirt with diamond cufflinks which twinkled in the bright lights with a matching diamond tie pin on a dark blue tie, and dark blue chinos. In essence, he had that indescribable charisma which would have been evident even if he'd been wearing a black plastic sack!

"Well, welcome Lisa," James said as held out his hand to shake hers. Quickly wiping her sweaty palm down her smartest dark denim Lee Cooper jeans, Lisa silently shook his offered hand. "Let's sit down," James said indicating two upright, pink and blue striped upholstered chairs. He thought Lisa was charmingly quiet, such a nice contrast to his last assistant, Tessa, who could irritatingly talk the hindleg off a donkey.

Before we begin, please let me take your jacket, and would you like a drink of something? Water? Tea? Coffee?"

"Er, no thank you, I'm fine," Lisa managed to squeak. Then clearing her throat and telling herself to get a grip, added more clearly, "I love your shop, and its name. So unusual!"

After James hung her jacket on a nearby hook, they both sat down, Lisa neatly crossing her legs at her ankles so only her part of her black Chelsea boots showed. She took a breath. It was interview time, and she must not mess it up.

"Oh, thanks. Yes. Er, yes," stumbled James. Gosh, he's inarticulate again thought Lisa. So sweet. And seeing what he looks and sounds like, so unexpected. She smiled encouragingly.

"Er, well," continued James. "It was my partner's idea."

"Oh, well done your partner!" Lisa exclaimed, "She's chosen a brilliant name!"

"Er, *he* not *she*," James said quietly. "His name's Simon." Looking at Lisa with a small smile, he continued. "He's the inspiration and I couldn't have this shop without him. I'm just the business part of it."

Lisa could see James wasn't used to explaining his private life to anyone, but then why should he have to? "That's brilliant, James. By the way, is it alright to call you James?"

James laughed, clearly relieved. "Yes, of course it is! Simon and I started this jewellery shop because we noticed there isn't anything like it locally. And people often don't know what they want so they'll say they're looking for 'Some*thing*...' From that we thought of the name '*Thingamabob*'. We specialise in the unusual and different type of present, so the name fits perfectly."

"I think it's great. Anyway," Lisa began in a confident voice which belied her nerves. "Your advertisement said the job is a full time, temporary position, so can you tell me how long I'd be working for?"

"Yes, of course. We're looking at having help for about six months and then we'll re-evaluate how the shop's doing. We hope to carry on until Christmas which obviously is the most lucrative time of year, but we don't yet know. Would that suit you?"

Lisa couldn't believe her luck; it fitted almost perfectly with her holiday dates. "Yes, that's perfect, thank you. I've got a holiday booked from 20th June to 3rd July." She wasn't sure if she'd stay on until Christmas, she'd have to see how things went.

James raised his eyebrows. "Oh, where are you going?"

"Greece. Well, Kefalonia actually. It's an island in the Ionian Sea."

"Oh, I've never heard of it. Sounds wonderful," replied James as he shifted in his chair slightly. "Anway, let's talk job. Now, I saw from your CV that you've experience in selling jewellery in a town called Argostoli?" James said questioningly, eyeing Lisa with his head on one side.

"Yes, that's the main town of Kefalonia. A friend and her husband own it," supplied Lisa. No need to go into any more details.

"Good. You clearly liked the job. What was your favourite part?"

Taking a moment to think, Lisa then replied, "Well, the customers I suppose, they were so diverse. And I enjoyed helping find the right piece for them, too."

"Perfect. Perfect. You'll suit us well as this is exactly what our shop is all about. So, money." James paused then went on to state what her salary would be which wasn't quite what Sue and Trevor had paid but was enough. She then gave James her national insurance, tax and bank details, they chatted a bit more about hours and agreed she could start work the following Monday. James showed Lisa around the shop which, because it was quite small, didn't take very long. She was really impressed with the many quirky and pretty things James and Simon were selling. This could be fun, she thought. Happy days!

In just over an hour the interview was over, and Lisa and James said goodbye. As she was getting into her car, Lisa decided that considering it had all happened so quickly, she was most probably the only person who'd applied for the job! Whatever, it would either work out or not, she'd just have to wait and see. Now it was time for tea and to ring Fifi-Rose. Then get all the jobs done she'd been putting off before she was a working woman again!

Chapter Twenty

Lisa adored her job at *Thingamabob* and quickly became used to her work routine. She and James got on well, and he and Simon were thrilled to have her in the shop because she was great with all the customers, was always punctual, polite, friendly and efficient, and was never scary or pushy. And all their customers loved her!

The year moved on, first to Valantine's Day when the shop became very busy with people looking for that special 'thing.' In just two days, Lisa sold three diamond and gold engagement rings, a faux diamond brooch in the form of a tiger, a cute, little jewel-encrusted handbag, and a very unusual, pre-loved and unique silver bracelet which had been made by a local silversmith. It had four, thick interwoven strands of silver with three small rubies set into the main band, and a safety chain at its pretty clasp. Lisa loved it.

Easter was also busy, and then after that James and Simon restocked the shop for the forthcoming summer season. James told Lisa that the shop was really doing well so they'd continue until Christmas when they'd re-evaluate again, and Lisa said she'd be happy to work until then. Time was ticking on, and the date when Lisa had to pay the outstanding balance for her Kefalonia holiday arrived. She rang the travel agent and spoke with Jenny who said she could send a cheque provided there were sufficient funds in her account, so that's what Lisa did. And so, it was done. She was returning to Kefalonia.

"That's epic!" screeched Fifi-Rose with excitement, and her long, red, dangly earrings swinging. "You are awesome, girl, and I wish I was coming with you."

Lisa sat with her hands round a large glass of wine watching her friend bounce up and down in her pub chair. Only Fifi-Rose could react like this! "Yes, well, I just hope I don't regret it. Last time I was there it wasn't exactly a fun experience, was it?"

"Bollocks. You'll be fine. And anyway, you'll have me to talk to on the phone. So, promise me you'll ring me as soon as you get to your hotel. Okay? Promise?"

Lisa laughed. She could always rely on Fifi-Rose to inject a bit of fun. "Yes, of course I will. There are telephones in the main square, I'll just need to get a phone card from the kiosk. The time goes quickly, though, so I won't be able to chat for long."

"Well, buy a couple then, that way you'll have more time to chat," replied the ever-practical and positive Fifi-Rose. "Anyway, cheers my friend. Here's to your magic island in the sun. It's a bit like a fairy tale, isn't it? You know, 'Once Upon a Greek Island'," she laughed. "Only an adult version!"

"Oh, honestly, you're as mad as a box of frogs," Lisa chuckled. "I know I'll only be gone two weeks, but I'll miss you, you mad cow," she laughed as she held her glass up to honour her friend. "Cheers!" She said as they merrily clinked glasses.

The two women chatted, and Fifi-Rose agreed to ask a letting agent to list Lisa's cottage if she decided to stay longer. "Although I bloody hope you don't," Fifi-Rose said with a deep frown. Having arrived by taxi, they booked another to take them home, and as Fifi-Rose would be the last to be dropped off, the friends said goodbye in the cab and As Lisa entered her cottage, her heart flipped when she saw her dark blue suitcase standing ready for her take to Kefalonia. This time her suitcase had yellow, red and blue ribbons tied to its handle, not just a popular pink one!

The following morning, the taxi arrived dead on time at five-thirty. As usual, Lisa wanted to get to Gatwick early, and the journey was quick and easy as there wasn't much traffic on the motorway.

After paying the cabbie, Lisa entered the airport pulling her case behind her. She scanned the Departures Board and saw her flight way down at the bottom, so she knew she had plenty of time for the usual pre-flight stiff whiskey she liked to have before flying. But first she needed to check in. With passport in hand, she went to her tour operator's desk, asked for a window seat, and then watched her case being tagged before it disappeared to baggage handling to be loaded onto the aircraft. It was too late now for a change of mind.

After breathing a sigh of relief, she went through passport control and security without any problems and into the Departure lounge where she found a surprisingly busy bar and ordered her whiskey.

Perched on a high stall, Lisa observed other passengers and wondered who else would be taking her flight. Everyone looked so interesting! People always fascinated her, and she loved airports where she could people-watch to her heart's content. It was like a goldmine for writers! Ah, yes, writing. She'd packed a large notebook in which she planned to make notes in preparation for writing her story. Now was the time.

Lisa sat for a while, watching either other passengers or the departure board until she suddenly saw her gate number. She quickly gathered up her bag and set off to find the gate.

After her passport had been checked, Lisa joined the other passengers and found a seat by the window looking out onto the airfield and her plane. She suddenly felt a fizz of excitement: not long now.

Eventually, everyone was called to board, and as Lisa walked out towards the plane, her heart began to bump with excitement. She waited with some other passengers to climb the aircraft steps and then, on entering the cabin, looked for her seat number. It was a window seat on the left-hand side. Good. She edged her way across the two other seats and made herself comfortable with her bag down by her feet. Her two fellow passengers, a young couple, came to sit in the other two seats. Lisa felt like she was in a dream, and that she'd wake up soon.

But she wasn't dreaming. This was real. Once all the passengers were seated and strapped in, the cabin crew showed the safety procedures and then strapped themselves into their own seats. The plane moved off onto the main runway where it waited before eventually edging forward as its engines began to roar. The noise got louder as the plane accelerated along the runway then slowly lifted gracefully into the lightening sky, flying east out over Sussex and Kent and across the Channel to the Continent.

Lisa was on her way back to her spiritual home.

Chapter Twenty-One

The deep blue Ionian Sea sparkled, diamond-like, in the sun as the plane banked round, dipped and banked again, its left wing seeming to almost touch the sparkling, crystal-clear water. Lisa's heart sang with joy as people waved from the beautiful Kefalonian beaches near the airport, and tears threatened as she saw Mount Aenos rising majestically and mysteriously into the clear blue sky, its many secrets hidden from view.

There was a slight thump as the plane's wheels touched down, and the cabin crew alerted passengers to stay put until the plane had stopped, but many started to unbuckle and get their things together ready to disembark as quickly as they could. The plane cruised to a halt and the sign to release safety belts lit up. Then there was a scramble as everyone tried to get in line. Lisa had to wait for the young couple next to her to leave their seats first, and then she joined the long line of passengers waiting to disembark.

With her heart in her mouth, Lisa reached the open cabin door and stepped out on to the top of the plane's steps. Taking in the heat and the unmistakable, beautiful scent of oregano, thyme and pine, she stopped and stared. Her spirit was home again at last! Tears spilled down her cheeks with joy as she descended the steps to join the other passengers as they made their way to arrivals, passport control and finally baggage reclaim.

This time, Lisa's case was the only one with multi-coloured ribbons on its handle, so it was easy to see. Luckily, it was amongst the first to appear on the creaking gondola, so Lisa was able to pull it off and make her way out into the arrivals area to find the rep of the popular tour operator she'd booked with. She quickly spotted a young man wearing several bracelets and long fair hair tied back into a ponytail waving a board with the company's name on it. No Sam this time. She was soon joined by other passengers who were staying at various places around the south of the island and once checked off the rep's names and accommodation list everyone boarded the cool coach, excited to be starting their holidays at last.

There was the usual stopping at various resorts along the way to drop off holidaymakers at their accommodation before the coach finally approached the hill leading down to Skala. Lisa was shocked to see that in such a relatively short space of time, several new apartment blocks and a couple of new hotels had been built along that road. Then the coach turned the corner into Skala's hilly main road where it stopped to let more people off before finally descending to Skala's main square and the nearby new Hotel Anabella.

Lisa looked out of the coach window to see that despite some changes, Skala village was thankfully still beautiful. Then, just before she looked away, a man's green eyes locked on to hers.

Christoph.

Christoph had felt strange all morning, as if something was about to happen but he couldn't think what. His life was very quiet now, no dramas or traumas, just ordinary - except for the changes the village elders had agreed to. He'd watched his village slowly change from being a traditional, sleepy place into one totally geared up for tourism; he wasn't sure he approved of, or liked, this new Skala. But then he'd also changed; the fire and its consequences had had an enormous impact on him, and he longer 'entertained' young female tourists, instead he was happy just being by himself. His family still urged him to marry, although not as insistently as they had before the fire, they appreciated that it had taken Christoph a long time to recover from the fire and his injuries which, as well as a badly broken ankle and terrible burns and cuts to his face and hands, had included severe concussion. This had affected his memory, and even though he'd begun to remember quite a few things whilst still in hospital, for a long time afterwards there was still a lot he couldn't recall.

For a long time, Christoph's parents, cousins, and friends deliberately kept all village events from him because he needed to concentrate on getting better. Then once his injuries and memory began to improve, he went to stay at one of his wealthy uncle Tony's hotels in Athens to fully recover and only returned to the village once he was as healthy as he would ever be. However, once he was back in Skala he was surprised to find that he missed his sister, Maria, and her husband Nikos, who lived in Athens, he'd enjoyed them popping in for a chat and taking him for regular medical checks.

He also missed Lisa. Every day. He frequently wondered what had happened to the beautiful English woman he'd fallen in love with. A cousin did tell him that, because of some sort of emergency, Lisa had returned to the UK very suddenly, but she'd not kept in contact with anyone, not even Daphne who was very upset about it because she'd loved Lisa like a daughter, so no-one knew anything about her.

Christoph discovered that a few weeks after angrily ending their engagement, Sam had also mysteriously left Skala - one day she just wasn't around and had left lots of her things in her rented house but with no forwarding address. He didn't miss Sam, and despite their relationship ending badly, he hoped she was happily getting on with her life. At the end of the day, two women had 'run away' from him. What a mess he'd made of things.

It was two thirds through June, and the weather was really warming up. It was also a Thursday which was a tourist change-over day in Skala. During the afternoon, Christoph decided a cold drink would be nice and strolled to *Rebecca's* for an iced lemonade. At least his favourite bar had stayed the same! Tracey made his drink which he took out outside to sit in the shade of a fir tree. First, Yannis joined him, and then Georgios; it was good to have such loyal, caring cousins.

After a while, the three men decided to walk up to their favourite bench in the shade of two tamarisk trees. Here, they could have an ice cream or maybe a beer at Michaelis' nearby café-bar. Christoph settled down on the end of the bench, chatting with his cousins and watching the comings and goings of tourists and locals. Tourist coaches were beginning to arrive, each of them disgorging their passengers onto Skala's hot pavements.

Despite being busy talking, something made Christoph look up just as a coach rounded the corner from the Argostoli road into Skala's main road. As he watched the coach stop near where he was sitting, a woman on the coach looked at him and their eyes locked. He gasped. No, it couldn't be! But it was. It was Lisa.

Just then, Lisa was called by the rep to get off the coach and retrieve her case because the minibus was waiting for her and the other holiday guests who were staying at the Hotel Anabella.

Dragging her eyes away from Christoph's, Lisa hurried out of the coach and looked to where he'd been sitting but he wasn't there, only two men who she recognised as Yannis and Georgios.

But there was no time now to think about Christoph because the minibus driver was impatiently waiting to get to the hotel, and back to the main street to wait for the next group of holidaymakers.

Lisa was delighted to discover that the Hotel Anabella stood amongst beautiful gardens directly opposite Skala's long beach and was painted white with brilliant purple and pink bougainvillea climbing up several walls. Added bonuses were the large, sparkling blue pool surrounded by palm trees, comfortable sun-loungers with umbrellas and a café-bar situated to one side of the pool.

Lisa's first-floor room was a spacious, smartly decorated double with a large shower room – with a shower curtain! – non-slip floor tiles, and a complementary fluffy white robe. The white-painted lounge was furnished with a tv and coffee table, a large, comfortable light brown fabric sofa with matching easy chair, and a kitchen area with all the usual basic amenities. Large patio doors with white vertical blinds either side opened on to a large balcony overlooking the beach and the beautiful Ionian Sea. A medium sized table and four chairs and two sun-loungers provided a place to eat or just relax. Pure heaven.

After quickly unpacking her case, Lisa changed into her black one-piece swimsuit, pink shorts and matching floaty sun top, and stuffed her bright red beach towel, suncream, water and squishy straw sunhat into her multi-coloured tote bag. Then, donning her Rae-Bans, she set off to recce the hotel pool, the gardens and the beach. Still reeling from seeing who she thought was Christoph, she decided to go to the pool bar first for a drink to calm herself down. Taking her white wine spritzer to a table under a palm tree on the patio area overlooking the beach road, she tried to think. If Christoph had recognised her, he'd probably have been just as shocked as she was, maybe even more so because he didn't know she was coming to Skala. She needed a plan. Firstly, why had she really come? Had she secretly been hoping to see Christoph? Was it because they had unfinished business? She told herself she needed to be prepared for him to have a new partner or perhaps married. If so, would that matter?

Her daughters, especially Tiffany-Mae, had thought she was bonkers returning to somewhere she'd had a lot of stress. But then they didn't understand the pull of the island, the longing to return, to become 'joined' with her spirit again. She reminded herself that was the main reason why she was here. Whatever else happened during the next two weeks she'd always remember that. And that she wanted to make notes in preparation of writing her story.

Lisa finished her drink and walked down the hotel steps to the beach road. She decided she'd walk up the main street first, look at the shops and then go for a swim. She noticed the beach was quite busy with families enjoying the lovely beach, sea, volleyball or just relaxing in the sun.

She turned up into the steep road which joined with Skala's main square and began to walk up the hill. There were lots of holidaymakers, more than she'd expected, and despite the heat, the village was buzzing.

Village? She thought. Hmm, it was now more like a small town! So much had changed since she was here. She glimpsed at least one other new hotel and two apartment blocks in the side roads, and along the main street a couple of new shops with apartments above had also appeared. Skala had been busy in a very short space of time; it made her feel quite sad. Stopping half-way up the main street, she looked towards the end of the village and the olive groves. She could see the forest and knew that beyond that up the mountainside was Old Skala. So many memories. Tears threatened, so she turned round and started to walk back down to the beach.

"Lisa?"

Looking round Lisa couldn't see anyone, and then, sitting in the shade of a fir tree, she saw Christoph. Her heart leapt in her chest. God, it really was him! "Christoph?" she managed to squeak.

Christoph stood up. Lisa just about managed not to gasp. He was so different! Thinner, greying, and with a long scar down his left cheek, he looked… Lisa couldn't decide how he looked.

"Christoph. I…" She faltered. She didn't know what to say. She'd often thought about this moment but the reality of it was very different. She swallowed. "I didn't expect to see you. So soon. That is, I guessed you'd be here but…well, you know," she finished, her voice trailing off.

"Yes, I know," Christoph said quietly. "It's been a shock for me, too. I never expected to see you back in Skala. Ever," he paused, then, after standing up, went on. "But why are you here? I'd have thought you'd have had enough of Skala. Yannis told me you left the island very quickly last year. Some sort of emergency. Are you okay?"

Lisa looked at this once very proud, arrogant Greek man who she knew had stolen her heart. "Christoph, I had to come back. You see it's my spirit. My spirit lives here. Can you understand?"

"Yes, of course. It's like that for many people who come to Kefalonia. The island has a sort of magic which pulls them back time after time." Stepping closer to her, he continued. "Can we meet later, say at the white stone bench overlooking the beach? Would that be alright?" He stopped, then added, "that is, if you're not busy."

Lisa looked at him. He seemed nervous; this was so unlike the Christoph she once knew. "Yes, how about eight o'clock?"

"Good. I'll see you then. I'll go now. Take good care. By the way, I hope you like the Hotel Anabella."

Lisa's eyebrows shot up. "Oh, how do you know I'm staying there?"

"Ah, well, as you know I have many cousins," Christoph laughed. "But I won't say which one told me. See you later."

Yes, Lisa knew Christoph had many cousins, and that not a lot escaped them! She watched him walk slowly down the hill, as upright and strong as ever even though he was thinner. Not for the first time, she wondered why he didn't work. And come to that, why Georgios didn't appear to, either. She knew Yannis and Michaelis worked in their respective bars, but

Christoph's and Georgios's incomes remained a mystery. Although she did remember once seeing Georgios accompanying some wealthy-looking men round Skala – so maybe he was some sort of upmarket rep.

Lisa spent the rest of the day swimming and relaxing although as it was late afternoon by the time she got to the beach, she didn't have very long. Seeing other people leaving, she decided to leave as well, thinking that now was a good time to ring Tiffany-Mae and also Fifi-Rose to let them know she'd arrived okay, and that everything was good.

Tiffany-Mae's phone went to answerphone, so she left her a message asking her to tell her sisters that she was okay. Then she rang Fifi-Rose who picked up immediately.

"Wow, the hotel sounds amazing, Lisa! And, oh my god, you've seen Christoph! You must keep me posted," she yelled making Lisa laugh. They chatted about Skala until Lisa's first phone card rang out, so she said goodbye to her dear friend because she wanted to save her other two phone cards for another time.

After the phone calls, Lisa went back to Hotel Anabella, showered and changed into a long, pale lemon, boat-necked sleeveless dress which fitted her perfectly. She let her long, dark hair hang loosely down her back. Then, gathering up her white leather bag, she went to the pool bar for a drink. Looking at her watch, she saw it was already seven-thirty, so she didn't have long to wait before she saw Christoph again. What would he say? What would *she* say? She began to feel nervous.

At seven fifty-five, Lisa started to make her way to the white stone bench. It was a popular place to sit in the daytime because it was shaded by tall fir trees, plus it had a good view of the beach and the beautiful sea. She crossed the square where the fountains played and sparkled in the light from fairy lights and lamps. Because there were lots of people wandering around or chatting, so although she was on her own, she didn't feel self-conscious.

Just like their last fateful meeting, she saw Christoph before he saw her. He was sitting slightly forward with his head down and his arms resting on his thighs and his hands clasped, making him look vulnerable. As she approached, he looked up and she noticed again the long, livid scar down his left cheek, and her heart went out to him.

Christoph stood up. "Lisa, you came," he said, just like he had once before.

"Of course. Why wouldn't I?"

"Well, I wasn't sure. Not after all you've been through because of me," he replied gently. "I owe you so much. Come, sit down," he said as he gestured to the space next to him.

Lisa sat down on the hard bench. She was suddenly lost for words. There were a million reasons why she shouldn't be here; a million reasons why she shouldn't love this man. But she was and she did. Yes, she'd thought he was emotionally dangerous right from the off, and how true this had been. But he was different now. She realised the difference that she hadn't been able to fathom before was his demeanour; he seemed softer, gentler.

Looking at Lisa with his green eyes, Christoph gently took her right hand in both of his. "It's three hundred and sixty-four days, three months and I think about four hours and ten minutes since I last saw you. And I have missed you all that time," he whispered as tears filled his green eyes.

Wide-eyed with disbelief, Lisa stared at Christoph. "What? Have you been counting? I mean, surely not. No-one does that!"

"Well, I have," replied Christoph. "That is, apart from when I couldn't remember anything."

"What do you mean, 'Couldn't remember anything'?"

"'Oh, well, you know I was injured. When I went to help. With the…the… fire," Christoph stuttered. "Thomas saved my life. I was in hospital a long time. I had concussion which wiped my memory for a while."

"And you cut your face?"

"Yes, and some other bits of me got cut, too. And burnt."

Sam's fury when she slammed down the ring in the Argostoli jewellery shop came flooding back to Lisa. How dreadfully unkind of her to reject this brave man just because he was scarred. But did he know about the baby? Did Sam stay in Skala or go home to have it?

"Oh, Christoph, I'm so sorry to learn this. You must have been through hell. All I knew was that you'd been injured and had gone to hospital, Thomas, too. I asked Daphne to let me know how you were getting on, but she didn't tell me very much, so I didn't know just how badly you'd been hurt. Sam of course didn't tell me because she hated me. Then Sue and Trevor closed the Accommodation shop, and I went to work in their jewellery shop in Argostoli which meant I didn't see anyone during the day except when Sue occasionally popped into the shop, but she never told me anything either," she paused. "Yes, I left the island very quickly because after Sam brought her engagement ring into the shop to be valued, and angrily told me I was welcome to you, I couldn't take any more stress. I'm sorry."

"Yes, Sam was angry when she saw I was so injured, and she called off our engagement. But I didn't know she'd taken her ring to your shop," Christoph murmured sadly as he held Lisa's hand more tightly. It was now clear to Lisa that Christoph didn't know about Sam's pregnancy because if he did, he'd have mentioned it. But she wasn't going to tell him, it wasn't her place to do that. She would keep it to herself for as long as she had to. And if Sam had gone home to have the baby, Christoph wouldn't know anything about it; also, very importantly, Sam wouldn't want Christoph claiming the baby especially if it was a son.

Lisa and Christoph looked into each other's eyes but didn't speak. There were no more words for now because they both had a lot to think about. People in the square chatted and laughed, dogs barked, children squealed, music played. Normal Skala life went on all around them, but neither was aware of it. It was as if time stood still for a few moments.

Then Lisa broke the silence. "Christoph, I've not seen Daphne and Thomas yet. I didn't keep in touch with them after I went home, I'm not sure why. In fact, I didn't keep in touch with anyone except my friend Janey who lives in Ratzakli, although she never told me anything. Actually, it feels like no-one wanted to tell me anything."

Christoph took a deep breath. "Lisa, I'm sorry to tell you that Thomas passed away in March. He's buried in the cemetery here," he paused then added, "maybe Daphne didn't tell you much about me because she didn't want to worry you. But also, this is the Greek way, we keep things amongst ourselves."

Shocked, Lis gasped. "Oh no! Poor, brave Thomas. And poor Daphne. I really must see her s soon as I can."

"Well, you can because she's the cook at your hotel!"

"No way! That's amazing!" Lisa exclaimed in astonishment.

"Yes, she took the position of cook to help her cope with her grief at losing Thomas. And you can imagine how I feel about Thomas dying, it was my fault he became so frail and ill."

"No! Don't think that!" exclaimed Lisa. "It wasn't your fault at all. Thomas would have done the same for anyone, he was that sort of man. He'd have helped anyone who was in trouble."

Shaking his head, Christoph looked sad. "I know he was, but it doesn't stop me feeling guilty. I asked him to help me, and he did."

Lisa took Christoph's hands in hers. "Look, I do understand but in time you'll come to terms with what happened. And remember, that you're the same, you'd have helped Thomas if it had been the other way round."

Christoph looked at Lisa in surprise. "Do you know, I never thought of it like that. And yes, you're right, I would have helped Thomas. Thank you, Lisa, for enabling me to see that." He bent forward and kissed her on the lips. "You are amazing, and I love you with all my heart."

Lisa savoured the kiss even though Christoph's lips were far from soft. "I love you, too, Christoph, so what are we going to do about it?"

Christoph didn't reply for a moment, then looking deeply into Lisa's eyes, said, "I guess we could live together. I've a cousin who has an empty house just outside Katelios village, so we could live there. What do you think?"

Crikey! Thought Lisa. This was sudden. Live together? And of course, he'd have a cousin with a spare house! "How would your family react, Christoph? Would we be safe? Would we be left in peace? And what about Sam? Is she here?"

"Yes, we'd be fine. And no, Sam hasn't returned from the UK. I heard she'd had some sort of operation. But anyway, I know that because of what happened here, she doesn't like Skala now, so she won't be back. So, what do you say?"

Lisa hesitated, "But what about my family and my job in England? And how would we manage for money? There's such a lot to think about."

"Lisa, I'm sure your daughters will understand, and anyway, we can invite them over to stay with us so they can see how happy we are together. Of course, you'd have to give up your job, but that's a decision only you can make. And regards money – I know I've never told you what I do, but I will now. I've two very wealthy uncles, my uncles Tony and Theo. As well as owning four hotels in Athens between them, they also both own shipping companies with headquarters in Greece and America. Oh, and they also own a property and restaurant in Launceston Place in Kensington. I am their liaison officer which means I seek out wealthy contacts who may be interested in having a shipping contract with them or want to rent their London house."

After taking a deep breath, Christoph continued, "Georgios and I work together on this because he knows a lot of people in America and goes there quite frequently. He also occasionally brings people here to have a look at Skala and the whole island. I'm mostly Greece-based but also occasionally go to the UK. As you can imagine, we both have highly confidential positions, which is why they're never discussed." Christoph stopped talking and looked at Lisa with his head on one side, waiting for her response.

Listening to Christoph, Lisa's mouth dropped open, and her eyebrows shot up. "Good god, I had no idea! But that explains why I once saw Georgios with some wealthy-looking men. And why you always seem not to have to worry about money," she eventually managed to say. Then, with wide eyes, she continued. "But ships?

Athens? Hotels? The US and the UK? Crikey, Christoph, you, your uncles and Georgios are international moguls!"

"Yes, well, I guess we are international," replied Christoph. "But it doesn't mean a lot to us because we've always known it this way. A lot of people in Skala have shipping and American connections, and the money from these are what helps keep the village comparatively wealthy." Christoph shifted his position on the hard bench. "Look, to be honest, I'm also wary about us. I'm scarred, my body's not the same and I often still have nightmares." Then, indicating his greying temples and with a wry smile, he continued. "I'm also going grey. And I'm thinner. I'm not exactly the best example of Greek manhood! Like Sam, you may find me repulsive. I don't know."

Gently touching Christoph's left arm, Lisa said quietly, "Firstly, I'm not Sam so let's not mention her again, okay? Secondly, you are still the same man, Christoph. Annoying, yes," she laughed. "But you're also kind, caring and very brave. Your scars are proof of your courage and natural willingness to help others, so wear them with pride not shame. Scars, greying hair and being slimmer doesn't bother me because they're all part of who you are."

Deeply moved, Christoph felt tears spring to his eyes. "Thank you, Lisa, that's most kind," he murmured. "But we still need to decide what to do. Maybe you should take a few days to think about things and then we can talk again?"

Thinking about Sam, Lisa didn't reply at first. Did Sam have an abortion operation? Or a post-miscarriage operation? Either would explain why she'd left Skala so suddenly and not returned. Poor girl. Whatever, Lisa gave thanks that she'd not mentioned Sam's pregnancy to Christoph because if he knew it would cause all sorts of extra problems, and they'd quite got enough to deal with already. Yes, she had a lot of things to consider, it wouldn't be easy to decide what to do.

But then, there is only one life… Was it time to move out of her comfort zone and take a chance?

Chapter Twenty-Two

Christoph took Lisa to *Rebecca's* for a drink and to catch up on what had been happening in her life since they'd last seen each other. Then, because neither of them had eaten, he took her to The Grapevine for dinner where Andreas was delighted to see them together again.

"I will make you a special dinner," he said with a wide grin. "Meanwhile, please accept this with my compliments," he said as, with a dramatic flourish, he produced a bottle of his best champagne from behind his back and poured them each a glass.

Lisa laughed. Christoph told Andreas he shouldn't have but then thanked him warmly for his generosity. Touching Lisa's glass with his own, he said, "Here's to us. Whatever happens."

"Cheers Christoph," Lisa said with a smile. "Yes, to us and to whatever happens."

After dinner, Christoph walked Lisa back to her hotel, then after saying he'd see her at *Rebecca's* the next day at ten thirty in the morning, kissed her on the cheek. Lisa agreed with the arrangement and then watched Christoph walk away, unsure whether she felt relieved or sad that he'd not even hinted that he might like to stay over. But then maybe not yet, and anyway, she had a lot of thinking to do.

The following morning, Lisa rose early and sat on her balcony with a cup of tea. She wanted to make her decision because there was no point in hanging it out. Weighing up her options, she thought she'd ring Fifi-Rose and then after that, her PA daughter Scarlett. She knew Scarlett would have her own private work phone line, although using Skala's public phones would mean Lisa couldn't have an in-depth, personal conversation with her girl.

"Well, darling," Fifi-Rose said confidently, "No contest, really, is there? You clearly love this chap, and he loves you, so why wait? You've already been through a lot together which would test any relationship, and have come through it, so in my view it's time to give the man a second chance. Just go for it, girl!" Then when Lisa mentioned the age gap, she told her not to be ridiculous, it meant nothing!

Scarlett was a bit more cautious. "If that's what you want to do Mum, then do it. But only if you're totally sure that's what you want," she countered. "Anyway, whatever happens, remember we three are here for you if you need ever us. Just be careful, that's all."

Lisa thoughtfully ended the call. She couldn't chat for long because it was a Friday, and other, newly arrived holidaymakers, were lining up to use the one useable public phone, probably to reassure their families they'd safely arrived.

Lisa went for a coffee at a new café bar where no-one knew her. Sipping her drink, she thought about what she really wanted to do. She knew that if she was truly honest with herself, she wanted to be with Christoph. So that's what she would tell him. And then she'd have to tell her girls, and James at *Thingamabob*. And of course, Fifi-Rose, plus, out of courtesy, her parents, Patricia and Brian. Not that they'd be bothered as they were now happily living in a posh retirement village in the Yorkshire Dales.

Feeling relieved that she'd finally made her decision, Lisa hurried back to her hotel room to change. She chose a mid-length, loose-fitting, slashed neck, sleeveless pale coral shift dress with flat sandals to match, and tied her hair long, thick hair back with a coral ribbon. Then she lightly applied some lip-gloss and a quick spray of Mugler's new 'Angel' perfume before checking herself in the mirror. A curvy, blue-eyed woman stared back at her. *Hmm, not bad for your age girl.* She thought as she tucked a loose strand of hair back over her left ear. Then hoisting her black tote bag onto her shoulder, she set off down the marble stairs and out into the bright sunshine on her way to meet Christoph.

This time, Lisa was the first to arrive. Tracey made her an iced coffee which she took to a shady table looking out into the main street. She was a few minutes early, so immersed in the warm evening scent of herbs and the sound of cicadas, she felt quite happy just watching people coming and going. But after waiting twenty minutes, Lisa began to feel a bit concerned, thinking, *oh, no, please not again. Please let him be here soon.* Then, just as if he'd heard, Christoph rushed up full of apologies.

"Oh, Lisa, I'm so sorry," he panted. "I had a phone call to deal with, and as it was important, I had to take it. Sorry." He sat down with a bump and extended his hand across the table to touch Lisa's.

"Oh, no problem, although I was beginning to get a little worried," Lisa said as she curled her fingers round Christoph's scarred right hand. "But you're here now, that's what matters." She could see Christoph had got himself in a bit of a flap about being late. It must be difficult juggling work with private time, she mused, but then before the fire Christoph would have taken it all in his stride; he'd most definitely lost some of his old confidence.

Christoph also ordered an iced coffee, then taking a deep breath, looked across the table at Lisa. *How beautiful she is, and what a lucky man I am,* he thought.

Lisa, in turn, looked at Christoph. He was wearing a smart white t-shirt with an elegant gold chain just skimming his neck, and pale grey chinos. His thick, dark hair was swept back as usual, but now his temples were attractively greying. They stared at each other for a few moments before Christoph said, "Shall we talk? If you want to, that is?"

"Yes, let's," Lisa said, then after clearing her throat, went on. "I've made my decision. I think we should give ourselves a chance to be happy, so do contact your cousin about the house in Katelios!"

Christoph's eyes widened. "Are you sure, Lisa? One hundred percent sure?"

"Yes, I am, so let's not waste any more time. I'll tell my daughters and my boss James that I'm staying here. I'll also tell my friend who's got a key to my cottage in case of any emergencies and ask her to organise the letting of my cottage as furnished and to get my post forwarded. I'll also need to ask her to clear and store all my clothes, towels and personal items. And I'll tell my parents. Oh, and I'll tell Sue and Trevor as well, I wanted to see them anyway, to apologise for rushing back to the UK - I do hope they've forgiven me for that. I also hope Daphne's forgiven me, too. I saw her the other day at the hotel, but she was busy so I couldn't talk to her."

"Wonderful!" grinned Christoph. "I'll contact my cousin Kostas after we've had lunch. And yes, I'm sure Sue and Trevor will have forgiven you, and Daphne," he said as he leaned across the table to kiss Lisa on the cheek; he no longer cared who saw them together.

It was the beginning of a new chapter, but one which would have consequences beyond anything they could ever have imagined.

Chapter Twenty-Three

The Katelios house was a substantial, three bedroomed, whitewashed, bougainvillea-clad Greek villa standing slightly elevated in beautiful, well-maintained gardens full of brightly coloured flowers, oleander, and fir and palm trees, with a long path bordered by bright geraniums leading up to the large front door. A small ornate iron balcony leading off the front bedroom allowed views over an olive grove and countryside.

When Lisa first saw the house, all she could say was, "Oh." It was nothing like she'd imagined it would be. Slowly walking into the vast entrance hall, she was amazed to see a huge modern interior with floor tiles throughout, and whitewashed beamed ceilings. The living room was lit by wall lights, and huge patio doors to one side lead out into the garden. There was a large brick fireplace in front of an enormous, black sofa, two easy chairs and a coffee table, and an archway lead into a vast modern kitchen with a huge cooker, modern sink unit and lighting, and all the cupboards and marble worktops anyone could wish for. A large, farmhouse table with six wooden chairs round it stood in the centre.

Lisa silently wandered from the kitchen into yet another beamed room with an impressive glass chandelier suspended over a large, shiny dining table with six elegant chairs.

Upstairs were four spacious ensuite double bedrooms, three with a small balcony. The main bedroom had glass doors out onto a larger balcony overlooking the garden and the *pieče de resistance*, the pool, around which were several sun loungers and umbrellas. A bar stood in one corner of the pool terrace, with a barbecue next to it. Beyond was the countryside and olive groves and a breathtaking view of Mount Aenos.

Although the interior was modern, the house had a cosy, friendly feel. It was a happy family house, and Lisa was beside herself with joy. Turning to Christoph who'd silently followed her as she'd explored the house, she said, "It's perfect, Christoph. Far too big for just us of course, but perfect."

"I'm glad you like it, my darling. Kostas built it himself for his wife and two children, but they've now moved to another property which he's also built so he lets this one out, and we can have it for as long as we want it. I hope it's not too remote for you, I know the shops and beach aren't on the doorstep, but you'll have your own car so everything's only a few minutes away. A local man, Nikos, comes to look after the pool and garden every day, and his wife, Alexandra, does all the cleaning so all you'll have to do is the washing and ironing!"

Lisa looked at Christoph wide-eyed in astonishment. "Wow! No housework? At all?"

Laughing, Christoph said, "No, only minor stuff that you might want to do."

"Well, yes. I'd prefer to clean my, I mean our, bedroom. I don't want anyone going in there and possibly having a poke around."

"That's okay, I'll let Alex know. But she is very discreet, and anyway, it wouldn't be to her advantage if she spoke to anyone about our house. Or us."

"Hmm, that maybe true but then you never know, and you and I have had quite enough gossip to deal with. We just want a quiet life now," Lisa said thoughtfully. She'd learned not to trust anyone except her family and her very close friend Fifi-Rose.

Just before she moved into the house with Christoph, Lisa found Daphne and told her how terribly sorry she was to learn that dear Thomas had passed away. Daphne, now dressed in widow's black, thanked Lisa for her kindness and went on to say she forgave her for not keeping in touch even though at the time it had upset her. Then she reassured Lisa that she was beginning to settle a bit better now that she was working in Hotel Anabella, and also still making cheese pies!

When Lisa told Daphne she and Christoph were moving to Katelios together, Daphne smiled and said, 'See, I knew you loved each other, and I'm so happy for you. Now you must take good care of each other.' They then hugged goodbye, and Lisa promised to visit Daphne again soon.

After talking with Daphne, Lisa saw Sue and also asked for her forgiveness, which Sue readily gave because she knew Lisa had had a rough time with Sam and then Christoph's terrible accident. "Forget it now, Lisa, but don't forget *us*. Maybe you'll ask Trevor and me to dinner one day?" She laughed.

"Oh, bless you, thanks Sue. And yes, we certainly will invite you to dinner. Soon. I promise." The two women hugged each other warmly and Lisa left her former employer, now friend, with a smile, happy knowing that she'd always be welcome in Skala.

Just before leaving the village, Lisa rang James to tell him her news. He was surprised and said he and everyone would really miss her, but he wished her well, adding that if she ever wanted a job in the UK again, she'd be most welcome back at *Thingmabob*.

Then she rang her parents who didn't pick up, so she left a message to say she was in Skala for the foreseeable future and would ring them again soon. And so, it was done.

Christoph kept his own house in Skala because there he could make highly confidential phone calls and store important documents. He also wanted to keep his working life and his private life separate.

Lisa and Christoph's first night together was tentative – they were both nervous because it had been a long time for either of them since they'd slept with anyone. The next morning, Lisa woke first. She turned to look at Christoph who was still sleeping. What a gentle lover he'd been. And when she'd stroked the scars on his face, back, arms and hands and told him he was beautiful, he'd cried like a baby. Then they'd held each other tight, all past traumas gone. It had eventually been a night they'd both remember for the rest of their lives.

Lisa got out of bed and pulled aside the long blinds to see the sun was up bathing the garden in glorious sunshine. What a wonderful day!

There were many more days like that. Occasionally, Christoph went back to his house in Skala to work, sometimes having to go to Athens for a night or two. Their lives fell into a routine of a relaxing breakfast in the garden when the weather was good, going to the beach, swimming, socialising, occasionally working and generally being happy. Christoph even invited people to the house, something completely new for him. Their first dinner guests were, as Lisa had promised, Sue and Trevor who were bowled over by the house.

"Gosh, it's stunning Lisa," said Sue as she gazed around. "I'm so pleased for you both. Are you happy now?"

"Thank you, yes I'm very happy," replied Lisa as she hugged her friend. "In fact, I never knew I could be this happy!"

And so it continued. In Late November Lisa told Christoph it would be her fiftieth birthday on December twelfth, and she was thinking of having a party. He looked at her in amazement. "That's such a coincidence, my birthday's on December fourteenth!"

"Crikey," exclaimed Lisa. "And how old will you be then?"

"Er. Thirty-eight actually," he grinned, adding, "I'm getting old!"

Lisa laughed. "You daft thing, that's not old! Anyway, we can celebrate our birthdays together."

"Well, I had been wondering if a Christmas drinks party would be nice so we could still do that if you like," Christoph said. "What do you think?"

"I think it's a brilliant idea so let's get planning," replied Lisa happily.

They decided to have the party on Lisa's fiftieth birthday and to invite Kostas and his family, Nikos and Alexandra, Daphne, Sue and Trevor, Dimitri and Helen, all Christoph's cousins and their partners and families, and the local priest. An open invitation was also extended to all Skala and Katelios residents and their families.

The party was a huge success, and for the first time in a very long time, the house was filled with music, dancing, laughter and happy people. Alexandra bought four banners from Argostoli emblazoned with 'Happy 50th birthday' and hung balloons everywhere she could. Rebecca made a birthday cake topped with the number 50 and Yannis bought numerous bottles of champagne to toast both Lisa and Christoph. The priest blessed the couple and

their house and drank a fair bit of Robola before being driven by a sober Michaelis back to his house near Skala's church.

Lisa cut her cake to rapturous applause and cheers, and Christoph gave her an elegant diamond necklace which he placed round her neck whilst everyone looked on, many in tears. It really was a very special time for everyone.

Once they'd settled down after the party, Lisa and Christoph bought a huge Christmas tree in Argostoli which was delivered on the back of a truck and then hoisted into place in the main entrance hall by two burly Greek men. They also bought lots of tree decorations and presents for family and friends. Because of their respective work commitments, Lisa's daughters were coming to see them in the week between Christmas and New Year, and Lisa couldn't wait, she missed them so much.

Lisa and Alexandra decorated the Christmas tree with hundreds of fairy lights, filling the room with light and colour, then after struggling with wrapping paper and Sellotape accompanied by a lot of giggling, Lisa and Christoph eventually placed their Christmas presents underneath it, excitedly grinning at each other like children. Christoph had secretly bought Lisa a gold bangle from Sue and Trevor's jewellery shop, and Lisa had asked Rebecca to get Christoph a gold watch from a different shop.

Lisa and Christoph went to the Christmas Eve service in Skala's old church, and when Lisa saw the Nativity scene, the gold, the icons and smelt the incense, she was quite emotional, it was all so moving and utterly stunning. The church was packed, and everyone was pleased to see them, happily hugging and kissing them and wishing them *'Kala Christoúgenna'*.

Lisa and Christoph spent Christmas Day at The Grapevine which was packed to the hilt. Andreas and Sophia arranged the restaurant so that as many people as possible could sit down, and cooked a very traditional, rather splendid Christmas lunch of turkey with all the trimmings which everyone loved. There was lots of chatting and laughter, especially when crackers were pulled and coloured paper hats donned; Christoph even had a small glass of Robola to toast the very special occasion!

After the toast, the music changed from British Christmassy tunes to typical Greek music, and without any prompting, four Greek waiters started dancing. Soon, others joined in, and it became very Greek with lots of 'Opa' and clapping. Lisa loved it, especially when, thanks to Yannis' encouragement, Christoph eventually joined in; she'd never seen him dance before and was mesmerised by the grace and emotion he displayed as he moved, kicking and dipping in time to the music.

Over the next two days, Lisa and Christoph were busy clearing up and getting ready for Lisa's daughters to arrive. They were due to land on Monday the twenty-seventh at two o'clock in the afternoon; Lisa could barely contain herself and insisted she and Christoph arrived at the airport early even though she knew they'd have to wait a while.

It was a bit cold, but the sun was shining as the plane touched down. Lisa was very excited to be seeing her daughters again and to show them where she was now living – she felt the house was proof that she'd made the right decision to be with Christoph, although she did wonder how her daughters and Christoph would get on.

The girls eventually appeared at baggage reclaim and Lisa ran through from the main airport to hug each one in turn. Christoph hung back as he wasn't sure how he'd be welcomed; it was potentially a tricky time. But he needn't have worried for when Tiffany-Mae saw him she squealed to her sisters, "Cor, look at him girls, what a hunk!"

"Sssh," scolded Bella. "He'll hear you."

Bella was the last to go forward for a hug with Lisa, and to shake hands with Christoph. Looking at him with knowing grey eyes, she said, "great to meet you at last Christoph. We've all heard so much about you."

Christoph felt her reservation and knew he'd have to be sensitively careful. "Thank you, Bella, it's nice to meet you, too. I trust you had a good flight?" He asked politely as he gently let go of her hand.

"Yes, it was pretty good really. It's always spectacular coming into land here, isn't it?" Bella replied.

"Yes indeed. I know it feels like the plane's wing's about to touch the sea!" To which all three girls laughingly chorused "Yes!"

After the girls had retrieved their cases from the gondola, they followed Lisa and Christoph to the airport's car park where Christoph had parked the BMW. The journey to Katelios was full of Lisa and the girls chatting and laughing while Christoph drove and listened. He felt deeply moved by the obvious closeness the four women shared and which he was now privileged to be a small part of.

The conversation dwindled, and tapping Christoph on the shoulder, Tiffany-Mae said,

"Excuse me Christoph, hope you don't me asking you something while you're driving. Is that okay?"

Christoph blinked in surprise. "Er, yes. Of course. How can I help you?" He asked feeling slightly worried.

"Well," began Tiffany-Mae, "Mum has told us that you've got lots of cousins, so just how many is 'lots'?"

Relieved, Christoph laughed. "Yes, I do have several cousins. I've got ten, three on my Mum's side, and seven on my Dad's. My Dad, Vasilis, has three brothers who each have two boys. My Mum, Thalia, has a brother and a sister – her brother and his wife have a boy, and my aunt and her husband have two girls and a boy. By the way, I've also got a sister and a brother-in-law who've got a little boy," supplied Christoph, adding. "They live in Athens and are the ones who looked after me when I went to my uncle Tony's Athens hotel to recover from the fire accident." Christoph felt it was important to be honest and open about himself. Well, that is, as much as he wanted to be.

Having received so much unexpected information, Tiffany-Mae couldn't speak. All she could think was, what a man! Not only was he a hunk, albeit a bit of a scarred one, although that didn't matter, but he was also interesting. No wonder Mum fell for him! Smothering her instinct to ask more, she sat back. Scarlett looked at her sister and silently mouthed, "Are you okay?" To which Tiffay-Mae nodded yes.

Bella quietly stared out of the car window. She'd heard it all but felt there was more to Christoph than he was letting on, and she was determined to find out exactly what it was.

Chapter Twenty-Four

Christmas at the Katelios house was wonderfully full of fun, love and laughter. Lisa adored having her daughters with her and taking time out just to be with them. After present-opening before yet another Christmas dinner - which Lisa cooked with Christoph's help - the four women went for a long walk along Katelios's beach, and then out into the countryside.

Bella, Scarlett and Tiffany-Mae were delighted to see their Mum living such a lovely, stress-free life in such a glorious place. Lisa also took them to Skala where they walked along the beach, after which they had a coffee with Andreas and his wife Sophia. They also went to see Daphne who was over the moon to see her beloved Lisa and her three daughters, and, with a kiss on the cheek, she gave each one of them one of her famous cheese pies!

All too soon, it was time for the three girls to return to the UK. Lisa took them to the airport where she bid them a very tearful farewell with a promise to come and see them in the UK as soon as she could.

With a very heavy heart, Lisa watched their plane elegantly take off into the winter blue sky. Had she made the right decision to stay in Skala? Yes, she and Christoph were very happy, but she did miss her daughters, especially now Bella had quietly told her she and Alan were hoping to have a baby next year. This would be her first grandchild! Such mixed emotions: Christoph versus family. What a choice.

But Lisa didn't yet know that the choice would very soon be made for her.

The new year heralded in nineteen ninety-four and things jogged along nicely. Lisa got used to having someone else do her housework. Alexandra was a delight, so attentive and respectful, although Lisa ensured she wasn't made to feel like a 'domestic', always having a coffee and chat with her, just like she would with any female friend. After all, she was no better than anyone else, she just happened to live with a very rich man in a big house. And Fifi-Rose was due to come and stay for three weeks in June; life couldn't be any better!

Christoph became very busy. He also became a little withdrawn. Lisa tried hard to get him to talk but he always apologised, smiled and reassured her that it was just work pressures because rich people could be very difficult at times, so Lisa had no reason to disbelieve him.

One Sunday in late February, Christoph unexpectedly announced that he had to go away the next day for five days. First, he had to go to Athens to see his uncle Tony, then to the UK to see his uncle Tony's UK counterpart, Clive. Lisa wasn't at all happy about this, she hated being left alone in the large house which wasn't particularly close to any neighbours, but she had no choice; after all, Christoph's work is what kept them going.

The next day, Lisa took Christoph to the airport early and waved him goodbye with misty eyes. She so loved this man. She returned to the house, made some phone calls and then went to do some shopping in the village supermarket. As it was late February, it was getting dark by the time she got home. After parking her black Audi, she hurried up the brightly lit front path, unlocked the large, white wooden door and slammed it shut behind her. Home! What a relief! Dropping her shopping bags on to the floor, she pulled off her black puffa jacket and long, black leather boots, hung her jacket over a nearby chair and went into the kitchen to unpack her shopping. *Thank goodness the house has underfloor heating*, she thought, as she padded to the fridge. A glass of wine was in order!

Settling down in a corner of the large, floral sofa with her legs tucked underneath her, she felt relaxed and happy. What a lovely life she had: a beautiful home, a handsome, loving partner plus precious friends and family in the UK. She felt very blessed.

Sipping her wine, she slowly became absorbed in the UK period drama she'd been following and so didn't hear the door softly open behind her.

The knife point against her throat was sharp. As her heartbeat went up, Lisa told herself not to panic. Do not panic. Whoever it was would hopefully calm down in the end and everything would be alright again.

Lisa realised who her attacker was as soon as she spoke. It was Theresa, the Italian girl who'd fallen in love with Christoph.

"Well, English bitch," she hissed into Lisa's right ear as she grabbed her round the chest from behind, pushing the knife even harder onto Lisa's throat. "You think you have him now, don't you? Was it not enough to take him from the other English girl? No? You want it all? You want his body, his mind, everything about him? You think you know him? Well, you don't. I am mafioso and that man knows this. He pays me a lot of money to keep quiet about our affair because he knows that if he doesn't pay me, I will tell everyone he raped me. And that would destroy him and all his family. He also doesn't want people to know about the boy-brat. Do you understand?"

Terrified, Lisa nodded. *Jeez, I must be in a nightmare*, she thought as her mind whirled with fear. Boy-brat? Mafioso? What did the girl mean? Was she going to die? Because of a Greek man? Why did Christoph have to go away just now?

Looking sideways at her attacker, Lisa realised the girl was Theresa, the Italian girl Christoph had had an affair with several years ago. She'd been angry when they'd first met, but for some reason, she was even angrier now.

Theresa pulled Lisa up, hurting her chest. "Stand, bitch," she ordered. Then, moving around the end of the sofa while still holding the knife to Lisa's throat, chuckled. "Ah, I see you don't know what I mean. Well, I'll tell you. The boy is Christoph's son. And my son. He's now three years old and lives with Christoph's sister Maria in Athens. I didn't want a kid, and they can't have any kids, so they adopted him." She stopped, waiting for what effect this startling information would have on Lisa.

Seeing Lisa's look of horror, she went on, "Oh, yes. Your Mister Wonderful is a daddy. The brat's name is Sebastion." Theresa stopped and pulled Lisa even harder against her body. "My *Nonna* has the Elleniki mafioso power now, but when she dies, I will have it, not my mother or my father," she said as she spat on the floor. "Poof, such weak people. But I am strong."

The room swayed. *Don't faint, hang on. If I faint this poor, mad girl might stab me to death*, Lisa told herself as she clenched her fists against her rigid body. Then, still holding the knife to Lisa's throat, Theresa moved round to the front of her to stare into her face with huge, black, crazed eyes.

"Christoph pays me well to keep quiet about our affair and our brat," she spat. "He loved me, but his family said no. And so, he said no to the boy and to me. He is weak." She stopped, then went on, "Lisa, isn't it?" Lisa nodded silently. "Lisa. A nice English name. Well, Lisa, you think the fire started naturally? No, I started it. And I started the one near Argostoli, too. The fires were meant to frighten people, especially Christoph. That is my power."

Suddenly, the outer door banged, making both women jump. Lisa took the opportunity to smack the stubby, black-handled, short-bladed knife from Theresa's hand and then stand on it so it couldn't be picked it up. Then she punched Theresa hard in the face, knocking her to the ground. The girl moaned and closed her eyes for a moment before screaming in fury.

Lisa quickly picked up the knife, charged out of the front door and then ran, barefoot, like the wind. She ran like she'd run to get help for Christoph and Thomas, only this time it was her life, not theirs, which depended on her speed. She didn't hear Kostas calling out to her.

It was dark outside, but Lisa knew the road well and made for the next house where she could see lights were still on. She knew an English couple, Jenny and Andrew, lived there.

Gasping for breath, Lisa banged on the front door, shouting, "Help me, please help me!"

The door shot open to reveal Andrew standing in the doorway framed by the hall light behind him. Seeing how distressed Lisa was, he worriedly asked, "What the hell's happened, Lisa? Do come in. Jenny, quick, come here, it's Lisa from up the road." Then noticing Lisa was clutching a knife, said in horror, "And, oh, god, she's got a knife." After swallowing hard, he nervously reached out his right hand and quietly said, "Lisa, please give me the knife." But struck rigid with terror and exhaustion, Lisa couldn't move.

Just then, Theresa skidded to a halt near Lisa. Looking at Andrew she screamed, "You help her, and I will kill you. And her."

Bloody hell, thought Andrew, *I'm in the middle of some sort of bizarre, surreal film.* Then putting up his right hand in a stop position, he looked at Theresa and calmly and firmly commanded, "Stop. Whoever you are, just stop."

Theresa stared at Andrew. How dare a mere man tell her to stop? Who does he think he is? Seeing Theresa hesitate, jolted Lisa into action. Discreetly sliding the knife along the ground to Andrew, she whispered, "Use this to defend yourself, if necessary, Andrew. I'm so sorry you've got involved in all this."

Andrew picked up the knife and threw it into his house. "Thanks, but that won't be necessary. I'll deal with her." He started to move towards Theresa but stopped as Kostas panted to a halt just behind the crazed woman, and as she turned to see who it was, Kostas hit her hard across the face, felling her to the ground. "Call the Police, Andrew," he shouted as he bent down to check Theresa's pulse. "She's still alive but won't be going anywhere."

Jenny slowly appeared from behind the front door. "I'll do it. You three keep an eye on the woman," she said in a small, frightened voice. "Take care."

Within fifteen minutes, policeman Spyros arrived, donned his cap, and after carefully listening to Lisa's account of what had happened, cautioned Theresa who was slowly coming round. After nudging her into a kneeling position, he angrily pulled her up before pushing her into his police car. "Okay. She'll be charged with aggravated assault, or maybe even attempted murder. Whatever, she'll probably be taken to the psychiatric hospital," he stated importantly. Then turning to Lisa, gently asked, "Are you okay, Lisa?"

Lisa fainted before she could reply. Thankfully, Kostas caught her just before she hit the ground and helped Jenny and Andrew carry her into the house and onto to their sofa. Then, after making sure she was coming round, he shrugged on the jacket he'd gone to Lisa's house to retrieve, said goodbye to Jenny and Andrew, and left. He had a lot to tell Alexandra.

Seeing Lisa's eyes open, Jenny called to Andrew, "Quick, Andrew, she's awake."

Andrew rushed in from the kitchen where he'd been making that very English of things in a crisis, a cup of tea. "Thank goodness, how are you feeling, Lisa? I've called the doctor, and he'll be here any minute."

Unable to talk, all Lisa could do was to look at the young couple who were worriedly staring at her. Then suddenly, she started to violently shake all over.

"She's in shock, Andrew," Jenny stated as she pulled a throw over Lisa's legs. "Is there sugar in that tea? Here, give it to me." She carefully took the mug of hot tea and gently held it to Lisa's lips, telling her to take a sip because it would make her feel better.

With some effort, Lisa managed to do as she was told. Her swimming head was pounding and full of thoughts. What had happened? Had it been Theresa? What did she say about Christoph? And a small boy? She shook her head to try to clear it, but it made her feel dizzier. Where was she? Her neck hurt and her eyes couldn't focus because everything was blurry. She tried to speak but no words came out.

"It's okay, Lisa, don't try to talk, just rest," Jenny said kindly. Lisa gratefully sank back against the soft cushion Jenny had put behind her head just as there was a knock at the front door.

"I'll get it," called Andrew. "It's probably the doctor."

Doctor Anapolous examined Lisa all over and declared that she was suffering from severe shock and needed to rest for a couple of days. He gave her an injection which calmed her down and made her feel sleepy and told her that her bruised neck and ribs and injured feet would recover in time; she just needed to keep her feet clean and dry with the sterile dressings he produced from his medical bag.

A couple of hours later, Andrew drove Lisa back to her house, making sure that all doors and windows were securely locked before helping Lisa crawl upstairs to the bedroom where she fell, half-dressed, into bed, assuring Andrew who was waiting outside the door, that she'd be okay. Then, after hearing him say he'd check on her the next day and slam the front door shut, she turned over and fell into a deep, dreamless sleep.

Lisa woke with a start to the sound of a cockerel crowing in the distance. It was just about light. Everything that had happened the night before came flooding back to her. Why was she attacked? What was Christoph keeping from her?

She stumbled out of bed, standing still for a moment to allow the room to stop sliding and her head to stop pounding, then with shaking hands, she slowly dressed and went downstairs to put the kettle on. It was seven o'clock, and Christoph should be awake by now. She looked at their pinboard next to the fridge where Christoph had put two telephone numbers for Lisa to use should she need to contact him whilst he was in Athens or the UK. With a shaking hand, she dialled the Athens number.

The phone made that familiar 'brrrr, brrrr' sound which Lisa always found slightly irritating. Why can't Greek phones ring like British ones?

"Kalimera," said a male voice.

"Christoph?" asked Lisa. But it didn't sound like him at all.

"Yes. Is that Lisa? Are you okay?" Christoph asked more clearly.

"No. I mean yes, it is me. But no, I'm not okay. I want you back here immediately."

"Why, what's wrong?" asked a puzzled Christoph. "Tell me."

"No, I won't bloody tell you. Just get your Greek arse back here on the next flight," Lisa said in a loud, angry voice. Then she slammed the phone down.

The telephone rang three times, but Lisa ignored it. She was determined not to talk to Christoph until they were face to face and she could see if he was telling the truth or not.

Lisa busied herself cleaning things which didn't need cleaning even though it exhausted her and her hurt body and feet. She then phoned Alexandra to say neither she nor Kostas were needed for a few days and that she'd phone again when they were. She suddenly felt she had to get out. Feeling nervous, she pulled on the softest shoes she could find for her sore, torn feet, and gently put her arms into the sleeves of her comfy black puffa jacket, then after easing it over her bruised ribs she pulled up the zip to just below her sore neck.

Once ready, she gingerly climbed into her car and drove to the little taverna overlooking Katelios beach where she ordered a coffee. As it was a Tuesday, she knew that even though it was still early, Christoph would be working so wouldn't be able get back from Athens for at least a couple of hours, or maybe even more if he had things to sort out before getting the next domestic flight to Kefalonia. He'd then need to get a taxi to Katelios as he'd not taken his own car to the airport. It would all take time.

The wait seemed endless. Lisa ordered two more coffees before deciding it was time to return to the house. Unlocking the front door with a shaking hand, she stepped inside and stood still. It didn't feel the same, it felt alien. Feeling slightly sick, she removed her coat and shoes, padded across the entrance area, then slowly ascended the grand staircase to her bedroom. Their bedroom. Their sanctuary from the world. Only now it no longer felt like a sanctuary. She felt like an intruder.

With an ashen face, Christoph stared at Lisa. "She lied, Lisa. The boy isn't mine. She was already pregnant when I first met her, but she didn't tell me immediately. That's why I ended the affair."

Lisa bit her bottom lip. How could she believe this man? "Can you prove it?" She snarled.

"No, not unless I take a blood test and she wouldn't allow me to do that, not even after Maria and Niko adopted him." Christoph looked at Lisa pleadingly. "You have to believe me, Lisa, I wouldn't keep something like that from you."

"Yes, well you have. You've kept all that from me. Supposing I'd never find out?"

"Look," Christoph began miserably. "Theresa blackmailed me. She told me that if I didn't take the child and pay her a lot of money for the rest of my life, she'd tell everyone I raped her, and that the boy was a result of that. That terrible lie would have destroyed not only me but also my family. Forever. I had no choice. Even worse, she told me she'd been raped by a stranger, but she couldn't tell her family because it was such a disgrace. And she claimed that the little boy is a result of the rape."

Lisa gulped. If that was true, then poor girl. No wonder she'd become unhinged. "So that's why she was angry with you when I met her in Skala?"

"Yes. But she became even angrier when I told her a few weeks ago that I couldn't pay her anymore because I have a new life with you. She threatened to harm you, but I didn't believe her, I thought she was just trying to scare me. But clearly, she did mean it," Christoph whispered. "And you could have died. How can you ever forgive me, Lisa?"

Lisa didn't answer at first. Her heart was pounding with stress and her mouth was dry. "Did you know she started the fires In Skala and near Argostoli?"

Christoph gasped. "What do you mean she started the fires?"

"That's what she told me. She claims to be mafioso and started the fires to scare everyone including you. To show us all how powerful she is. I know you don't mess with them."

"Oh, my god. Mafioso. I heard a rumour that her *Nonna* was involved but not Theresa. It's well known that when *Nonna* passes that'll be the end of the Mafia in that area of Italy."

Christoph stopped talking, took a breath, and continued, "Lisa, Theresa isn't mafioso, that's her twisted mind thinking that. I know she's done terrible things, but she is ill, she needs help. I think maybe having a baby she didn't want especially as he may have been the result of rape, made her ill. But I don't know, I'm just guessing. But what I do know is that there are some people you just don't argue with, and if she'd somehow crossed those people then she's lucky to be alive, that it was only rape."

Lisa closed her eyes. *Only* rape? Good god, it was one thing after another and all too much. Her initial instinct that Christoph was dangerous had been oh, so right.

A strained silence filled the air for so long that it became palpably painful.

"Talk to me, Lisa. Please," pleaded Christoph eventually.

Lisa opened her eyes and looked at him. "I don't want to stay in this house, Christoph. I'm scared because you talk of frightening things that I don't want to know about. And clearly, Theresa had been spying on us for ages, so she knew our movements. Then, when she knew you'd left, she came here and just walked in the back door - which obviously was my fault for leaving it unlocked. But how do you think all this makes me feel, Christoph? And why was she on the island at this time of the year anyway?"

Ignoring Lisa's question about how she felt, Christoph murmured, "I don't know. But she's an adult and can travel whenever and wherever she wants; she doesn't have to explain herself to anyone." He paused thoughtfully, then continued. "When I broke up with her, she went crazy. Do you remember me telling you that she ran away up into old Skala village and hid without any food or water?"

"Yes, I do. I hate her but I also feel sorry for her. I hope one day she becomes well again."

Moving slightly nearer Lisa and putting out his scarred, right hand to try to touch her arm, Christoph quietly said, "Lisa, please stay. We can work this out…"

"No!" Interrupted Lisa loudly as she snatched her arm out of his reach. "I am not staying. In fact, I'm going right now," she said firmly as she moved towards the staircase. "I'm going to Skala to stay with Daphne, I know she'll put me up until I can arrange to go home. Do not try to stop me, Christoph. I've had enough and I need time and space away from you, from here, from everything and everyone. Now get out of my way and leave me alone."

Sidling past Christoph so she didn't have to touch him, Lisa walked up the stairs as fast as her hurting body and feet would let her to the bedroom where she threw a few basic things into her suitcase, including her notebook that she'd almost filled with notes for her story, which ironically was becoming truer by the day; it was almost as if she'd had a premonition. Then, despite the pain, she dragged the case downstairs, put on her puffa jacket and soft shoes, pulled up the handle of her suitcase, opened the front door, and climbed into her Audi parked outside. Without even a glance at Christoph or the house she then swiftly drove off in a screeching cloud of dust.

Stunned, Christoph could only silently watch her leave, his green eyes filled with tears. His beloved Lisa had left him – but for how long? He knew he could stop her getting on the plane if he wanted to, his contacts would see to it, but he didn't want that for Lisa, he deeply loved her, she was his first and only true love, and he just wanted her to be safe and happy. Anyway, he couldn't cope with another English woman having an unfortunate 'accident' on a mountain road because of him….*Nouno* Uncle Theo had said that woman asked too many questions about his business in Athens when Christoph took her there. Christoph was told he wouldn't see her again because after the 'accident' she'd quickly returned to the UK – and he knew better than to question his powerful uncle about that, or about anything.

Christoph shuddered and shook his head. It was time to change, to move on, to live a different, better life. But what to do now? Was this really the end of him and his beloved Lisa?

Chapter Twenty-Five

Daphne welcomed Lisa with open arms, although when Lisa told her why she was there, she became very sad. "But I thought you were both so happy, Lisa. This is terrible, it's such an awful thing to happen to you, you poor girl, and I can understand why you want to go back home," she said as she put her arms around Lisa's rigid body.

Feeling the warmth of Daphne's love, Lisa broke down sobbing in her old friend's arms. She'd still been too shocked and worn out to cry when leaving Christoph. "I loved him, Daphne, and I trusted him. We were so happy. But I can't live with this. And what's next? Will there be something else I don't know? Christoph hinted there were dangerous people around. Is that true?"

Daphne didn't reply at first. "Lisa," she began carefully. "There *is* something else about Christoph, but it won't directly affect you. And yes, there are some people who…who aren't very nice, but we don't talk about them."

"Oh, god what now?" Asked a tearful Lisa as she closed her eyes. "But you must tell me what you know, Daphne. Please."

"Well, Christoph isn't who he seems to be," began Daphne. "He's really his uncle Tony's son; he has Tony's green eyes. Tony and Thalia had an affair a long time ago, but Vasilis stayed with Thalia and raised Christoph as his own. Then they had Maria."

Open mouthed, Lisa stared at Daphne. Ah, so that would explain why Tony was so good to Christoph, and why he chose him to be his agent - blood being thicker than water. "Oh, well, that's not so bad," she replied. "After all, that sort of thing happens, but isn't openly talked about. It wouldn't make any difference to me, but Theresa's attack and the reason for it, does make a difference to me, and I need time to think about what to do next. And you don't say how Christoph knows about the not-very-nice people – who are they, Daphne?"

Daphne nodded but didn't respond to Lisa's question. Instead, she told her she was welcome to stay for as long as she wanted to. Lisa thanked her and said she was going home as soon as she could get a flight, adding that she'd leave the Audi with her, and she could do with it what she wanted.

Daphne nodded again whilst saying, "Go home, Lisa, go home and be safe. Please."

Leaving Daphne in the kitchen, Lisa telephoned Olympic Airways to book a flight back to the UK. It being out of season, she was able to book one to Heathrow leaving at ten o'clock the following morning. Then, after phoning for a taxi to take her to the airport, she phoned Fifi-Rose and left a message to say she'd be home the next day. She also asked her friend to stop forwarding her mail and to tell the letting agent to take her cottage off their register immediately. Lisa knew the cottage was between tenants so thankfully she could go straight home.

After a tearful goodbye to Daphne the next morning, Lisa climbed stiffly into the taxi with her multi-ribboned suitcase. As the taxi drove away, she tried hard not to look back at Daphne and the village she loved but she just had to. And then, just as the taxi turned right to go up the hill out of Katelios, there she was: A slightly out of focus, smiling young girl dressed in grey, waving and mouthing goodbye. Lisa gulped, looked away and then back again, but the girl had gone. Lisa shivered. Had it been the ghost of Ariadne-Rose? Or had she imagined it? She'd never know. Maybe she was losing her mind because of all the stress.

Shaking her head, Lisa looked down but then couldn't resist the urge to look up once more at the beautiful, rugged scenery she'd grown to love. She tried hard not to cry as her beloved, rock-strewn Mount Aenos soared to her right, but soft tears fell as pretty village after village slowly disappeared, and the taxi finally drove down the hill to the airport.

Wiping her eyes, Lisa paid the taxi driver and, without a backward glance, hurried to check-in before going through the usual security and into the departures lounge where she found a seat beside the large window through which she could see the aircraft that would take her home. She felt unreal, as if she was dreaming and would wake up any moment. But it wasn't a dream, and soon the call came over the loudspeaker for passengers to Heathrow to go to their boarding gate. Without thinking, Lisa found herself climbing the plane's steps and looking for her seat. She didn't care where she sat so long as she got home soon.

The journey was uneventful. Lisa had a coffee but no food. She closed her eyes and tried not to think about what had happened. She must have dozed off because she suddenly became aware of the plane slowly dropping in stages as it prepared to land. Then it gently thudded down on to the tarmac at Heathrow and halted at its stand. She was home.

Baggage reclaim was easy, and Lisa was soon out of the airport looking for a taxi. She didn't care how much it cost to get back to her cottage in Iden, nor about the cold UK weather. She just felt numb, as if her body had been scooped out, removing all emotion.

Glancing out of the taxi window, everything looked strange. It was grey and small and unfamiliar. How long had she been away? She couldn't remember. Everything in her body hurt and her brain was tired, so she wearily closed her eyes to shut it all out.

Making Lisa jump, the taxi driver called out, "We're just coming into Iden, love. Can you tell me where to go?"

Lisa dragged her eyes open. "Oh, er, yes, turn right at the next crossroads, then first left into a lane. My cottage, Wisteria Cottage, is a few yards down on the right. You can't miss it, it's the only black and white one."

With an exhausted sigh, Lisa stepped inside her cottage. It smelled empty and strange. She didn't know if she felt pleased or sad to be back. Looking round, she saw a white envelope addressed *'Lisa'* in Fifi-Rose's handwriting propped up on the coffee table. She tore it open to find a note inside saying: "*Welcome home dear friend. I let myself in so there's milk, cheese, eggs, butter and wine in the fridge, pizza in the freezer, teabags and coffee in the cupboard and bread in the breadbin. The cottage has been deep-cleaned at one hours' notice by a kind friend, all bedding's new including the duvet and pillows (purchased at same time as very early morning supermarket shopping!), and there's no washing or anything like that so everything's tickety-boo. We'll get your clothes and stuff later. Love you and see you asap. F-R xx.*"

Clutching her kind friend's note in her hand, Lisa sat down on the nearest chair with a bump and cried until she had no tears left.

After unpacking her suitcase, making a cheese sandwich and a cup of tea, Lisa sat looking out of her cottage window at the bleak, leafless Sussex countryside. She needed to light the fire – that would cheer her up. It took two attempts, but she was soon sitting in her favourite floral armchair beside the blazing logs with her legs tucked underneath her.

The log fires' flames threw long, sad shadows across the beamed ceiling and bumpy walls, even the old floorboards seemed to creak with sorrow. Silence fell like a heavy blanket around her. It was too quiet. Lisa decided to turn on the tv for company, then as she was watching a boring late afternoon programme, Fifi-Rose arrived with her usual flourish.

In sharp contrast to Lisa's black jeans and jumper, Fifi-Rose's colourful ensemble of wide, bright red trousers and a loose, red jumper with long earrings to match, clashed dramatically with her short, spiky pink hair. "Darling!" She stage-whispered as she hugged her friend. "I'm so pleased to see you! But I'm guessing you're here so suddenly because of something that's happened in Kefalonia? Again?" She ended questioningly.

"Yes. Thanks for coming round so quickly. Let's sit down and I'll get us some wine."

Leaving her discarded bright blue coat and black boots in the small hall, Fifi-Rose followed Lisa into the living room and sat on a stool beside Lisa's armchair in front of the log fire.

Lisa poured them both a glass of wine, then handing Fifi-Rose hers, said, "Fifi, I can't take any more. It's all a disaster."

"Whoa, hang on. Take it slowly. From the beginning."

Perched on the edge of her seat, and clutching her glass of wine, Lisa bit her bottom lip and whispered, "It's Christoph."

Ah, thought Fifi-Rose, now there's a surprise. Not. "Yes? Carry on. In your own time."

Lisa started slowly but then the whole story rapidly came out about the old village and the ghost, the coach saga, Mark turning up, his nastiness and then his accident, Sam and the ring, the fire, Christoph being hurt and how she'd run to get help for him and Thomas, she and Christoph deciding to live together, and finally ending with Theresa's attack.

Stunned, Fifi-Rose very uncharacteristically couldn't say a word.

Lisa looked at her friend. Even to her ears, it all sounded utterly unbelievable. "There were many good bits, too," she said, hoping to sound more positive. "Christoph and I were very happy in Katelios, and everyone in Skala, including Christoph's many cousins, was lovely and I made some wonderful, very kind and good friends there, especially Daphne and Thomas, and Rebecca and her husband Yannis. I loved working in Sue and Trevor's Accommodation Shop in Skala, and in their jewellery shop in Argostoli town. Also, it was brilliant when my girls visited. Despite how it sounds, Fifi, it wasn't all doom and gloom."

But Fifi-Rose wasn't convinced. She felt everything that had happened to her friend must have taken a terrible toll on her.

Seeing Fifi-Rose's hesitation, Lisa added. "But I can't help still loving the island, it's such a magical, beautiful place which will always be in my heart, it's where my spirit lives and I feel whole when I'm there, the true me, if that makes sense? It's well known that lots of people have their special 'place', and Kefalonia's mine. In fact, I was often told by the locals that lots of people return to the island many times, especially to Skala, because there's something about it which keeps drawing them back. So, I'm not as potty as I probably sound. One day I'll return, I feel I need to reconcile the past, and to join with my spirit for one last time."

"You're nuts," scoffed Fifi-Rose, totally not understanding what Lisa meant. "I can think of dozens of other Greek islands, or any island, which you could go to! But anyway, you seem to have made up your mind. So, what about Christoph? Do you still love him?"

"I don't know. I think I'll always be fond of him but it's different now. He deliberately withheld important things from me, so how could

I ever trust him again? Trust is so important. I don't care that he's really Tony's son, that's not important to me. But it's the boy. And the money. And also…" she hesitated.

"And also? What?" asked Fifie-Rose sharply. "What is it, Lisa? Tell me?"

"I don't know, it's probably just my imagination, but I…I… I think there's something a bit more sinister going on that's been kept from me, that I must never ask questions about. I had a feeling that Daphne knows but she'd not say."

"What makes you think that?"

"It was just something she said firstly a vague hint about some bad people and then asking me to go home and be safe. It didn't click at first, but I think she was trying to warn me of something without actually doing so. It's just a feeling but a strong one.'"

Fifi-Rose stared at her friend. What the bloody hell? Something was very wrong here, and a shiver went down her spine. She moved forward and took both of Lisa's cold hands in hers. "Look, you're better off at home, Lisa, and I beg you never to return to that island. Please promise me you won't go back."

Lisa looked into her friend's wide, concerned eyes. "I can't promise that, Fifi, I can promise to always be careful if I do return. But yes, maybe I do need to let go of Christoph and move on, even though he'll always be in my heart. If I do decide to see him again, I think

It would need to be in Argostoli. Not in Skala or Katelios."

Fifi-Rose thought Lisa was hedging her bets but didn't say that. Instead, she ignored what Lisa had said and agreed that trust is vital, adding. "But only you know if you want to see Christoph again, and if so, where that might be. Just take some time to think carefully, Lisa, don't rush into anything. Ok?"

Then, keen to lighten the mood, she smiled broadly and raised her glass to her friend. "Anyway, cheers and welcome back!" Whilst secretly doubting if she could ever have coped with all that Lisa had been through.

For a few minutes, the two women sat in companionable silence. The day was sombre, heavy and encompassing, only the log fire seemed to bring any comfort. There was no sound from outside, not even a dog barking; it was if everywhere was holding its breath.

After taking a long drink of her wine, Lisa suddenly continued. "Remember I'd planned to write a story?" Fifi-Rose jumped a little and nodded yes. "Well, the story was originally about a woman of a certain age who goes to a Greek island, meets a dangerous chap and has many adventures. It was by pure chance that I initially went to Kefalonia, but once I was there, I felt completely at home. I also soon knew that, without realising it, I'd outlined my own personal Greek story with my fictitious story outline before I'd even got there. How odd is that?!" She finished.

"Well, yes, that is very odd, Lisa! Thing is, how does your fictitious story end?"

Lisa didn't reply at first. Then very slowly said, "Well, I'd thought my heroine would return to the island and tell the Greek chap that he must marry and have children because that's the Greek way. But he's devastated because he loves her. Nonetheless, she goes home to the UK but returns many years later when she's older. I haven't planned the absolute end yet, that's what I was hoping to do when I was in Skala."

"Ohhh," sighed Fifi-Rose, with eyes so wide her false eyelashes almost touched her perfect eyebrows. "That's, that's…really moving, Lisa."

Lisa laughed. "Yes, well, it is only a story, Fifi, it isn't real life. It's just coincidence that my story idea became real life for me in some ways, and although I had thought my heroine would have some adventures, I hadn't planned for her to experience what I've had to deal with!"

After declining another glass of wine, Fifi-Rose sipped water and stayed with her friend until it was getting dark - she couldn't stay any longer because she had to work the next day. Wednesdays were always full of business meetings, so she needed to get a good night's sleep. The two women chatted about everything that had happened, about what Lisa might do about Christoph and how she'd cope being back in the UK. In the end, Lisa decided to ring James and Simon the next day to see if they had a job for her at *Thingamabob*.

Lisa also decided she'd talk with Christoph and tell him she'd not be back to Kefalonia for a while although she would occasionally contact him. But that was all. Other than that, she couldn't even begin to think about him, nor the house which had been their wonderful, happy Greek home, nor about everything, both material and emotional, she'd left behind. She couldn't even think about the other people she cared for, and everything she knew and loved about her Greek island. She needed time.

Fifi-Rose agreed Christoph would have to pay for Lisa's legal representation in the case against Theresa, and that Lisa might have to go to Greece to give evidence. Lisa decided she'd cross that bridge when, or if, she came to it. However, first she needed to rest and let her body and mind heal. But she knew that it was also time to accept how things were, to let go of the past, and to move on – no more Skala. And no more Christoph, the ghost of Ariadne-Rose, or those unknown not-very-nice people whom no-one must speak of.

Chapter Twenty-Six

Lisa's daughters were quick to respond to her messages telling them she was home for the duration. Bella wasn't at all surprised, Scarlett was shocked, and Tiffany-Mae was upset.

Due to their respective work commitments, the girls couldn't get to see Lisa for a few days, Scarlett being the first to visit after having had a busy day in meetings as PA to her Corporate Law firm boss, Lamont. Tiffany-Mae was away on a long-haul flight, and Bella was working nights on a busy paediatric ward, so neither of them could visit for a while.

Lisa opened the door to her daughter feeling very relieved that at last she was with one of her precious girls. Scarlett threw her arms around Lisa, suddenly becoming aware of how thin she was. "Mum! It's so lovely to see you!" she exclaimed. "Are you okay?"

Burying her head in her youngest daughter's mop of dark, thick, straight hair and breathing in her delicate, but expensive, perfume – Chanel? - Lisa didn't reply for a moment.

"Yes, yes, I'm fine," assured Lisa, blinking. "I'm just pleased to see you, that's all. It seems to have been a long time, and such a lot has happened."

"God, yes, hasn't it just!" agreed Scarlett. "Look, let's go and sit down. I've brought wine and pizza so we can eat, drink and chat. You need to eat, you're too thin."

Lisa was full up. How kind and thoughtful her youngest child was. "That'll be brilliant. I'll put the pizza in to cook, it won't take long. And I'll open the wine. Now you go and make yourself comfortable by the fire."

"Okay, that sounds good, see you in a moment," replied Scarlett as she eased off her black jacket and high heeled long, black leather boots. "You sure you don't want any help?"

"No, no, I'm okay."

Half an hour later the two women were sitting in front of the blazing log fire eating pizza and drinking white wine.

"Mum," began Scarlett as she turned, slice of pizza in her hand, to look at her mother.

"Yes?" Lisa asked warily. She knew her daughter could ask awkward questions. And there may be a lot of those.

"Well, I just want to say that I'm sorry things didn't work out for you, especially as you and Christoph seemed so happy. But also, if there's any legal stuff which needs to be sorted then let me know because I can ask my boss Lamont to deal with it for you."

Ah, Lamont, thought Lisa. Scarlett had often spoken about him; he sounded such a nice, caring man. Very bright and interesting, too, and very young to be a senior partner in a law firm. She knew he was the eldest of four brothers in a Caribbean family, and that his parents had come to the UK on HMT Empire Windrush when they were very young. His dad had been a bus driver and his mum a nurse, and both were now happily retired somewhere in Surrey. Lamont was their pride and joy.

"Well, there could be, so if there is I'll let you know," replied Lisa thinking of what she and Tiffany-Rose had discussed as she reassuringly patted her daughter's hand.

"He's very good at what he does," continued Scarlett. "And he's a good boss, too."

Lisa looked at her daughter; she knew that tone of voice: softer, with a slightly dreamy edge. Her daughter was falling for her boss – the age-old story! "Is he handsome?"

"Hmm, well, yes, I suppose he is. He's tall, broad-shouldered and has a lovely smile. But most importantly, he's kind and caring, loves his mum to pieces, and looks up to his dad who he's very close to. All his younger brothers know he's always there for them, too. It's a close family."

"Have you met them all?"

"Yes, Lamont invited me to his parents' retirement party a couple of years ago. It was wonderful! Full of joy and laughter and fab Caribbean music and dancing! Loads of relatives were there, all dressed in the most amazing outfits. I loved it," Scarlett grinned. "Defo not your usual retirement party with the clock or wristwatch as a present!"

"What are his parents' names?" Lisa was intrigued by this very different family life.

"His dad's called Idris and his mum's name is Simone. His brothers are Jamal, Davy and Anton but I can't remember who's who!"

"You seem to be very fond of Lamont and his family, Scarlett. Is there more to the boss-PA relationship than you're saying?"

Scarlett didn't reply at first. Looking down thoughtfully at her hands she screwed up her nose. "Well, maybe. But it's early days, Mum. For now, we're just as we should be in a very busy law firm, so that's it for now."

"Okay, just asking," Lisa knew when not to push her daughter. "Anyway, what do you think about Christoph and me?"

"In what way?" asked a puzzled Scarlett. "You said you're home for the duration which implies you may not return to Kefalonia, or to Christoph. And what does Fifi-Rose think?"

"More importantly, what do Tiffany-Mae and Bella think?" Countered Lisa. She knew they all often talked on the phone, and that they'd definitely have been asking each other what they thought of their Mum's latest situation. "Not that anyone's opinion will change things, I'm just keen to know."

"Why? Are you thinking of going back?"

"No. Well, yes. But no," stuttered Lisa. "I'm not sure. I would like to go to see Daphne, Sue and Rebecca because they're good friends who've all been very kind to me, but I don't want Christoph getting the wrong idea."

"Well, put him right then, just tell him there's no way forward for you both so he can't misunderstand then. Easy-peasy, Mother."

"Don't call me 'Mother'," snapped Lisa. She took a deep breath. "Sorry, it's just that I'm still recovering from the attack which really shook me up. I'm not myself, I need some time."

Scarlett took her Mum's hands in hers. "That's okay," she said gently. "I can understand because it was a terrible thing to happen to you. Basically, you had your very life threatened and that would unsettle anyone, Mum, so, yes, give yourself time. And don't make any decisions yet."

"Yes, you're right. I still don't sleep very well and often dream she's chasing me and I'm running but getting nowhere. But I would like to go back to the island sometime. Meanwhile, I'm going to ring James and Simon to ask them if I can go back to work in *Thingamabob*."

"Well, that's brilliant, Mum, let us know how you get on!"

"I also miss Christoph," continued Lisa. "I loved him, we were like soul mates, but he didn't trust me enough to tell me the truth about Theresa and that hurt me very deeply. I can't live with someone who doesn't trust me."

"He must have had his reasons, Mum. But I get what you're saying. Trust is everything in a relationship and once broken it's hard to get back."

"Yes, it is. Anyway, I'm getting too old to be worrying about such things, I need to live my life without that sort of stress and worry. Also, Christoph needs to marry and have children because that's the Greek way, that's what his family expects and although they've been very kind to me, I know they'd wished I could have had his children, especially a son, to carry on the family name."

Scarlett looked at Lisa. Was Mum over her menopause? She wondered. It wasn't something she and her sisters had ever even thought about! But then being over fifty Lisa may well be over it, and even if she wasn't, she certainly wouldn't be wanting any more children. Perish the thought!

Keen to change the subject, Scarlett looked at her watch. "Hmm, okay. Look, I'm sorry I can't stay very long, I just wanted to check you're okay, but I've got to go, now, Mum. I need my sleep as I've another busy day tomorrow. The money's good but I damn well earn it," she laughed.

"That's alright. It's been lovely to see you, and we can meet up again soon," Lisa said as she stood up to hug her daughter.

The two women went into the small hall where Scarlett donned her jacket and boots, and after another hug and promises to contact each other soon, Scarlett left.

Over the couple of weeks, Lisa saw her daughters more than she'd seen them in the past two years! Once they were all satisfied that she was coping they decided not to see her so much and happily returned to their usual daily and work routines.

Lisa missed Christoph more than she ever thought she would. She missed his presence, his kindness and the smell of him. Had she made a mistake? She decided to phone him, and he was thrilled to hear from her, but she told him she couldn't stay long on the phone because it was expensive, so Christoph promised to ring her the following week. Which he did.

"I still love you, Lisa. You know that and you know I always will," Christoph stated after they'd exchanged the usual social niceties.

"Yes, I do know, Christoph. I'm very fond of you, too…" she began.

"'Fond'? Is that all? Just 'fond'?"

"Oh, please don't question me, Christoph. I want us to be friends without any issues about anything."

Christoph was silent for a moment. If it was possible to hear a heart breaking, then Lisa would hear his right now. "Yes, of course. Anyway, how are you? Are you working?"

"I'm better, thanks, but still not right. It's taking a long time, Christoph. Yes, I'm working. I've started work in the jewellery shop in Rye, James and Simon are being very kind to me.

And I've had a letter from Therea's family solicitor which I'm going to give my solicitor. I'll post you a copy."

"Oh, okay thanks. There's no need to worry about the costs of anything, Lisa, I'll pay for everything."

Well, so you should, chum, thought Lisa. "Thank you," she said, "I'll keep you posted."

They continued chatting for a short while longer and promised to keep in contact. But would they?

As the weeks turned into months, Lisa slowly recovered from the trauma of the attack, and the nightmares lessened. The Greek court case went ahead on the mainland, but Lisa didn't have to attend as there was a lot of first-hand evidence provided by the statements from Kostas, policeman Spyros, Andrew, and Lisa's own statement. Medical evidence from the doctor sealed the case and judgement was passed: Theresa would serve five years in a secure prison, initially in a psychiatric unit.

Lisa slowly came to terms with living without Christoph, had her personal belongings shipped back to the UK, and began to feel settled again. She loved working in *Thingamabob* and once again became every customer's favourite. She also joined a local writing group and made friends with Katie, Marie, Lilian, Oliver and Frank; they were a fun bunch and there was always lots of laughter when they met in the local pub's social events room.

Lisa immediately took to Oliver; they got on well, had a similar sense of humour, and, like most of them, he'd joined the group for support and advice with writing a novel; he'd already written a professional science book but wanted to branch out. Lisa's own book had stumbled to a halt because she couldn't think how to end it.

With Oliver, Lisa discovered she could laugh again without feeling an underlying sense of sadness. He was a widower of indeterminate age having lost his beloved wife Annie a few years before, but there wasn't any hint of romance between him and Lisa, just a good, stress-free and honest friendship, rather like she had with Fifi-Rose. Plus, they liked the same things, shared story ideas and characters, visited art galleries, bookshops, pubs and cafes, explored countryside and coast, and once ventured to London where they took in the sights. Fifi-Rose sometimes joined them, making Oliver laugh at having two beautiful women on his arm! Fifi-Rose thought Oliver was adorable and a real gentleman.

Oliver, who was a private scientific consultant to a paint manufacturer, wasn't a handsome man, but he had a round, open, kind face, twinkly brown eyes, a lovely laugh, and a stocky, reassuring figure. He always dressed smartly whether it was in casual clothes, or the occasional three-piece suit which he wore to big meetings. It didn't matter that he was losing his greying hair and occasionally got backaches. What was most important to Lisa was that he was trustworthy and made her feel safe. She knew that Oliver would be someone to lean on if ever necessary, and that they would be friends for life. Her daughters also liked the sound of him, although they were slightly disappointed that Lisa didn't view him romantically!

Lisa was thrilled when Bella announced she was expecting a baby in September: she'd be a nanny! Summer came and went, then early autumn arrived in a burst of defiant orange, gold and brown, and sometimes bonfire smoke filled the air. But Bella's baby, adorable Clementine, decided to arrive a little early by making her appearance without any problems in late August. *Thingamabob* became very busy, and in early December the writing group enjoyed a jolly Christmas meal at a local pub.

For the first time in several years, Scarlett and Tiffany-Mae had three days free at the same time, and as Bella was on maternity leave, the four women, plus Bella's adored husband Alan, and little Clementine, were able to enjoy Christmas Eve and Christmas Day together at Lisa's cottage.

Wisteria cottage looked chocolate-box perfect. There were twinkling fairy lights everywhere, and a large Christmas tree which Oliver and Fifi-Rose had helped Lisa put up and decorate, stood in a corner by the inglenook fireplace. Whilst hanging the lights on the tree, Lisa brushed aside the memory of her and Alexandra decorating the tree at the Katelios house; that was in the past, now she lived in the present.

The ancient cottage glowed. Its old beams seemed to sparkle with joy, the bumpy walls cast happy shadows on to the old, wooden floor, and the inglenook really came into its own with a non-stop log fire casting warmth and brilliant light into the living room. The old, black wooden front door was adorned with a huge Christmas wreath of holly, ivy and a red ribbon bow, and the garden plants lying darkly dormant until their Spring resurrection twinkled with the fairy lights which Lisa had hung along all the hedges.

Lisa adored Clementine, so named because clementine's were Bella's favourite fruit! The baby quickly became known as Clemmie, and with her halo of blonde curls she looked like her daddy, although she had huge dark blue eyes like Lisa, plus dimples in her cheeks and a mischievous little smile like her mummy! Her soft, chubby body was a joy to hold and her 'baby smell' was like nectar to Lisa who never wanted to put her down! Clemmie made everyone's Christmas special - after all, children are what Christmas is all about, whether from a religious point of view or not. Happy days!

All too soon, Christmas came to an end and the cottage was once again too quiet. Lisa stayed with Fifi-Rose for the new year, and they went to the local firework display to watch nineteen ninety-six arrive in a shower of magnificent colour and noise, both wondering, in their own ways, what the new year would bring.

January was cold and February brought snow which Lisa hated. She struggled and slid into work as best she could, but then James told her to go home and not come back until the snow had gone because they had no customers.

During all this time, Lisa and Christoph continued to talk regularly on the telephone. Lisa always asked after Daphne, Sue, Trevor and the others. But then one Sunday afternoon in March, she sensed something was changing, that somehow Christoph was different.

"Christoph. Is everything alright?" She tentatively enquired one rainy Sunday afternoon as she gazed out of the leaded light sitting room window at raindrops plopping on to her yellow daffodils.

"Why do you ask?"

"Oh, it's just that…I don't know…you just don't sound yourself recently. I hope you're okay."

"Yes, I'm fine thank you," replied Christoph politely. "Look, I can't stay long today, Lisa, I only wanted to make sure you're okay, and from what you've told me, it sounds as if you're getting on with a good life which is brilliant. I'm so pleased for you because all I want is for you to be happy." He paused, then continued, "Sorry, but I need to go now as I'm rather busy. You know how it is. Anyway, bye for now. Take good care and we'll chat again soon." Then the phone went dead, leaving Lisa staring at the receiver. Oh, yes, she knew how it could be alright. But she also knew he wasn't telling her the whole truth, there was something else going on, she could feel it in her bones.

But what Lisa didn't know was that she wouldn't talk with Christoph again for a few months, and that when she did it would change her life yet again.

Chapter Twenty-Seven

Two months later, Lisa decided that it was time to invest in one of the new mobile phones, or cell phones as the Americans called them. So, on her Wednesday half day, she drove into Rye to find the shop selling the new devices.

Walking into the shop, Lisa encountered a confusing array of black phones in all shapes and sizes lying in glass-topped display cabinets. Each phone had a description of its make, how it worked and its price. Good grief, she thought, how are people supposed to understand this sort of stuff?

But clearly many did because the shop was rapidly filling up with eager customers.

"Can I help you?" enquired a young, black-clad female assistant who'd noticed Lisa's obvious confusion.

Startled, Lisa looked up from the display cabinet she'd been staring into where a black device was cradled in its holder like a tiny new baby. She'd noticed it didn't have a long antenna like the phone she had at home. And it was a lot smaller.

"Oh, yes. No. Well, yes. I was just looking. That is, I'm thinking of getting one of these. I've seen them before, and I've got one but not like any of these."

"Ah, yes, you've probably got one of the very first ones. We call them 'bricks' because they're so big!" laughed the girl. "Does it have an antenna sticking up out of it?"

Lisa smiled. "Yes, it does. But to be honest I rarely use it. It's too bulky for me so it's in a drawer somewhere. I use my landline instead. I know what I'm doing with that."

"Okay. But you'll find that cell or, as we call them now, mobile, phones are the thing of the future, and landlines will eventually become defunct. Let me show you this one," she said as she lifted the display cabinet lid. "I'm Avril, by the way. And you are Mrs…?"

"Ms," corrected Lisa primly. "Barat." This Avril was way too familiar for her liking.

"Oh. Ms Barat," said Avril as she looked at the phone she'd taken from the cabinet. After clearing her throat, she went on to describe the phone, how it worked, and its price, but Lisa lost all concentration after only a few moments. Feeling stressed and waving her hands in the air, she said the phone was way too expensive and asked if there was a cheaper, less complex one.

"Yes, there is, just here," replied Avril patiently as she moved to the next cabinet. "Here's the latest one which you'll see also doesn't have an antenna. These are the very latest modern phones," she said as she pointed to a relatively small, neat black device. It looked vaguely comforting and when Avril gave it to her to hold, Lisa found it fitted in her hand perfectly. This was the one.

After being told how it worked, and its price, Lisa was directed to the desk to sort out her price plan. Thinking things were done and dusted, Lisa prepared to leave but then the assistant said she needed phone insurance, going on to explain in great detail what could go wrong with Lisa's new phone.

After what felt like hours, and hot with anxiety, Lisa eventually left the shop with her new mobile phone in her bag. She needed coffee. Then, with downcast eyes, she hurried along the pavement thinking how, as a successful senior project manager and a senior salesperson, she could feel so dim. She needed to get a grip. Deep in thought, she turned the next corner and abruptly bumped into someone coming the other way. Frowning with annoyance, Lisa looked up and saw it was Oliver.

"Oh, Oliver!" she exclaimed with relief. "I'm so sorry but I didn't see you. Are you okay?"

"It should be me apologising and asking you that!" Laughed Oliver. "Anyway, you seemed to be elsewhere. Is everything okay?"

Lisa sighed. "Oh, yes. Thank you. It's just that I've bought a new mobile phone but hadn't realised just how complicated it could be, or how expensive! I've bought one because I think it's time that I got more modern. I do have a mobile phone, but I haven't used it for…let me think…about four years? Apparently, it's basically a dinosaur now!"

"Oh, yes, it will be," agreed Oliver. "The mobile phone market has moved on in leaps and bounds in the last couple of years. Anyway, if you're free shall we go for a coffee and then you can show me your new acquisition. What do you think?"

When Lisa didn't reply straight away, Oliver tilted his head to one side and regarded her through slightly narrowed eyes; he thought she looked tired. "Lisa, you probably need a break of some kind. When was the last time you had a holiday? I mean, like a *proper* holiday?" he asked kindly.

"Holiday? I don't need a holiday!" Lisa protested. "I'm fine," she added whilst mentally batting away long-buried memories of Kefalonia, Skala and Christoph.

Holding up both hands in surrender, Oliver said, "Whoa, just asking. But bear it in mind. Anyway, coffee?"

Lisa nodded, and the two friends resumed amicably chatting and laughing as they walked with linked arms down the road to the coffee shop.

The holiday brochure which had come through the post in January showed a ten-day holiday in Skala in mid-September. September was always a good month to take a break because thanks to holidays and the expense of children returning to school, no-one had any money to spend in *Thingamabob*.

Lisa wondered if she should. The voice on her shoulder told her she should. The voice in her heart told her she should. But the voice in her head told her she shouldn't. She asked herself why she wanted to go back to the island. Oh, yes, her spirit. She needed to feel 'joined' again. For the third and last time? She also needed to know why Christoph didn't tell her the whole truth when they last spoke on the telephone. And why he hadn't trusted her enough to tell her about Sebastian. Could there be something a bit more sinister going on after all?

"Hi, is this the travel agent shop?" Her heart had won. So be it.

"Yes, it is. Marion speaking. How can I help you?"

"Oh," Lisa swallowed. "I'd like to book the ten-day holiday in Skala for mid-September so can I come in tomorrow to pay please? And will you keep it reserved for me until then?"

"Well, I'll certainly ensure you'll have first dibs, but I can't guarantee to hold it for you. You need to be here as soon as possible. Sorry."

Lisa thought Marion was nowhere near as helpful as the girl she'd dealt with before but politely agreed to get to the shop as soon as she could before putting the phone down. *Oh, bother, why didn't I use my mobile?* she thought. Then she realised she'd need to ask about taking it abroad, charges for using it and all that palaver. Modern technology certainly wasn't simple.

After parking her little car in the multi-storey car park at the top of the functional shopping mall, Lisa took the escalator down to the next floor where the travel agent shop was situated, and taking a deep breath strode confidently inside.

"Hello," smiled the pretty girl behind a large desk as she pushed large, red-rimmed spectacles up her nose. Lisa noticed they matched her bright red uniform dress. "How can I help you?"

"I rang you yesterday about the ten-day holiday in Skala," replied Lisa. "I'm Lisa Barat."

"Ah, yes, Ms Barat. I looked you up on our system and see you've been to Kefalonia before. You obviously must have liked it to want to return," she laughed, adding, "I'm Marion by the way."

"Well, yes, er…Marion. I was there for a while, as it turned out. I love the island and want to return to see some friends I have there," responded Lisa whilst at the same time thinking *Too much information, Lisa. Shut up. Just book it.*

"Oh, how lovely!" exclaimed Marion over-enthusiastically. "Well now, let's see," she said as she clicked on to the company's holiday site on her computer. "Ah, yes, here we are.

Availability for ten days in Skala is only from the fifth to the fifteenth of September. It's self-catering in a block called Sappho Apartments. Looks like it's just off the main street," she added as she peered more closely at the screen. Lisa thought Marion's bright red spectacles might need changing. Then, bringing herself back to the task in hand, replied. "Okay that's fine. I know my way round Skala." *Don't I just,* she thought. *Like the back of my hand.*

Marion looked up enquiringly. "Everything okay for you with this holiday? Would you like me to book it? Transfer is included, and I expect you know the luggage allowance. Have you got travel insurance? And spending money? We do money exchange here so I can order for you. I can also book you a hire car of you'd like one."

"Yes, to all that, except the hire car which I won't need, thank you," Lisa replied briskly, keen to get the whole booking over and done with before she changed her mind. Her heart seemed to be beating at such a rate she thought she might faint at any moment. "How much do I owe you?"

After paying for the holiday and spending money with her credit card, Lisa thanked Marion, gathered up her bag and walked swiftly out of the shop, totally unaware of Marion watching her with raised eyebrows whilst thinking what an odd customer she was.

It was a dull April day. The sky and buildings were grey, and Lisa felt grey. It didn't help that she was wearing a grey greatcoat with matching scarf to keep out the early Spring cold. She hurried back to her car, keen to get home to the cottage and light the log fire for some much-needed warmth and cheer. She suddenly felt very lonely. It was all very well being an independent woman with a good job, and her own house and car, but she couldn't help wishing she had someone nice to go home to, someone she could curl up with, share stuff with, laugh or cry with. Oliver suddenly sprang to mind. She felt sad that there wasn't anything more than a good friendship between them; he'd make an ideal partner, but he was more like brother than a lover. *Lover?* She thought with a start. She didn't need another one of those thank you very much!

Shrugging off her greatcoat and scarf and hanging them on the peg behind the solid oak front door, Lisa went straight into the sitting room to light the fire. Very soon the whole ambience of the cottage was lifted with light and warmth. She then made a cup of tea and sat in her favourite flowery armchair beside the fire. The chair had belonged to her aunt Peg and was quite old, but it was the only thing she'd wanted from her deceased favourite aunt's bungalow when Peg's only son had invited her to have anything she fancied. The bungalow had been stuffed with knick-knacks and objects d'art, probably some of them quite valuable, but Lisa had only wanted to keep the memory of her aunt sitting in the chair.

After sipping some tea, Lisa looked again at the brochure advertising the Skala holiday in September. The three storey Sappho Apartments looked really pretty, with purple and pink bougainvillea climbing up its white walls and a hint of the sea in the distance. She wondered whether it was anywhere near Sam's house which had been similarly situated. September was five months away so there was no point in thinking about all that now.

"Really?" Exclaimed Fifi-Rose as her raised eyebrows disappeared under her over-long pink fringe: she was growing her hair out of its usual spiky style. "You mean, you're actually going back? For a third time?"

"Yes, I'm going back so don't start with the questions," replied Lisa defensively. "I need to know why Christoph isn't telling me the whole truth. And for him to tell me once and for all, exactly what was behind his decision not to share his difficulties with Theresa with me. Then I can tell him it's finally over between us which will mean we can both move on with no more contact," she finished, pursing her lips defiantly.

Fifi-Rose regarded her friend. "Okay, okay," she said as she held up her hands in a gesture of surrender. "I get it. I suppose I can understand you want answers and to move on, but I thought you'd 'parked' him anyway because you'd not heard from him for ages."

It was a hot mid-August day, and the two women were sitting in their usual café-bar having an after-work drink. Lisa had been very busy in the shop and was also overseeing the opening of another one in Tunbridge Wells, which meant she spent quite a bit of time going between the two towns. It was exhausting but she was being well paid for her efforts. Fifi-Rose had also had a busy day project managing a big building contract in her new job with a property developer.

"Have you told your girls?"

"No, why should I tell them? Bella's busy with Clemmie and Alan, Scarlett's away on a work trip with her boss Lamont, and Tiffany-Mae's on a lay-over in the US. They're all busy women and don't need to be worrying about their mother!"

"Yes, I get all that, but I still think you should tell them you're going away. Just for a holiday.

You don't need to tell them exactly what you've told me, although of course they'll probably ask why Skala. Again. Especially Tiff will."

Lisa surveyed the wine she was swirling in her glass. She'd thought of all this, but of course, Fifi-Rose was right, she should tell her daughters. After all, suppose something else happened? It wasn't as if she'd ever had a straightforward holiday on the island!

"Yeah, okay, I'll tell them I'm going for a holiday and to see Daphne and Rebecca. Which is true. But that's all. Now, let's have a coffee," she said, avoiding her friend's quizzical look. "Cheers! Here's to moving on!' she grinned. "And who knows, I might actually have an ordinary holiday this time!" she laughed with fingers mentally crossed and thinking she'd also need to tell Oliver she was going away. Lisa and Oliver were now very close - something which hadn't escaped the notice of the other members of their writing group, or Fifi-Rose. Was there more to Lisa and Oliver's friendship after all?

Chapter Twenty-Eight

September arrived in a blaze of unseasonal warmth and light autumn colour to the leaves. Lisa had packed for her holiday with the words of her daughter Tiffany-Mae telling her to be careful in her mind. Bella had distractedly wished her a lovely holiday, and Scarlett had texted her to say she'd see her when she returned to the UK at the end of the month, with a postscript saying: 'Have a lovely time mum, and no dramas this time please! xxx'

The day of Lisa's holiday arrived at last, and although it was only five in the morning, it already looked like it was going to be a bright day. The night before, Fifi-Rose had arrived with a bottle of wine, yet another pizza, and a pretty present bag containing two bottles of factor 40 sun cream lotion and a tube of insect bite treatment, which had made Lisa chuckle.

The taxi was on time and Lisa was soon on her way to Gatwick. As the airport came into view her stomach did somersaults but there was no time to be nervous, she had to get out, pay the driver and get into the airport to check in, get her boarding card and then go through passport control and security and into the departures lounge where she could have her usual pre-flight whiskey.

Thankful that the alarms hadn't gone off when she'd passed through the security scanner, Lisa collected her small cabin case and strode into departures where she looked up at the nearest information board to see her flight was the last one listed. This meant she had plenty of time to get a whiskey and have a mooch round. The airport was very busy with queues at every café and restaurant. Even the retail outlets were busy. It always amazed Lisa that people could be so wide awake so early in the morning. She had a good look round but didn't buy anything, then, yawning, found a seat near another departures board. Setting her cabin case down she looked up to see her flight had shot up to third and had a gate number.

With her heart pounding, she pulled up the handle of her case and quickly followed other passengers making their way to the gate. It seemed that every yard they walked, yet more people joined! After what felt like a very a long trek, Lisa eventually arrived at the appropriate gate, and after being checked in found a seat near a window in the small departure area.

Looking out at the newly bright day, she saw the aircraft which would take her back to her magical island. And to the man she'd loved. She allowed herself to wonder how he was and how he'd be when they met. It had been a long time. In fact, it had been two years; a lot can happen in two years.

Lisa found her window seat on the left-hand side of the aircraft and fastened the safety belt. Once everyone was seated and the necessary checks had been carried out, the plane was towed off its stand and on to the runway. The engines began to quietly roar as the aircraft slowly moved forward. Gradually, the roar got louder, and Lisa could feel the familiar exciting thrusting force of the engines as the plane gathered enough speed to take off. And then she was in the air. She could barely stop herself from laughing out loud with joy – how she loved this part of flying! The pure exhilaration was indescribable. To her, it was heaven. She was leaving everything and everyone behind. Now, it was *her* time, and she could be herself once again - not someone's ex-wife, ex-lover, mother, grandmother, daughter, employee, friend. Just her. Her and her spirit could be at one again.

The flight was uneventful, and eventually her beloved Kefalonia island nestling, stark and dark in the deep blue, twinkling Ionian Sea, came into view. The plane began to descend bit by bit on its approach to the island, then banked round twice to get the correct angle to land on the airstrip. As usual, Lisa was stunned to see the plane's wing tip almost touch the sea as it banked, and people on the beaches waving.

Emerging from the plane, Lisa halted at the top of the plane's steps as a wall of heat hit her. Breathing in the familiar aroma of herbs, pine trees and flowers, she felt her whole body relax. She was home again at last.

After the young, green-dressed smiley female holiday rep named Janey had checked that all her passengers were present, the air-conditioned transfer coach headed off to Skala, dropping off passengers at various resorts along the way. Lisa smiled to herself as she heard the island's 'newbies' oohing and aahing at the passing beautiful scenery.

The coach eventually descended slowly down the hill to its final stop in Skala's main street. Lisa gathered her cabin case and stepped off the coach steps on to the familiar pavement. The sun was glaringly hot and bright, so she donned her Rae-Bans to stop herself from squinting. The rep checked her name off her list and then took her and two other passengers, all of them self-consciously dragging their cases, down to the end of the road, where she turned right into a small side road and stopped as she pointed to the newly built Sappho Apartments shining whitely in the bright sunlight.

"Here we are folks. This is your holiday home. One of the newest apartment blocks in Skala which our Company is privileged to look after. Okay, follow me."

Lisa remembered that not too long ago, two old goats had grazed on this land, often with the old goatherd sitting near them in the shade of ancient olive trees. It was also the goatherd's job to open the rickety gate leading into the area where the remains of a mosaic floor belonging to a long-ago Roman villa was situated. There was a rather faded notice in bad English precariously pinned to the falling-down fence telling tourists to ring the bell on the nearby stool for someone to come and let them in the gate. Then, if people were lucky, and the goatherd was awake and in a rare, good mood, he'd grudgingly unlock the rickety gate for them. It was always trial and error, but no-one ever complained. The goatherd would have been of a similar generation to the old man who'd lived and died in the shack on the beach.

But now there was no land, no goats, no goatherd and no olive trees. Lisa felt a lump in her throat. Change. She swallowed. What else had changed? She wondered. Was the mosaic floor still there?

Even though she'd sensibly worn a sleeveless pale pink cotton top with matching easy-fit pale pink crop pants, Lisa felt sweat drip slowly down her back. She shifted the dark green linen jacket she'd brought with her from her right arm to her left and licked her lips. Water! She needed water!

"Here we are!" trilled Janey who, to Lisa, looked about twelve years old. "Ms Barat you're in number four here on the ground floor. And you two," she said as she leaned sideways to peer at the young couple standing quietly behind Lisa, "are on the next floor in number eight. Anyway, do make yourselves comfortable and have a lovely holiday, and don't forget the welcome drinks at six o'clock in Rebecca's Bar!"

The girl toothily grinned as she made to hurry away, leaving them to sort themselves out.

Lisa said goodbye to the shy young couple, then turning the key in the door of her holiday apartment door let herself into a bright, clean and airy apartment with all the usual basic facilities. Much to her relief, the shower had a curtain and a mat to step out on to. Two large glass doors in the living room area opened out onto a generous, shaded patio. There was a table and four chairs, and beyond the low hedges surrounding three side of the patio, Lisa could see beautifully maintained grass, trees and flower beds. Also, what looked like a small café/bar. And a swimming pool! She'd forgotten about the pool. It was all just perfect.

After unpacking the few clothes and bits and bobs she'd brought with her, Lisa pulled on her new dark blue one-piece swimsuit and tied the matching dark blue and cream wrap sarong-style round her waist. Then she crammed her cream baseball hat on her head, slipped on dark blue flip-flops, donned her Rae-Bans and hoisted her straw beach bag onto her shoulder before heading for the pool café/bar. It was already late afternoon, and she wanted to make the most of what was left of her first day.

Lisa ordered an iced coffee and wandered to the pool where she saw several vacant sun loungers and parasols. She chose a lounger in the corner in the shade of an olive tree which she thought would have the best view of the pool one way and the beach road just beyond a hedge the other way.

After laying her bright orange beach towel on the sun lounger and loosely tying her wrap to the parasol's struts, she settled down to sip her welcome iced coffee. This was the life! After a few sips she put the drink on the small table beside the lounger, pushed her Ray Bans up into her hair and lay down. Despite the lovely parasol and the slight wind, she could feel the sun warmly beating down and thought maybe she'd go for a swim…

"Madame? Madame?" Lisa heard a heavily accented male voice ask through a sleepy fog. Was she dreaming? Lisa forced her eyelids apart. No, she wasn't dreaming. Standing beside her dressed in bright yellow shorts and a white t-shirt was a male person. Male person? Lisa heaved herself up onto her elbows. "Yes? What? Who are you?" She croaked as she shaded her eyes with one hand.

"Sorry to disturb," the male voice said in a rather sexy, deeply accented voice. He's not Greek, thought Lisa groggily. He sounds French. French? What's a French man doing in Skala?

"Yes?"

"It's your er… how do you say…beachwear garment. It blew into the pool. I rescued it."

Lisa's eyes flew open. Beachwear garment? Oh, he must mean her wrap! Then she remembered she'd loosely tied the wrap round the parasol's struts, but the wind must have blown it off. Sitting up with bent legs primly clamped tightly together, and feet close to her bottom, she lowered her Rae-Bans to see who had disturbed her. She was startled to find herself looking into deep brown eyes surrounded by ridiculously thick, long dark eyelashes. *Good lord, he's beautiful*, she thought. *And I know where he got those gorgeous bright yellow shorts – Italy, probably Versace.* She knew this because Christoph had bought a pair when they'd moved into the Katelios house. He'd liked Italian clothes which is why he'd always looked so smart.

Clearing her throat, Lisa managed to whisper, "That's very kind, thank you, Mister…?"

"Monsieur Pierre Benoit. And you're very welcome, Madame? Madam?" That accent again. It made Lisa feel slightly weak at the knees.

Lisa knew he'd be aware that it was courteous to address a 'mature' lady as Madam, so he was just being flattering saying "Madame."

"Madam. Thank you," Lisa corrected as she swung her legs, still clamped together, off the sun lounger and stood up. "Well, thank you for rescuing my wrap. I can see it's very wet," she smiled. "I'll re-hang it on the parasol struts again to dry." She didn't really have much choice if she wanted to use the wrap to ensure she'd be modestly dressed away from the pool area.

"My pleasure," said Pierre with a slight bow. Then after hesitating for a micro-second, added, "Might I have the pleasure of buying you another drink? Perhaps a coffee, or maybe a glass of the wonderful Robola wine? Do you know it's made here on the island? In fact, there are several vineyards here."

Lisa realised that Pierre seemed to know a lot about wine. It made him seem even more attractive. She checked herself - she was probably old enough to be his mother and decided to politely decline his kind offer of a drink.

However, instead she heard herself saying, "Er, well, thank you, that would be very pleasant." Bloody hell, where did that come from? She was doing a 'Christoph' all over again. What was wrong with her?

Pierre beamed the most beautiful smile Lisa had ever seen, making his lovely eyes crease at the corners and his olive skin and white teeth glow. "It is my pleasure; shall we go now, or later?"

"Well, my wrap's still wet so how about in half an hour?"

"Oui. C'est magnifique. Au revoir for now and I'll see you in half an hour," Pierre agreed politely. Then he strode off with Lisa admiring the back of his tall, athletic physique and his bum clad in its bright yellow shorts before he disappeared behind the café-bar.

Lisa decided that instead of using the parasol's struts to dry her wrap, she'd tie it to the back of the sun lounger which she'd move into the sun. She didn't want her wrap blowing away in the wind again, that would be much too embarrassing!

Half an hour passed quickly, and thanks to the wind Lisa's wrap was soon dry. This time, she used it full-length, knotting it sarong-style above her bust, not around her waist. She fluffed up her hat-hair and applied some pale lippy which she always kept in her bag, then sat on the edge of the sun lounger with her ankles crossed demurely to one side, to wait for the handsome Frenchman.

Pierre appeared exactly on time, greeted her warmly, and whilst extending his hand to help her up, which Lisa politely declined – after all, a woman does have her pride, and she needed to demonstrate that she could stand up elegantly on her own – gave Lisa another dazzling smile before accompanying her to the café-bar.

Lisa would later discover that the young man behind the bar had seen everything which had taken place and would soon be telling a certain interested person all about it.

The Robola wine was delicious, light and slightly acidic with a hint of herbs. Lisa decided that as it was now approaching early evening, just one glass would be okay. Pierre turned out to be both interesting and interested, asking questions about herself as well as telling her things about Kefalonia which she already knew but was too polite to say so; she didn't want to appear a know-all.

"So, Pierre, how do you know so much about the vineyards here?" She asked as she put down her almost-empty glass.

"Well, I'm interested in the wine industry, it's my job. Or should I say, my passion. I already work in a large vineyard in France and am interested in what goes on here as I've heard it's becoming very popular. I understand there's a wine co-operative for all the local growers."

"Really?" Lisa was intrigued by this information as she'd only ever thought of the island as a tourist destination with a historical background. "Where?" she asked.

"Well, you may know that the vineyards are in the hills of the Omala Valley near St Gerasimos church. The grape harvest starts in August and ends in September, so it's almost finished now. It's an ancient industry here but with modern techniques, although the actual harvest is still undertaken manually." Pierre was pleased Lisa showed so much interest because not many people did, they were usually only interested in drinking the wine!

Lisa digested this information. Did she want to know more? No. Changing the subject, she looked at her new Motorola mobile phone to see what the time was. "Pierre, it's approaching six o'clock and I need to go. I've had a long day, was up at three o'clock this morning and I'm tired." Standing up, she held out her hand. "It's been lovely to meet you and have a chat, and thanks again for rescuing my wrap from the pool!"

Pierre also stood up. "Oh, going so soon? Well, I can understand you must be tired after such a long day. Thank you for your wonderful company, and hopefully we'll meet again?"

Erm, maybe not Mr Frenchman, thought Lisa. *I've got a Greek man to see and talk with and don't need any distractions to prevent me from doing that.* But instead, she smilingly said aloud, "Well, Pierre, au revoir, have a good evening." Then, after picking up her bag and the hem of her wrap, walked away from the handsome, polite Pierre thinking, *if only…*

Lisa returned to her apartment to shower and change. She needed to eat and decided to check out The Bay. After pulling on white jeans and a black shirt, she slipped on a pair of black canvas flats, put her black canvas bag over her right shoulder and set off to see if the restaurant was still there.

It was. As Lisa approached, memories of Christoph and Theresa and her family came flooding back making her feel nervous. Was this a good idea? Maybe she should go elsewhere. But it was too late, as a waiter had spotted her and called out asking if she'd like to see the menu.

Too tired to go elsewhere, Lisa said yes and was shown to a small table overlooking Skala's main street. From here she could see everyone passing by. As it was still early to be eating there were only two couples in the restaurant, but there were plenty of people strolling around, many of them locals. Lisa knew that most of the tourists wouldn't be aware that some of these Greeks would be 'promenading' as was the custom in Greece before eating –it was all about seeing and being seen, so therefore everyone dressed in their smart, second-best clothes.

However, the tourists were often dressed in their never-to-be-worn-again holiday clothes which usually meant the men sported bright coloured, patterned shirts, knee length shorts and trainers, with the women wearing long, floaty, trip-hazard dresses, or too-tight tube tops and shorts or skirts; they also often slopped along in espadrilles, or worse, flip-flops.

Lisa thought she was being snobby - after all, people were on holiday, so anything went, and it was none of her business anyway. She scanned the menu, and decided stuffed tomatoes would be nice, then just as she was about to order she heard a woman's voice shout, "Lisa! Lisa!"

Looking round she couldn't see anyone at first, but then she saw Rebecca getting out of a small red car parked opposite. "Rebecca!" She exclaimed. "I don't believe it!" She waved to her to come over, and as Rebecca approached Lisa could see that her friend was clearly very pregnant. "Oh, look at you! A bubba on the way!" She laughed.

Rebecca chuckled as she threw her arms around Lisa. "I know! Not planned but it doesn't matter, Yannis and me always wanted a family – and here we are! I'm just glad we got married first."

"No way!" exclaimed Lisa as she ushered Rebecca to sit down. "When?"

"Last summer. Yannis had been ill, so we decided to get married, his illness made us realise that time can be short."

"Oh, my dear, that's both sad and wonderful. Can I ask what was wrong?"

"Yes, he had a spot of heart trouble but he's okay now, thank goodness. We had a quiet wedding by Greek standards - only a hundred people," she laughed. "You know what Greek weddings can be like, usually feels like half of Greece has been invited!"

"Yes!" agreed Lisa with a grin. "Anyway, when are you due?"

"In November, so not long now."

Just at that moment the waiter returned. Lisa asked Rebecca if she'd like to join her in a meal, but Rebecca said she had to go to cook for Yannis, so Lisa ordered the stuffed tomatoes and a small carafe of Robola.

"Lisa, why are you here? Are you on holiday? Where are you staying?" enquired Rebecca as she shifted uncomfortably on the hard wooden chair.

"Whoa, lots of questions!" laughed Lisa. "I'm here on a ten-day holiday, staying at the new Sappho Apartments. While I'm here I'd like to see Christoph and Daphne. And also maybe Sue if she's around."

"Oh, okay. Well, good luck with all of that. Daphne's still in the same house but Sue, Trevor and their family now live in Argostoli, they sold the Accommodation Shop at the end of last season, I'm not sure why. There have been lots of changes Lisa, not all of them welcome but then I suppose that's progress. Georgios has also moved away, and

Michaelis got divorced and lives quietly in a small house on the Katelios road. We don't see much of him now, either."

The unspoken subject of Christoph hung in the air like a heavy cloud.

"Gosh, that is a lot of change," Lisa sighed.

"Yes, but we have to adapt, don't we? Anyway, I must go," said Rebecca as she stood up with some difficulty. Patting her swollen belly, she said, "The little one's kicking so it must be time to eat!" Then kissing Lisa on both cheeks, she said, "It's so lovely to see you, Lisa, and I'm sure we'll see each other again while you're here. Bye for now."

"Bye," smiled Lisa as she waved her friend off. "Take care."

Fortunately, Lisa's stuffed tomatoes and wine arrived shortly after Rebecca left so Lisa didn't feel lonely for long. Then, after finishing her meal and wine, she suddenly felt very tired but decided to have a short walk along the sea front before returning to her apartment for an early night. It was another day tomorrow, and who knew what that would bring?

Lisa woke to the sound of a cockerel crowing in the distance; there aways seemed to be one! After a cup of tea courtesy of the tea bags which had been left in the kitchen, she went out on to the patio.

The air was still, and sun was already well-risen, bathing everything in a soft, apricot glow before it got too hot. Lisa decided she'd have a swim in the sea before going for breakfast and then go to see if Daphne was at home.

The beach was deserted. Lisa lay her beach towel down on the gritty sand near the water's edge, then slipping off her denim shorts and flip-flops, walked slowly into the glistening, clear water as little fishes flashed like silver darts around her ankles. Taking a soft breath, she ventured further out into the mill-pond calm, twinkling sea until she could swim, closing her eyes to the warm sun as the water softly enveloped her body like deep blue and green liquid silk. Floating gently, her spirit soared as she gave thanks for being able to return once more to this beautiful place.

Lisa longed to swim to the distant horizon, light sky shimmering against dark sea, but she knew she couldn't and had to return to the safety of the beach - and to reality.

Returning to her towel on the sand, she lay down to let the sun dry her, closing her eyes behind her Rae-Bans. Pure bliss! After a while, she heard children's voices and turned her head to see a family had arrived nearby, the squealing children holding the hands of laughing adults as they paddled. Such a happy scene. Lisa could hardly remember any similar family times which she and Mark had shared with their three girls. *I must have been a dreadful mother*, she thought. Always preoccupied with keeping things on an even keel, never wanting to upset anyone. Never having enough energy for the children.

She decided it was time to get a shower and have breakfast, so she reluctantly left the beach and walked slowly back to her apartment where, after showering, she donned a loose, sleeveless, cream cotton dress which just skimmed her knees, and comfortable cream flat sandals. She knew it would be hot again, but the weather could soon become unpredictable, so she needed to get a move on and do the visiting and the talking as well as some sunbathing and relaxing before her holiday time ran out!

Walking up the main street, Lisa noticed a few new shops and another car hire business had appeared, then going past the kiosk she inwardly shuddered as she remembered the fire. She didn't want to think of that – but then what did she think would happen when she got here? Of course, she'd remember.

Daphne screamed with delight when she opened the door and saw Lisa. "Lisa! Lisa! You've come back! Come in, come in, my dear! Oh, how wonderful to see you!" She cried as she threw her arms around Lisa's shoulders.

"Hello, Daphne, it's lovely to see you, too. I'm here on a short holiday, but I also wanted to see you and a couple of other people. How are you?" Lisa asked as she tried to disentangle herself from Daphne's bear-hug. "Are you well?"

"Yes, yes, I am well," replied Daphne, beaming. "And I have cheese pies!"

Lisa chuckled, "Well, of course you have, Daphne. I wouldn't expect you *not* to have your lovely cheese pies!"

Daphne was beside herself with joy at seeing the dear surrogate daughter she'd missed so much. But she was also curious. With her head tilted to one side, she looked at Lisa questioningly. "Lisa, why have you really come back? I thought you said you'd never return."

Ah, thought Lisa, here's the big question. Nothing escapes Daphne. "Well, as I said, I wanted to see you, also Rebecca who I did see briefly yesterday evening. I'd also hoped to see Sue and Trevor, but Rebecca told me they've gone to live in Argostoli."

"Hmmm, yes, they have. So, you know their shop isn't open now? Things have, and are, changing, Lisa," replied Daphne. She paused, and taking Lisa's right hand lightly in her own, work-worn hands looked into Lisa's eyes and quietly asked. "And what about Christoph, Lisa? Do you intend to see him?"

Lisa's heart started to beat faster. "To be honest, Daphne, yes, I do. I need some answers. He hasn't been totally truthful with me, and I need to know why before I can fully move on with my life."

The old woman didn't reply at first, then, after a few moments, said, "I can understand that. But when you do see him be prepared for him to have changed. And do not expect anything from him other than the answers you seek," she advised wisely.

"Thank you. I won't ask how he's changed because I know you probably won't tell me. But I can deal with whatever happens. Anyway, let's change the subject. How have you been, and what's been happening in Skala that's nice and positive." She was keen to keep the conversation light.

Daphne told Lisa about the increase in tourism which had lifted Skala's economy, and the many nice people, especially the English, that she'd met and made friends with. She was pleased about Rebecca and Yannis' baby. They drank Daphne's homemade lemonade and ate two of her cheese pies, each woman savouring the company of the other.

Eventually, Lisa decided it was time to go, reassuring Daphne that she'd see her around whilst she was in Skala and would certainly visit her again before she went home. Lisa was very aware that Daphene had aged and had become slower in her movements. She also noticed her dear friend had a slight limp which Daphne had brushed off as 'old age,' ignoring Lisa's plea for her to see the doctor.

Lisa felt quite sad after leaving Daphne and decided to have a coffee before doing some necessary grocery shopping at the nearby supermarket. She wasn't sure what to do after that but knew something would come to mind. After hoisting her canvas bag onto her shoulder, she pushed her Rae-Bans up her nose and started to walk down the hill to a new café-bar. But then she abruptly came to a halt, for there, just a few yards in front of her, was Christoph.

Chapter Twenty-Nine

"Lisa."

"Christoph."

They stared at each other, unsure of what to say next. Lisa swallowed. "I...er...I'm on holiday," she stuttered. "For ten days."

"I see," murmured Christoph feeling as if he was in some sort of dream. Right in front of him was his beloved Lisa looking as beautiful as ever.

"Christoph!" Called a woman's voice in Greek. "Can you come here a moment please?"

The owner of the voice moved out from behind a parked car. She was petite, rounded and wore black leggings and matching t-shirt. Her abundant, shiny black hair fell around her shoulders, and on her right hip clung a round-eyed baby boy the very image of her. Both the woman and the child stared silently at Lisa.

"Who is this?" the woman suddenly demanded in Greek. "Do you know her?"

"Hush," scolded Christoph quietly in Greek. Then in English continued, "let's be polite to a visitor to our village. Please."

"Of course," the woman replied in English, then turning to Lisa said, "My apologies. I didn't mean to be rude. Welcome to Skala. You obviously know my husband Christoph. I'm Ariadne-Rose. And your name is?"

Stunned, Lisa froze. Ariadne-Rose? But that was the ghost-girl's name; the girl who'd hidden the Italian soldier! No! Christoph married? When? This was too much. Lisa's mouth was so dry she couldn't speak.

"Are you okay?" Asked Christoph kindly. "You've gone very pale."

Pale? What the hell did he expect? Why hadn't he told her? Ah, yes, of course, now she knew what he'd meant by 'being busy', this is why he hadn't contacted her. What other secrets were there? Had he known this woman all this time? Was this why he'd not been honest about Theresa? And what about this child?

Lisa looked at Christoph. He was thinner, greyer, smaller somehow. The scar on the left- hand side of his face had faded to silver but was still visible. What had life done to him? Was this the effect of being married to…to…*a ghost*?

Oh, for god's sake stop being ridiculous, she told herself crossly. *This woman isn't a ghost, she's real. Bloody man up, Lisa, and get a grip.*

"Pale?" She asked. "Must be the factor forty suncream I'm using." She gave a small laugh. "Not being Greek, I'm not used to the hot sun." Then looking at the woman, she asked, "Are you named for the legendary Skala girl who hid an Italian soldier in the war?"

The woman screwed up her face. So, this English woman knows things. And clearly also knows Christoph. She shifted the silent, round-eyed baby onto her other hip. "Er, no, not really. It's a family name. My original family lived in the old village," she said quietly. "My *yia-yia* was Ariadne-Rose, she was named for her mother Rose and grandmother Ariadne. They all died but the combined name has been kept for other family girl babies. Long story," she added dismissively. "So, what's your name?"

It was her eyes. Eyes like endlessly deep brown pools. Lisa swallowed. "I'm Lisa."

Sensing the tension between the two women, Christoph coughed politely and told Ariadne-Rose it was time to go. Looking at Lisa apologetically, he bowed his head and said, "Nice to see you, Lisa. I hope you have a good holiday." Then, taking the woman's arm, said goodbye and walked away with her and the silent baby.

The rest of the day had a slightly unreal feel about it. Lisa swam and slept on the beach until deciding it was time to go back to her apartment to change and go for dinner. She was finding eating on her own difficult. It had never bothered her before, but it did now.

She remembered a new, attractive-looking restaurant, Gabriel's, which offered a mix of British and Greek dishes and decided that was where she'd go.

After a stroll round the village shops, she arrived at the restaurant and was invited to take a table overlooking the road. She chose a Greek salad and a carafe of Robola and sat watching the comings and goings of the early evening village until her food and wine arrived.

The staff were attentive and kind, but they didn't stop Lisa from feeling very lonely. She wasn't used to eating in a restaurant on her own anymore; she either had Oliver, Fifi-Rose, or one of her writing friends to chat to. She suddenly felt tears well up, so leaving some of her food she asked for the bill, and after paying, left.

Walking back down the main street and being amongst people made her feel less lonely. She made her way to the bottom main square and chose a seat facing the street so she could see people casually strolling and children playing in the warm evening.

Deep in thought, she wasn't at first aware of someone sitting beside her. Movement made her jump. "Oh, gosh, I didn't know anyone was here. *Christoph?*" she asked incredulously.

"But why are you here? I didn't see you arrive, where did you come from?"

"Sorry, I didn't mean to make you jump," Christoph said quietly. "I came up from the beach road over there," he said pointing to behind the trees. "I wanted to see you. To explain."

"Explain!" exploded Lisa. "Yes, please do explain. In fact, you owe me a lot of explanations."

Christoph held up his right hand. Lisa noticed the scars on it had faded. "Okay, okay, I will. Please just give me a moment."

Lisa looked at the man she'd loved. Daphne was right; he'd changed. And it seemed so had his life. She wasn't sure she wanted to know all the details. She suddenly had an urge to run away, get on a plane and go home. But she'd come to Skala to get answers so she couldn't do that.

Christoph could see Lisa was struggling. "I'll tell you as quickly as I can. Ariadne-Rose is the daughter of Theo, a friend of my Uncle Tony's. I was asked to marry her because she'd had a bad relationship and needed looking after. I couldn't refuse because Uncle Tony's friend is not, how can I say, someone you argue with. He has connections. People you don't argue with. I can't say any more than that," he said, looking at Lisa pleadingly. "My family is very complicated, so I won't even begin to try to explain it to you."

Lisa couldn't say anything. This man got more complex as time went on. And, of course, she understood about Uncle Tony who, Daphne had revealed, was in fact Christoph's real father. Christoph would do anything for Tony. And it sounded like Tony would do anything for Ariadne-Rose's father Theo. So here was the conundrum: there were other, powerful forces at play here which Christoph was caught up in; who were these people?

"And is the baby yours? But before you answer that, how did you know I was here in the square?"

"Stephanos, the barman at Sappho Apartments, told me he'd seen you talking with a Frenchman not long after you arrived - something to do with your beach wrap?" Christoph queried. Totally amazed, Lisa could only nod. "Then when he was in the main street today, he saw you walking down to the square and phoned me to tell me that, too," Christoph said quietly whilst looking at Lisa intently. "From the moment we met, you've been watched, Lisa. Sorry, but that's just how it is. Certain people, especially one, have become very protective of me because of the fire and how it was started. Then because Sam left me after it, and then because you also eventually left me, they've become more so. But I've never asked them to be protective, they've just wanted to be."

"Uncle Tony?" quizzed Lisa.

Christoph looked at Lisa miserably. "Yes, Uncle Tony. People don't refuse him."

"I see. And what about the baby, is it yours?"

"Yes. It's a little boy. He's very delicate because he was born early. We named him Thomas for Daphne's Thomas who saved my life."

"Oh, that's a nice thing to do Christoph," Lisa said kindly. Then, after taking a breath, she continued, "But now, what about Theresa? Why didn't you tell me about her?"

"I didn't because she was linked with Uncle Tony's friend Theo, and his friend's Italian 'friends', if you know what I mean. Half of Theresa's family are related to those people. I was told to keep quiet about how Theresa had behaved, her child Sebastian, and her mental illness. I had no option, Lisa. I'm so sorry. I wanted to tell you but just couldn't."

Bloody hell's bells, thought Lisa, *this gets more like a Le Carré novel every second*. She didn't comment.

Sighing, Christoph carried on. "I couldn't tell you about my wife Ariadne-Rose for the same reason. You need to understand that I owe Uncle Tony everything, and in Greece loyalty to family is paramount. It comes above everything else. There are also some people, family or not, you just don't argue with." Christoph looked down at his hands, then looking up, said, "It's been hard on you, and you deserved, and do deserve, so much more."

"Well, thanks for that," Lisa managed to say. "Yes, it's a bit of an understatement saying it's been hard on me. You didn't share extremely important things with me, didn't trust me enough to keep quiet if you did, and I can't live with someone who doesn't trust me, no matter what the reason for that lack of trust. And I was almost killed because of you. And you were almost killed because of Theresa." Feeling slightly sick, she took a breath before adding, "It's not been good has it, Christoph?"

"No, it hasn't," Christoph agreed. "Except for Katelios. I've truly never been happier in my whole life than when we lived in Katelios. Please believe that."

Lisa looked at Christoph's sad face and tear-filled green eyes."Yes, I believe you, Christoph. I agree they were happy times. Until Theresa ruined it. I think we'd probably still be in Katelios if she hadn't tried to kill me," she said sadly. "I miss Skala, Christoph. I miss Kefalonia. I did miss you, too, but don't anymore. Sorry. Anyway, thanks for explaining. It's now best that you get on with your life and I get on with mine. I'm going back to the UK after I've seen a couple more people and had a bit of a holiday. I had booked ten days, but I've now decided not to stay any longer than a week, so I'll get an earlier flight back. I need to be with my own family, my daughters and little granddaughter, Clemmie. And my friends. I now need to ask you not to talk to me if you see me around again because it would be wrong. So, Christoph, this is our final goodbye," she said, adding with a small smile, "Be happy." After all, she thought, he now had the son his family had always wanted for him, and a pretty young wife, so he wouldn't be lonely.

"Oh, Lisa, I miss you, too. You have no idea how much. I still love you and always will," Christoph murmured as he stood up, holding out his scarred right hand. Lisa also stood up and took his hand in hers. Then she gazed into his teary, green eyes for the last time as he whispered, "Goodbye, Lisa. And thank you for the good times. I'll never forget you. You be happy, too, my love, you deserve it." Then, proudly ramrod straight as ever, he walked away from Lisa to his new life.

Well, that was surreal, thought Lisa as she walked down the steps to the beach road. She felt numb with shock that Christoph had been put under so much stress but wasn't able to share anything with her. Did all this really happen? It felt like some sort of horrible dream. She badly needed a shot of reality, to go home, away from this beautiful place once and for all.

After having a strong coffee, Lisa went to the tour operator's office and was relieved to find her rep there. Without any preamble, she immediately said she wanted a flight home in three days' time. Surprised, the girl asked if something was wrong.

"Plenty, but you don't need to know what," Lisa replied brusquely. "Now, a flight please. I don't care which airline it's with."

The girl pulled a face. Rude. But, hey-ho, the customer was always right. Not. She found an Olympic Airways flight for three days' time and booked it. "There. It's done. Collect your ticket and boarding card at our airport desk. Safe flight Ms Barat. Nice to have met you."

"Thanks," replied Lisa, then after paying an exorbitant amount for her flight, she walked out of the office feeling like a weight had been lifted off her shoulders. She was going home to her lovely Wisteria Cottage, her beloved family and her friends.

But despite the relief of knowing that she now had the answers she'd sought, was free of Christoph at last and so could now move on, part of her couldn't help wondering if she'd ever return to her beloved Greek island. It wasn't something she wanted to wonder but she did; the 'pull' of her Greek Island was still there.

Chapter Thirty

On the day she was due to fly home, Lisa said goodbye to a tearful Daphne who hugged her before giving her a package. "Some cheese pies, Lisa, in case you feel hungry on the plane," she said with a brave smile. "Please keep in touch, don't forget me. You know I'll miss you but maybe you'll come back one day, who knows?"

Lisa hugged the dear friend who had helped her and meant so much to her. She felt very sad that she might never see her again. "Thank you for the pies, Daphne, and I promise I'll keep in touch. Maybe ask Yannis to help you with your mobile phone, show you how to video chat? Then we'll be able to see each other when we talk. Anyway, don't worry about that now, just keep in it in mind."

Lisa left with a heavy heart. How she'd miss this lovely woman. But now it was time to go and see Rebecca who was waiting for her. She bid Daphne goodbye and walked back down the main street to Rebecca and Yannis' house in a side road. They welcomed Lisa with open arms and a large glass of wine.

"Yamas!" Said Yannis as he touched Lisa's glass with his, Rebecca doing the same with her glass of water, saying, "We'll miss you, Lisa. And we're so sorry you've had such a difficult time here because of

Christoph. But we hope you also remember Skala as a nice, pretty place," she smiled.

"Oh, yes, I will," assured Lisa. "Skala will always be in my heart, Rebecca, and so will you and Yannis. Anyway, here's to your baby!" She ended, raising her glass in the air. "Yamas to the next generation in Skala!"

After lots of chatting and goodbyes, Lisa left with tears in her eyes. She'd miss these nice people and felt sad that she wouldn't be around when their baby was born.

Walking slowly back to her apartment, she savoured the sights and smells of the village, the warm sun, people strolling around, chatting and laughing, and that wonderful Greek aroma of food, herbs, geraniums, oleander, oregano and pine trees. She wanted to breath it all in and store it in her heart forever.

Walking down to the stone bench overlooking the beach, she remembered Christoph's words. Why did it all have to go so wrong? She looked at the beautiful beach where people played and sunbathed, and at the glistening Ionian Sea. Oh, how she'd miss all this.

Life went on around her; a dog barked, cars hooted, motorbikes roared, people shopped, ate, drank, laughed. A young, red shorts-clad man laden with beach stuff called to his children, two women walked past in flowing dresses, laughing, and several coaches drew up to take the long line of waiting holidaymakers on board, making her remember her own traumatic coach trip. This was her beloved, vibrant Skala, and everything she saw and smelt reminded her of her chequered times here.

And oh, yes, old Skala village. Was it really haunted? Had she really seen the ghost-girl, Ariadne-Rose, or had she just been a figment of her imagination?

And the fire. That dreadful fire that had changed everyone's lives. Lisa's mind jumped to Sam - what had happened to Sam? Bless that girl and her baby, whatever must she have gone through? Then her own near-death at the hands of Theresa. Oh, the very sad complications of that poor girl, of that whole family, of the Italians, especially *Nonna*. Lisa knew she'd never find out what, or who, was behind so much in that family. Likewise, in Christoph's family. She could only guess who the 'friends' were that he'd spoken of. Christoph. Such a complex human being. She'd loved him once and was thankful for that. She knew that when she was old, and despite what had happened, she'd still remember him with affection, and wonder what his life was like with little Thomas and his own Ariadne-Rose, she of those deep, dark, pool-like eyes.

Lisa realised that, although she'd found and loved a fairy-tale island, sadly there hadn't been a Greek island 'Once Upon a Time' happy fairy-tale ending for her.

All too soon, Lisa's taxi arrived to take her to the airport. The journey was a very emotional one. Tears streamed down her cheeks as every yard she travelled reminded her of something or someone. Then, as the taxi climbed up the hill towards Mount Aenos and the main Argostoli road, coming to a halt at the junction, there she was, standing so close to the road that Lisa could see her very clearly: a young girl dressed in black with large round, dark brown eyes like deep pools.

Shocked, Lisa leaned forward. "Goodbye, Lisa," the girl mouthed as she waved a small, delicate hand. "See you again one day. And thank you for…"

The taxi accelerated forward. With her heart racing, Lisa sank back into her seat with a thud. No. No, it couldn't have been. Could it? And 'thank you' for what? For believing? For seeing her? Was she real? Yes, of course, the girl was real, she'd seen her and looked into her eyes. To double-check, Lisa quickly turned round to look out of the rear window. But the girl had gone.

Lisa spent the rest of the journey drying her tears and telling herself to be strong. The girl had been another fantasy, that's all. She wasn't real, it was just this magical Greek island playing tricks on her mind again.

Lisa's plane had arrived, and in no time at all she was through security and walking out in the brilliant sunshine across the tarmac to her plane. After reaching the top of the aircraft's steps, she turned round for one last look at Mount Aenos and, whispering goodbye to her mountain, felt the tears threaten once again.

She found her window seat in the middle of the plane but was determined not to look out in case she cried. Then, as the aircraft soared up into the cloudless, deep blue sky to take her home, she took a deep breath and told herself to stop being so emotional. She also decided that she'd write about this special place, and that her ghost-girl Ariadne-Rose would be a major part of her story; this would be her 'Once Upon a Greek Island' tale. Then, with that thought, she closed her eyes and fell asleep.

"Welcome home but why are you a week early. Also, why so early in the day?" asked a surprised Fifi-Rose loudly when Lisa rang her to say she'd been home about two hours. "Anyway, I hope the cottage is okay – and you, too. Something's obviously happened, so we must have a catch-up as soon as."

"Well, obviously, but not today, I've got things to do. But thank you for leaving everything nice for me. How about meeting up tomorrow evening if you're not busy?"

"Fab, say about seven-thirty? I can't come any earlier because I've got a late meeting."

"Yes, that'd be fine, so see you then. Bye for now." Lisa put her mobile phone down. Back to normal. Normal. Would she ever be and feel normal again? She knew she wanted to write, to get her story done and dusted as soon as she could but doubted it would ever get into print. She was just an ordinary woman of a certain age dabbling in writing. Not for the fame of being a successful author. And most definitely not to make a fortune! She knew there was stiff competition in the literary world because both Oliver and a neighbour were published authors, not that either ever talked much about their achievements. Anyway, it all sounded rather terrifying to Lisa.

No, she'd just finish her story and keep it on her laptop. Maybe it'd be a legacy of some kind? Old girl writes a novel - be inspired, all you women of a certain age!

The following day, Lisa rang James at the shop. He was delighted to hear from her but insisted she still take the leave she'd booked. But being the ever-respectful James, he didn't ask why she'd come home early; he knew she'd tell him if she wanted to.

Next, she rang her daughters, leaving each of them a message saying she was home and would chat soon. Then she phoned Oliver. "Oh, Lisa, you're home. What happened? No, you don't have to tell me. Look, are you okay? Do you need anything?" he asked in his usual kind way. *Why haven't I noticed how caring he is?* thought Lisa. He's such a sweet man.

"No, I don't need anything, thank you, Oliver. But it would be nice to see you for a coffee and catch-up later this week. If you're not busy, that is," she added carefully. She didn't want to seem pushy.

"Great! How about Saturday lunch time? We could go for lunch at the Harvest Moon in Castleford village. It's a lovely old pub which does good food, so if that sounds okay, I'll book a table."

"Sounds wonderful! Yes, please do book a table. Thanks Oliver."

They chatted more until Lisa said she had to make some more phone calls. She urgently needed to contact her bank to sort out a couple of direct debits before it closed, also to check her savings – she couldn't go on spending willy nilly, she'd soon run out of money if she did. She'd forgotten what it was like to have a partner to share such things with. It was all very well being a capable independent woman but sometimes it would be nice to have someone else do a bit of sorting, too. Sometimes the sole responsibility of doing everything herself weighed heavily upon her.

Fifi-Rose brought two bottles of wine with her. Lisa laughed, saying she didn't intend to get merry! "Ah, but the good old vino oils the cogs, so to speak," chuckled Fifi-Rose. "Anyway, you can keep what we don't drink until next time. Now, where are your glasses?" She said as she shrugged off her bright orange cardigan and eased off her black wedge sandals. Then, after twiddling one of her large gold hoop earrings back into place, and swishing her long, black dress under her bottom, she plonked herself down on Lisa's squidgy grey sofa. "Spill," she jokily ordered as Lisa poured wine into her glass. "The goss, not the wine!" She laughed, adding in a more serious tone. "Anyway, do tell me what happened, Lisa."

Fifi-Rose thought her friend needed to get something off her chest because she wouldn't have left that wretched island so early if something big hadn't happened there yet again. She smoothed her growing pink hair back over her ears and parted her too-long fringe so she could see Lisa clearly, and so Lisa could see that she was looking at her and listening to her properly. There was nothing worse than sharing something personal with someone and then the other person distractedly not paying attention.

"Well, the bottom line is that Christoph and I are over once and for all. He's now married with a little boy," began Lisa.

Fifi-Rose made a silent 'O' with her mouth. "Blimey!" she finally exclaimed. "That was quick!"

"Yes, it's a long story, Fifi, which I won't go into right now, but his wife's younger than him, but seems okay. Pretty. Their son's the image of her. They've named him Thomas after brave Thomas who saved Christoph's life."

"Yes, I remember you telling me about Thomas. Is that it?"

"Pretty much. He also told me the reason why he didn't share a load of stuff with me. It seems he was under strict orders from his Uncle Tony. Daphne told me Tony is Christoph's real father, but I don't think Christoph knows this," Lisa sighed.

Fifi-Rose's eyes flew open. "Really?! Bloody hell, what a mess!"

"Yes. The whole family is complicated. It's a long story, Fifi, which I'll tell you one day. Or you can read about it in my book!" Lisa added. But she was determined not to mention the Ariadne-Rose phenomenon, or her concerns about the hold Christoph's uncle had over him. She felt she'd already revealed more than enough for now. Also, she still found it odd that the middle name of both the Skala girl and her best friend was Rose. And that Christoph's wife was named Ariadne-Rose. It was all a strange coincidence.

"Book? What book? Crikey woman, you're full of surprises!"

"No, I'm not. I told you I was writing a story set in Kefalonia," retorted Lisa. "You probably didn't take it in."

"Yes, but I thought it was just, you know, a 'thing', not a book as such."

"Well, my 'thing' as you call it, will one day be a book. Not that it'll ever be published, it'll just stay on my laptop. But I will write it. Not sure about the ending yet, though," laughed Lisa. "Anyway, I'll probably be fairly ancient by the time I do finish it."

Fifi-Rose regarded Lisa thinking what an amazing woman her friend was. She'd been through so much in the past couple of years, yet here she was, still smiling and laughing. Tipping her glass towards Lisa's, she said, "well, here's to you, my friend. Here's to many happy times. And here's to your book, too! Cheers!"

Over the next few days, Lisa caught up with her daughters. Tiffany-Mae told her she wasn't surprised because she'd always thought there was something about Christoph which she didn't quite trust. With Clemmie noisily shouting in the background, Bella claimed she was pleased Lisa was home okay, but sorry, she had to go.

But Scarlett asked for more details. "There aren't any, Scarlett," replied Lisa. "Christoph's married with a little boy. End of. And I now know he was under a lot of stress from his uncle when we were together. Nothing too dreadful. I've also said goodbye to Daphne and other friends so will probably never go back."

"Probably? What d'you mean 'probably'? Better you say 'never,' Mum. And mean it this time," she scolded, making Lisa think how their caring roles seemed to be suddenly reversing!

"Well, yes, never. I don't want to go back, Scarlett, I've got other things to do with my life, work's busy especially with the new Tunbridge Wells shop, and my friends and I have lots of things planned. Plus, you girls and I will see each other at times, and hopefully spend a few days together more often. And, of course, I'll be seeing Bella and Clemmie. It's all good so don't worry," she finished, glad the subject was now closed.

Saturday arrived and Oliver came in his Ford Taurus to collect her looking very smart in a pale grey, lightweight suit, with white open-necked shirt. Lisa chose to wear a dark blue shift dress with a pale blue cotton jacket and dark blue leather pumps. She'd had her dark hair styled into a long bob which she thought really suited her: a new haircut to suit her new life.

Although it was a sunny day, it was beginning to get cooler, turning leaves gold and orange which shone in the sunlight. Pretty Castleford village had lots of stone and thatched cottages round its large Green, and a new build which stood out like a sore thumb was crammed on a small piece of land near the village shop. The old, black and white timber framed pub near the village pond and children's play area, had hop-bine decorated beams, and a large inglenook fireplace. Brass ornaments shone brightly amongst candles of all sizes in various nooks and crannies.

Oliver had booked a table beside a window through which Lisa could see the Georgian-style cream painted village mansion with its sweeping, curved drive. It was all perfect, and sighing contentedly, she thought how lucky she was.

Their meal was delicious, and Oliver was good company. He didn't ask her about Skala. As they were finishing their ice cream dessert he coughed slightly before asking Lisa if she'd like to go out for a day. Not with Fifi-Rose or any of the writing group, just the two of them. "Maybe to the coast?" He suggested tentatively.

Lisa looked at him. She instinctively felt he was saying more than she was hearing. She thought this could be the beginning of a relationship - if he got the courage to ask her! Would she want that? She wasn't sure.

"Lisa, you and I get on well, don't we?" Oliver continued. Lisa nodded in agreement. "Erm, so…so…I just wondered. And you don't have to agree," he added quickly, holding up one hand. "I just wondered if you'd like us to, er…to…"

"Become a couple?" Interjected Lisa with a smile.

"Well, yes. No pressure, though. Do take time to think about it if you want to. No need to answer right now. And I wasn't thinking of us living together, just to continue as we are but more, er, sort of *solid*, if you see what I mean?" He finished with a smile that crinkled the corners of his twinkly brown eyes.

"Well, that's very sweet of you Oliver, and yes, I see what you mean, and I will think about it. Anyway, let's have a coffee now, shall we?" She didn't want to rush into anything. She'd already done that too many times.

"Yes, yes, of course," Oliver said with a sigh of relief. At least he'd got it off his chest! It had been a long time since he'd lost his beloved Annie and felt he wanted to spend time with someone else. Not that anyone would ever replace Annie, no-one could do that, but even though he'd got several friends and two adult sons – who he didn't see very much - he was lonely and felt it would be nice to have someone to share things with again. It was time to move on.

They finished their meal and decided to go for a walk round the village Green and then explore a couple of the pretty lanes. It was a wonderful day, full of easy chat and laughter. By mid-afternoon they both felt like a cup of tea so went to the little teashop next to the mansion house intriguingly called 'Snowhill.' Looking at it, Lisa felt there was something not quite right about it. Was it more modern than it appeared, trying to be something it wasn't?

"Do you think the owners of the house also own the teashop, Oliver?" Wondered Lisa. "I mean, it would make sense."

"To be honest, I've no idea but maybe they do."

Just at that moment, a tall, distinguished looking man wearing a cravat and dashing handlebar moustache, came in the teashop. Lisa and Oliver looked at each and bit their lips to stop themselves laughing, both thinking he looked like someone from the forties! The day was getting more interesting as it went on! Lisa couldn't help thinking what a contrast it was to her life with Christoph in Kefalonia. She suddenly missed it all over again, but squashed the feeling down, very aware that it wasn't good to ponder. Nor compare Oliver with Christoph. But where was the excitement? Was there part of her that needed that 'edge'?

Looking down and fiddling with her delicate China teacup in its matching saucer, Lisa suddenly felt lost. So much had happened. Could she be happy with Oliver? He was such a kind man, so caring and attentive. And, after all, she was no spring chicken now so what did she want and expect out of life?

"Penny for them," Oliver said. Then when Lisa didn't look up or reply, he asked, "Lisa? Are you okay?"

"Oh, sorry, Oliver. I was miles away."

"Yes, I could see that," replied Oliver solemnly. "Where were you?"

"Erm, just thinking about stuff. You know, work and the family," Lisa lied. She couldn't possibly tell this lovely man she missed someone and somewhere else. Was she wary? Was her anxiety because any moment she half expected something to go dreadfully wrong, or someone to burst in on them and spoil it all? Was she experiencing the after-effects of trauma? Maybe she should talk to someone. A doctor? God, no, she hardly ever went to see a doctor, hated any kind of illness or being unable to do things. She'd see how she got on and if not feeling any better in a couple of weeks, then maybe she'd phone the surgery.

Holding out his hands across the table, Oliver took both Lisa's hands in his. "Look, Lisa, I understand. I know you think I don't, but I do. You've had a tricky time, and you need to recover. And I've asked you something potentially life-changing for both of us, so there really is no need to worry or stress about it. I just want you to know that."

Tears filled Lisa's eyes. What an understanding human being this man was even though he really had no idea of everything that had happened to her. "Thank you, Oliver," she whispered as she dabbed her eyes. "I'm okay now, it was just a blip."

But the mood was broken. No longer easy and relaxed, they both decided it was time for them to go home.

Lisa spent the evening watching a gardening programme and then, suddenly feeling rather exhausted, went to bed. It was another day tomorrow.

Sunday brought rain. Lisa rather expected Oliver to ring but he didn't which made her feel sad. Never mind, a new week was approaching, and she'd be very busy going back and forth between Rye and Tunbridge Wells.

After two weeks, Lisa realised her mood hadn't changed, and in fact she was beginning to feel worse with more flashbacks of Theresa with a knife, and often disturbed sleep. So, she reluctantly phoned the surgery and got an appointment with a female doctor who turned out to be very nice. The doctor listened carefully to Lisa's abridged version of the events of the last couple of years.

"Lisa, firstly, that's a lot to have gone through. Not least of which is that you had the trauma of your life being threatened. So, the fact that you said you're having upsetting flashbacks and sleep disturbance, suggests you may have a mild case of a condition we call PTSD, or post-traumatic stress disorder. As the name implies, it's a reaction to trauma; it often happens to service personnel who've experienced distressing things, and it was first discovered in 1980. It doesn't always manifest itself straight away and can begin any time after the trauma, sometimes even quite a long time after the upsetting event."

The doctor continued to explain things and offered Lisa some tablets for anxiety which she declined. She also declined the doctor's offer of joining a group or to see a counsellor to talk things through with, saying she was sure those services really helped lots of people, but they weren't for her. Then, after agreeing to join a relaxing yoga class, do breathing exercises and go for daily walks, she thanked the doctor for listening, for her time, and left the surgery telling herself she'd get through this with the agreed strategies, plus Fifi's and Oliver's support.

That evening, Lisa phoned both Oliver and Fifi-Rose to invite them round on Saturday evening for a chat and a drink. Oliver was pleased she'd contacted him because he was secretly beginning to think she'd gone off him, that he'd scared her off by suggesting they become 'solid', a couple. Fifi-Rose jumped at the opportunity, but then suddenly felt something wasn't quite right with her friend. "Can I bring anything?" She asked. "And are you ok?"

"No, just bring yourself, thank you. Oliver will also be here. I could be better Fifi, which is why I want to chat with you both."

This is not like Lisa, thought Fifi-Rose. At all. She'd never known her friend to virtually ask for help. Ever. Oliver also began to wonder what Lisa wanted to chat about and couldn't wait for the next few days to go by.

Saturday came and Oliver was the first to arrive. No sooner had he taken off his coat than Fifi-Rose arrived in a flurry of voluminous multi-coloured woollen cape which she dragged off over her pink hair, making it stand out at all angles.

As it was now October and the evenings were cooler, Lisa had lit the log fire which threw warming light and shadows round Wisteria Cottage's old, uneven walls. Then she pulled her sofa in front of the fire and angled Aunt Peg's armchair so that she was properly facing her two friends. Oliver sat on the end of the sofa nearest her.

After making sure her guests had a soft drink and could reach the nibbles which she'd put on the small tables either end of the sofa, she clasped her hands together and leant forward. "Thanks for coming you two," she began. "I know it seems a bit mysterious but it's not really. It's just that I need your support with something," she said as she looked from one to the other. "As you both know, I went through a difficult time in Kefalonia, and unfortunately it's had a bit of an effect on me."

Fifi-Rose blinked. This so wasn't like Lisa. She waited. Oliver cleared his throat before quietly managing to murmur, "Oh." They both looked at Lisa intently.

Lisa looked at her guest's expectant faces. The only thing to do was to tell them directly what the problem was and what she needed, so that's what she did, finishing with, "I hope that's okay with you both. But please don't feel pressured, I'll understand if you feel you can't help."

"Can't help? Of course, we – well I, anyway – can bloody help. That's what friends are for," cried Fifi-Rose.

"Same here, Lisa," Oliver said as he shifted slightly towards Lisa. "Like Fifi I'm here for you. Always." Then turning to Fifi-Rose he said. "We can be on tap, can't we, Fifi?" Fifi nodded. "So, Lisa, call us whenever you need to talk, or things are a bit rough, and you just need to know someone's there. But also, there's no need to talk if you don't want to." What he really wanted to do was take Lisa in his arms and cuddle her, to comfort her and make her feel better. And safe.

Lisa's throat was tight with emotion. What wonderful friends these two were; she felt very blessed. "Thank you so much both of you, you've no idea what this means, and I'm sure I'll soon feel better with your support. And with the yoga, breathing exercises and walking. I know talking and exercise can help with stress."

The three of them continued to chat until Fifi-Rose said she needed to go as she was busy with her voluntary work the next day. She worked in charity shop in a popular part of Rye which sold clothes and bits and bobs, and which, unlike many such shops, was open on a Sunday. It was a side to Fifi-Rose which many didn't know about, but she loved her voluntary work and also loved being able to spot and buy the occasional designer bargain!

Lisa joined a Thursday evening yoga class in her village hall which she found challenging at first, but she did what she could. The teacher was very understanding and sensed there was more going on for Lisa than she said – there was nothing obvious, it was just her instinct. Lisa also started walking. Initially, she just walked round her village main lanes, then after a few weeks she began to venture further until she was walking for an hour or more, but always in safe places like the local park and public green areas. Eventually, walking became necessary to Lisa, it lifted her mood and made her feel she'd achieved something.

Fifi-Rose and Oliver arranged to ring Lisa on set evenings, and both were on hand to chat, or just listen, at any time, and were with her every weekend. Oliver often took her in his car up on to the South Downs, and to many pretty Sussex villages where they walked together in the countryside, in woods and on the rolling Downs. Fifi-Rose sometimes joined them on a Saturday, but as she became aware that their friendship was developing into something more, she started to limit the times she spent with them.

Slowly, Lisa started to confide in Oliver, firstly telling him about her marriage to Mark, and what happened when he came to Skala. She also told him about how Sam had hated her, and about her relationship with Christoph, the good and the not so good, and the trauma of Theresa's attack which was the major cause of her problems now. She also shared what had happened when she'd last returned to Skala and had seen Christoph.

In turn, Oliver told Lisa about his beloved Annie and how he'd not wanted to live after she died but had found strength to carry on with the support of a male friend and his two sons.

Lisa and Oliver would sometimes cry together, or hug each other comfortingly, but more often they would laugh together, releasing any tension. It was a healing time for them both, and a strong, caring and understanding bond was gradually formed.

Fifi-Rose listened intently to everything Lisa told her, said all the right things, was quiet, when necessary, dried Lisa's tears, took her out, occasionally slept over in Lisa's spare room, hugged her and told her she loved her, and would always be there for her dear friend. She'd never felt so humble or inadequate in all her life.

Lisa's daughters were unaware of what their Mum was going through. This was because she chose not to tell them, thinking they had enough on their plates with their own lives, especially Bella with little Clemmie, who, although utterly delightful, was a very demanding child. As a mum and a nurse, Bella was conflicted about sending her beloved little girl to nursery when she returned to the paediatric nursing which she also loved.

During this time, it gradually became clear to Lisa that Scarlett was becoming close to her boss Lamont, and she wondered where that would lead. Tiffany-Mae was the ultimate career girl although she did often mention a Flyjet pilot she seemed to spend a lot of time with. All three girls were busy and so telephone conversations and meet-ups were sparse. But it would soon be Christmas, so Lisa insisted they spend at least some time together then, even if it was only for a few hours on Christmas Eve. Unusually, all three girls could agree to this because Tiffany-Mae had a week off, Scarlett had two weeks off, and Bella's husband Alan said he'd look after Clemmie.

By late November, Lisa was feeling lots better. The flashbacks had almost stopped, and she was sleeping well. She was convinced that being able to talk about things with her two dear friends, plus the yoga, breathing exercises, walking and being busy at work, had all contributed to her recovery. She was beginning to feel more like her old self every day.

The one thing Lisa didn't do during this time was write. She was afraid that writing about life in Kefalonia would bring the trauma back and she didn't want that to happen, so she put her story to one side, maybe to finish sometime later, she'd see.

For Lisa's fifty-sixth birthday on twelfth of December, Fifi-Rose bought her a spa day at a local hotel, which they both enjoyed. During the day, they enjoyed the pool, sauna, steam and jacuzzi as well as a long, leisurely lunch. It was just what both women needed, and they vowed to do it again as soon as possible!

Wisteria Cottage came into its own at Christmas – the log fire, and a tall fir tree decorated with lights and baubles, with prettily-wrapped presents underneath it, always made it quite magical. Lisa looked forward to Christmas Eve when her girls would be with her, and then spending Christmas Day with Oliver and Fifi-Rose – she felt she owed her two best friends a lot, and a Christmas dinner was one small way of thanking them. Both days were memorably filled with lots of fun and laughter.

On Boxing Day, Lisa drove to Bella and Alan's beautiful, old house in Firle on the South Downs. Alan was a successful City trader, and it showed in everything in the house. The large, tiled hall with its impressive staircase leading up to five ensuite bedrooms had a ceiling-height Christmas tree which shone and sparkled with hundreds of fairy lights, and pretty Christmas garlands were wound round the oak banisters.

The kitchen was huge with a range and a scrubbed table with six chairs round it. Bi-fold doors along one wall looked out onto a large, landscaped garden. The kitchen flowed into an impressive dining/sitting room with a beautiful old table seating twelve, and the room was complemented by a massive inglenook fireplace with a roaring log fire beside which stood another sparkling Christmas tree. Comfortable chintz sofas and armchairs completed the feeling of comfort and relaxation.

What visitors didn't see at first was the full-size swimming pool and tennis court in the garden, but Lisa knew about them and had spent many happy days in both. Alan might be successful, but he never made it obvious; he was the most affable, down-to-earth man who clearly adored Bella and Clemmie, and he always made Lisa feel very welcome. He also fully supported Bella's career as a paediatric nurse, even though they were very comfortably off and didn't need the money.

Clemmie was now four months old and sitting independently with a little support. She was very pretty like her mummy, with a cloud of blonde curls and blue eyes like her daddy. However, unlike either of her parents, she was a feisty little girl, and although she couldn't yet talk, she could make a lot of noise when she wanted something, and Bella often secretly thought her daughter was more like her sister Tiffany-Mae than her!

Lisa thought Christmas would be extra special with Clemmie in the family even though she wouldn't understand what was going on and would probably be more interested in the wrapping paper than anything else. But that didn't matter, Christmas was all about children and being with the family.

The day was full of joy, laughter and surprises. Bella and Alan bought Lisa a beautiful, long silver necklace, and she gave them a tall, cream ceramic vase decorated with an exquisite, raised floral design which complemented their décor; it was one of *Thingamabob's* best-selling non-jewellery items.

During the week after Christmas and before New Year, Lisa saw Fifi-Rose, James and all the *Thingamabob* staff in both shops, a long-standing friend, Carole, who was up from Devon seeing her family, and her writing friends including Oliver. The day before New Year's Eve, all the writing group friends had a very jolly time at a local pub celebrating the coming new year, and Fifi-Rose took the new Eurostar to visit her mother in Paris.

Lisa and Oliver spent New Year's Eve together, clinking glasses and giving each other a peck on the cheek as the clock struck twelve and fireworks went off in London to herald in the new year. They'd had quite a few glasses of wine, so at Lisa's invitation Oliver stayed in her spare bedroom. They both found it a bit unusual waking up the next morning to find someone else around - but not uncomfortable, in fact it felt quite natural when Oliver kissed Lisa 'good morning' on the cheek when they met for a cup of tea and breakfast in her small kitchen.

Life took on a familiar pattern: Lisa continued to work hard and became chief buyer for *Thingamabob,* and Oliver became a regular companion. Then, when they were out walking in nearby woods one Sunday morning, Oliver turned to Lisa and asked her if she'd like to become a proper couple now.

Without hesitating, Lisa said, "Yes, I'd like that very much, Oliver. So, what shall do? Would you like to move into my cottage? I know you've got a nice flat in Brighton but to be honest I don't think it's big enough for the two of us!" She laughed. "And you could bring your work stuff with you and anything else which is important to you."

"Well, yes, if that's okay, I'd love to, thank you," Oliver replied. He paused before continuing. "Er, will we share a double bed, you know, like a 'proper' couple?" He didn't need to say what that might imply.

"Of course, we will," Lisa smiled. "But let's just see how things go, there's no pressure to be any way other than how we are now," she added, keen to put him at ease because the poor chap was clearly a bit embarrassed. It was all very well being very good chums but living together was a huge step-change for them both.

As it turned out, their relationship was perfectly natural and normal and drew them even closer. Lisa's daughters were delighted to know their Mum was at last settled, and no longer on her own. Fifi-Rose was also pleased, especially as she'd decided to move to Paris to be near her mum who wasn't very well. She'd also met an artist, Antoine, when she was last there, and had discovered a whole new way of life which perfectly suited her flamboyant character. Lisa was very sad to hear about the move, but also happy for her friend who'd been on her own longer than she had. And she could always visit Fifi-Rose in Paris, so what was there not to like?!

Nonetheless, the tears flowed for both women when the time came for Fifi-Rose to board Eurostar. They'd shared so much over the years - school and all the trials and tribulations of growing up, the good and the not so good times as adults, laughter, tears, secrets, drunken hugs, everything. The two women clung together until the train was about to pull away, both feeling the almost unbearable pain of the coming separation.

"Thank you, my darling friend, I don't know what I'd have done without you all these years," sobbed Lisa into Fifi-Rose's now-auburn, and long, hair. "I'd never have survived without you. God bless you always. And be happy. Please be happy because you so deserve it."

"Oh, Lisa," cried Fifi-Rose. "You are the strongest, bravest woman I've ever known, and I want to thank you for being my friend and inspiration all these years. I can't say anymore but I think we both know what we mean to each other. We'll keep in touch, and you'll soon come to Paris so that'll be fun," she sniffed. "I've got to go now my darling. Take good care of yourself. And you be happy, too. If anyone deserves to be happy it's you. Bye for now." She said as, stepping into the train, she wiped her nose with the back of one hand and waved goodbye to Lisa with the other. Would they ever see each other again?

In nineteen ninety-eight, aged fifty-five, Lisa obtained an uncontested divorce from Mark, and she also decided it was time to cut down her working hours, so she negotiated with James and Simon to work three days a week to enable her and Oliver to enjoy more time together. Oliver earned very good money as a private consultant to a paint manufacturer so they wouldn't struggle financially, and Lisa still had her aunt Peg's inheritance, which had surprisingly arrived as a cheque in the post from her aunt's solicitor a long time after her aunt's passing. Following Fifi-Rose's advice, she'd put the money in a high interest savings account only to be accessed in an emergency; although not a huge amount, it was enough to reassure her.

Lisa delegated a lot of her work to a new young member of staff, Freddie, who was showing great promise even though it was only his first job after college. Tall and slimly built with grey eyes fringed by the longest dark lashes Lisa had ever seen on a man, and a short, dark blonde haircut, he had innovative ideas and seemed a lot older than his years. He was always friendly, smiley and respectful, smart in intellect and dress, always wore an immaculate dark grey or navy-blue three-piece suit, a pristine shirt, a tie with matching breast pocket handkerchief, and the shiniest of lace-up shoes. He was also fun and a joy to work with, as well as an absolute hit with all the customers!

Lisa and Oliver decided to pay Fifi-Rose a Springtime visit in Paris. It was very romantic, very bohemian and an absolute joy for the two women who, when they first saw each other, hugged so tightly that neither of them could breathe! Unfortunately, Fifi-Rose's mother,

Francine, was no better, and it became clear that she wouldn't make very old bones. Fifi-Rose's partner, Antoine, was a quiet, rotund, dark-haired artist who was friendly, welcoming, and a brilliant cook. Although younger than Fifi-Rose, that didn't bother him nor did the fact that she had three adult children somewhere. Lisa thought he was charming, very good-looking and had the most delicious accent when he spoke English!

Life for Lisa and Oliver was easy and relaxed. They saw Lisa's daughters whenever they were free, and adored Clemmie who was growing into a lovely little girl, full of life, energy and giggles. Oliver occasionally saw his two adult doctor sons who were now both married – the eldest, Ian, was married to a nurse, the younger, Howard, to a physiotherapist. However, much to Oliver's dismay, they all decided to move to Australia where they could earn much more in their respective professions. Oliver was deeply upset but knew his boys needed to live their own lives, and so, even though his heart was breaking, he wished them well.

Nineteen ninety-nine brought a huge change for Lisa. Now fifty-six, she was beginning to feel tired. Oliver was getting on for sixty and although still working and active, he also had less energy. But a long holiday with a couple Oliver knew who lived in the Spanish mountains near Almeria did them both the world of good, and they returned feeling stronger and fitter than they had for a long time.

Nonetheless, Lisa felt it was time for her to retire, so she reluctantly gave in her notice to James who was deeply upset to learn she was leaving. "But you're the very bedrock of *Thingamabob*, Lisa," he exclaimed. "What will we do without you?"

"Oh, bless you James," replied a misty-eyed Lisa. "Thank you, but you'll cope, and you've got the excellent Freddie at the helm now. You and I both know he'll go far."

James, Simon and all the staff at both shops gave Lisa a terrific send-off with party balloons, banners, cards and presents, a band, and lots of drinking, laughing and dancing. At one point Lisa took herself off to the Ladies room and cried because these lovely people, especially James, had literally been her salvation, her surrogate family, and yes, she'd miss them big-time. Saying goodbye was painful, but it was now time to do other things. She didn't know what, but she did know there'd be something.

Unfortunately, on top of her divorce from Mark, Fifi-Rose going to France and her daughters moving on, leaving work made Lisa feel bereft. She hadn't realised just how much her life had revolved around her job, and how important it had been to her. Oliver did his best to cheer her up, but there were some dark days which she struggled with.

The solution came in a Golden Retriever female puppy. Oliver brought the little ball of cream fur home on a cushion, and Lisa immediately fell in love with her and named her Emma. Gorgeous Emma was to prove to be an absolute godsend for both Lisa and Oliver in the next few years

Chapter Thirty-One

In Spring two thousand, and leaving Emma with a dog-loving neighbour, Lisa and Oliver went to Paris again. However, instead of staying in a boutique hotel in a quaint Paris side street, this time they were in the luxury hotel La Reserve Paris close to the Champs-Elysées, the Elysées Gardens and overlooking the Eiffel Tower, the Grand Palais and the Concorde obelisk. It was beyond anything Lisa had ever experienced before, and she was bowled over by its opulence. "Can we afford this, Oliver?" She asked worriedly. "I mean, it's so…so… *posh*"

"Yes, we can," Oliver replied as he put his arms round her. "Thanks to the good rent I get for my flat, I've got a bit of money put by and wanted to treat you. You deserve to be pampered, so here we are."

"Oh, bless you, you're such a kind man, Oliver," she sighed as she looked up into his twinkly brown eyes. "Thank you."

Fifi-Rose was delighted to see Lisa again and very happy that Oliver was so wonderful to her dearest friend. Fifi-Rose's mum, Francine, had gone downhill and it was a relief for Fifi-Rose to be able to go out and have some girlie fun with Lisa whilst Oliver and Antoine kept an eye on her mum.

Lisa and Oliver were booked to stay for ten days. The weather was glorious, the Eiffel Tower amazing and the Tuileries Gardens spectacular. Walking hand in hand along one of the main paths bordered by beautiful Spring flowers, Oliver stopped and drew Lisa close to his side. Lisa was surprised. "Is something wrong Oliver?" She asked with raised eyebrows. Oliver didn't reply, instead, he got down onto his right knee, drew a little dark blue box from his pocket and said, "I love you, Lisa. Will you do me the honour of marrying me so I can look after you for the rest of our lives? Please?"

Lisa was dumbfounded. Married? *Married?!*She stared at Oliver looking up at her pleadingly, unaware that a small crowd had gathered to watch. All she knew was that she loved this man, and that, as a now free woman, she could indeed marry him.

"Yes. I will," she beamed. "Yes, of course I will!"

The crowd cheered and clapped, making Lisa look round and laugh. "Oh, gosh, I didn't know you were all there!" She exclaimed. "Thank you!"

Laughing, Oliver got up and swept Lisa up in his arms before kissing her soundly on the lips and placing the solitaire diamond gold ring on the third finger of her left hand. Lisa immediately recognised the ring as being from one of *Thingamabob's* top ranges.

"Oh, Oliver, the ring is gorgeous, and I know where you bought it, bless you. What a lovely thing to do," she said tearily.

"Well, I thought it would be a nice reminder of your fabulous time there. It's also very beautiful, just like you!"

Fifi-Rose was over the moon to learn of Lisa and Oliver's engagement. "I am sooo happy for you both!" She cried. "This is the best thing *ever*! Let's celebrate!" She said as she opened a cupboard to find a bottle. In front of her was the bottle of Bolinger that she'd been keeping for a special occasion – and this was a very special occasion. Antoine opened the bottle with a flourish before filling everyone's champagne flute, and Fifi-Rose brought Francine from her bedroom into the sitting room to join in the celebrations so that she wouldn't feel left out. "Congratulations to Lisa and Oliver!" Francine beamed as she raised her glass. "And here's to a lifetime of happiness!"

The celebrations went on for the rest of the day, with Antoine cooking a lovely, surprise meal for them all. Eventually, Lisa and Oliver decided it was time for them to go, and after saying an emotional goodbye to Fifi-Rose, Lisa declared they'd be back to see her and Antoine before they left Paris in two days' time.

Lisa's daughters were overjoyed to hear of her engagement to Oliver, and they were all keen to know when their wedding would be.

"Not yet," Lisa told Scarlett who was the last one to ask. "We've got things to organise. But it's likely to be next Spring when Oliver's sixty. We thought it would be nice to have our wedding and to celebrate his birthday at the same time. But it won't be a big do, just close family and friends including my *Thingamabob* ones, and their families. I'll also invite Fifi-Rose and Antoine, as well as my writing friends, and Oliver wants to invite some of his work colleagues, plus of course, his two married sons who live in Australia. I know one of them also now has a child. And Bella and Alan will have their second child by then so there'll be quite a few of us. And that's without a couple of Oliver's cousins and their partners!"

Another chapter was about to begin.

The year was full of change. Scarlett surprised everyone by going to live with Lamont in a converted Oast house in Kent, and giving up her job as his PA. They agreed it might be a bit much to live and work together, so Scarlett happily became PA to an Ashford solicitor.

Tiffany-Mae also surprised everyone. When having coffee with Lisa and Oliver one Sunday morning, she suddenly announced that

Lawrence, the Flyjet pilot she'd been seeing for ages, and her were moving to France!

"France?" Squeaked Lisa, hardly able to believe her ears. "You mean, actual *France?!"*

"Yes, Mum," laughed Tiffany-Mae. "Actual France. Lawrence's family lives out there and they've got a house they let out which has become vacant, so we decided we'd have it."

Lisa stared at her daughter. Tiffany-Mae was often surprising, but this was something else.

"Oh, I see," she said even though she didn't. "But you've hardly ever been to France. And what about your jobs?"

"Well, as I said, Lawrence's family lives there so he knows it well. And we can get jobs working out of Avignon airport. Flyjet has a branch near the airport so it would just be a matter of transference for both of us."

Okay, thought Lisa, they've certainly got it all worked out. She suddenly felt bereft; all three of her children were moving on, leaving her behind. Tears threatened but she was determined not to cry. After all, her children had their own lives to live. And she was living hers, so it was no different.

Straightening her shoulders, she smiled and said, "That's brilliant news, and good luck to you both! You must tell us all about Lawrence's family, where they live and where you'll live," then after a pausing, added. "How exciting! It'll be a real adventure!"

It would indeed be an adventure because what Tiffany-Mae hadn't told Lisa was that Lawrence's parents, Marly and Ben, lived in, and managed, a Chateau hotel near the Cote d'Azur. Chateau d'Etoile was a ten bedroomed, turreted architectural masterpiece which could have come straight out of a fairy tale. They'd bought it ten years before when it was just a wreck and spent the next few years renovating it before finally opening it as a hotel.

It was agreed that Tiffany-Mae and Lawrence would rent the large, blue shuttered stone house in the vast grounds of the Chateau which was once used by the original rich eighteenth-century owner to accommodate his highly intelligent courtesans. However, all that disappeared in the Revolution, and before Marly and Ben turned it into a gite, it was a derelict shell used to house chickens and pigs! The chateau also had its own vineyard managed by the able and handsome Pierre. But Tiffany-Mae was reluctant to tell Lisa all this just yet, she felt her Mum had enough to take on board for now.

To cope with all the changes, Lisa often took Emma for long country walks, taking in the calmness of woodland, open fields and fresh air as she strode, green wellington-booted and Barbour-coated in wet weather, through grass and mud whilst allowing the sound of birds to fill her brain. Sometimes she'd hug a tree, firstly looking round to make sure no-one was around who might think she was slightly bonkers, because she knew that trees had a reputation for healing. Nothing fazed her, and as her shoulders relaxed, she smiled and slowly began to feel life was good again.

Emma loved their walks, happily sniffing and bounding around with her ears flapping and tongue lolling when she was safely off the lead. But she never took her eyes off Lisa for long and constantly checked she was okay because she could sense her sadness. Emma's rewards for being such a good companion were lots of strokes and some lovely treats! Emma went everywhere with Lisa, and they became inseparable companions.

Oliver made sure he was extra loving towards Lisa because having two sons living the other side of the world, he knew how hard it was when adult children moved on. Like Emma, he was a constant comfort to Lisa, and the three of them would often curl up on the sofa together. And Lisa and Oliver talked. And talked. About everything and anything. It was very healing for them both and drew them closer than ever.

The Thursday evening yoga classes also helped Lisa to relax and think more positively, and one Saturday morning she decided it was time to have a sort out. She'd kept so much from past years but now she was beginning a new chapter in her life, she felt a lot of it could go.

She spent ages standing at the dining room table delving into the three boxes which Oliver had heaved down from the loft. Inside the boxes were lots of mementos and some old clothes. There were also birthday and every-occasion cards which she spread out across the table to help her decide what to keep and what to throw away. In addition to all those, there were lots of photographs, some in albums, but many still in packets.

As she picked up a couple of the packets, one split open and two photos fell out. One was of the crystal clear Skala sea and little silver fishes, the other a rare one of a smiling Christoph standing beside the stone bench overlooking the beach.

Lisa's heart jumped. She so didn't need to see these, and as long-buried memories came flooding back, she silently screamed 'Noooo!' as she sat down hard on to a nearby dining room chair. Lying at her feet, Emma looked up and thumped her tail on the floor as if to ask what was wrong, then, sensing Lisa's distress, barked twice.

"It's okay, Emma, I'm alright," Lisa whispered as she leant down to stroke her faithful dog's head. "Don't worry." Emma thumped her tail again before laying her head down on to her front paws and watching Lisa with her big brown eyes.

Lisa stuffed the photos back into the packet, but it was too late to stop the memories, and the old longing to be in Kefalonia, for her spirit to be 'joined' once again, for her to be her true self.

"Lisa?" shouted Oliver from the kitchen. "Are you okay? Have you found anything interesting?"

"I'm okay, thanks," replied Lisa hurriedly. "I'm just sorting a few old photos and bits and pieces. But I'm stopping now, there's so much to look through and I don't really feel up to it today anyway."

Going into the kitchen, she smiled broadly as if she didn't have a care in the world, even though, in truth, she now had plenty.

Pushing the memories away, Lisa settled down to plan her wedding for the following Summer. Oliver would be sixty on July twenty-first two thousand and one, so they agreed it would be then. Although the wedding would be a small affair, it still took a lot of planning, contacting various wedding venues and companies, making lists and generally being busy. Like any bride, Lisa's biggest purchase would be her wedding dress. Never one to overdo clothes, she wanted something modest, perhaps a dress with a matching jacket.

"No, absolutely not," Bella said firmly as they discussed who'd wear what. She'd left Clemmie with Alan while she helped her Mum sort some things. "You're going full-on bridal, Mum!"

"Am I?" asked a startled Lisa. She had no idea about the latest bride and wedding trends, although she had looked at a couple of wedding magazines which had secretly terrified her – after all, it was a small wedding, not a state occasion like some people seemed to arrange!

"Yes, you are. You'll be a beautiful bride, Mum. You can't wear a dress with a jacket; they'll make you look like the bride's mother not the bride!" laughed Bella. "Obviously, you're a bit too ol...er...ol..," she stumbled uncertainly.

"Old?" supplied Lisa with a grin.

"No, not old, Mum. Mature," smiled Bella. "Clearly, you won't be wearing the traditional big white dress, but you can still wear something ivory, maybe a mid-length dress. What d'you think?"

"Mmmm, sounds okay, but I'll need to see and try on some dresses then I'll know what suits me."

In the end, Lisa chose an ivory silk, mid-length, cap-sleeved fitted dress with a slight 'train-dip' to the back hem. She chose a small modern, hand tied bouquet of cream and pink roses, and decided she'd wear pale pink and cream rosebuds pinned to one side of her hair. Guests would have corsages of the same colour roses. Lisa wanted her three daughters to be her maids of honour, also dressed in ivory silk dresses but in styles of their own choice. They'd each wear a cream and pink rose wrist corsage rather than carry a posy.

Oliver plumped for a grey tail suit and top hat, and asked his eldest son, Ian, to be his best man. His other son, Howard, agreed to be an usher, and both would also wear grey tail suits and top hats. Because her parents were now very elderly and in care, Lisa asked Bella's husband, Alan, if he'd give her away, a role he was delighted to accept; he'd also be wearing a grey tail suit and top hat.

The wedding guest list was modest by some standards. Oliver's parents had both passed some years before, and he didn't have any siblings, so there were very few guests to invite on his side. But he had his sons and their families, as well as his work colleagues and a couple of friends and their families. In the end, Lisa and Oliver invited sixty guests, which was an appropriate number seeing as it was Oliver's sixtieth birthday!

The wedding would take place in the beautiful garden of a posh hotel in the Sussex countryside so guests could stay over before and after the wedding. The wedding reception would also be a party to celebrate Oliver's 'big' birthday.

Lisa and Oliver went to *Thingamabob* for their wedding rings. They each chose a plain, twenty-two carat gold band which James said was their wedding present from him. He also invited them to choose an inscription to go inside each ring. Lisa and Oliver were overcome at such wonderful generosity and decided on, 'Eternal love from...' with whichever name was appropriate, plus the date of their wedding.

Lisa and Oliver's wedding day was full of sunshine, love and laughter. Lisa looked stunning and she took Oliver's breath away when he saw her. He couldn't believe how lucky he was that this beautiful woman had agreed to become his wife.

Oliver looked very dashing in his wedding suit, and Lisa's heart jumped when she saw him looking so handsome: how she loved this kind and gentle man who'd taken her to his heart without judgement or question. She felt very blessed, and suddenly also very nervous.

The sun shone, and the hotel's stunning wedding reception room was filled with beautiful cream and pink flowers. The ceremony in the hotel's garden was very moving, and as Lisa and Oliver stood under an arch of white flowers promising to always love and care for each other, there wasn't a dry eye anywhere.

Combined with the wedding reception, Oliver's 'big' birthday celebration was fun with a band playing many of his favourite songs, and to much cheering and clapping, he even very happily danced with his new wife!

After breakfast and waving goodbye to the last of their guests, Lisa and Oliver left for their honeymoon in southern France, returning a week later feeling relaxed and happy.

During one of their many long conversations, Lisa and Oliver had talked about how Lisa felt about Kefalonia, and her ongoing longing to return to the island. They eventually agreed to return together to the island for one last time so that Lisa could finally put it behind her and move on. So, in September two thousand and one, they set off for a week's holiday at the Hotel Paradiso overlooking Skala beach. Oliver had no concerns about returning to the place where his wife had once had a Greek lover because he was secure in the knowledge that she loved him and only him.

The flight was easy, and yet again, Lisa held her breath as the plane's wing tip seemed to almost dip into the beautiful Ionian Sea as it came into land. Their luggage was retrieved without any delay, and a taxi was waiting for them outside the airport to take them to their hotel.

On arriving at Hotel Paradiso, they were taken by a bellboy to their luxurious penthouse suite with its large balcony overlooking the sparkling swimming pool and Skala beach.

"Happy?" Asked Oliver as he took Lisa in his arms. "Just say if you're not my darling."

"Oh, Oliver, I'm very happy, thank you. How about you? Are you okay being here?" Lisa asked slightly worriedly. She didn't want her husband feeling uncomfortable in any way. But what she didn't tell him was that she'd not yet had that 'joined' feeling, and that she was wondering if she ever would again. Memories were beginning to flood her brain but not in the same way as they used to: now, the happy times came to the fore front rather than the sad and traumatic ones.

Lisa showed Oliver all her favourite places in Skala and Argostoli town, and they took a private taxi trip around the island. Oliver thought it was one of the most beautiful places he'd ever seen and told Lisa he could understand how she'd come to fall under its spell.

But when they drove their hire car up into Old Skala village, Oliver wasn't as impressed. "Lisa, this place feels like a graveyard, it's so sad," he shuddered. "I feel like an intruder."

"Yes, I know what you mean," agreed Lisa. "You may remember what I told you about the girl I thought I heard and saw here?" Oliver nodded. "Well, I often heard the locals say she's still here, and that sounds of someone crying can sometimes be heard." She shivered at the thought. "Bless all those who met their end in that earthquake. Anyway, enough of here, let's go and have a drink."

They drove back down to a new taverna located almost on the beach but slightly away from the centre of Skala. Soft Greek music played in the background and there were only a couple of people sitting looking out to the beach and sea, which suited them both perfectly; they didn't want loud music and loads of tourists around them.

After a long lunch of Greek salad, stuffed tomatoes, wine and delicious kataifi, the sweet cake with nuts and syrup, they walked hand in hand along the main street to look at the shops, some of them new since Lisa was last there.

Just as they were about to go into a dress shop, a voice called out, "Lisa? Lisa, is that really you?" Lisa turned round to see Rebecca with a chubby baby boy walking beside her.

The two women hugged each other, and Lisa introduced Oliver. "Rebecca, this is my husband, Oliver."

"Wow, a husband! Congratulations to you both! Pleased to meet you, Oliver."

"Likewise," said Oliver as he held out his hand in greeting. "I've heard a lot about you from Lisa," he laughed.

"I hope it was good," smiled Rebecca. "By the way, this is little Yannis. Named for his daddy of course!"

"Oh, hello, Yannis!" Lisa said as she bent down to greet the child. "Yes, I can see Yannis in him."

"He's like his daddy in lots of other ways, too," laughed Rebecca as she tried to pull the child from behind her legs where he was hiding.

The two women chatted for a while until Rebecca explained that she couldn't stay any longer because she had to open the bar.

"Oh, before you go, Rebecca, how's Daphne? And the others?"

Rebecca paused. "Oh, I'm so sorry, Lisa, but Daphne passed away earlier this year. Georgios lives a quiet life away from the village, and remember I told you that Michaelis moved away? Sue and Trevor still live in Argostoli and they rarely come to Skala now." Neither woman spoke of the one person who they both knew was on their minds: Christoph.

"Oh, that's so sad about Daphne," Lisa said softly. "I wish I'd known. But then I have been busy getting married." She paused before adding, "Er, how is…?"

"Christoph?" Asked Rebecca quietly as she looked sideways at Oliver.

Lisa took Oliver's hands in hers. "Don't worry, Rebecca, Oliver knows everything. So, how is Christoph and his family?"

Just at that moment, as if by magic, Christoph walked towards them, as upright as ever but looking much more mature with almost-white hair. He stopped, looked at Lisa, then at Oliver, and nodded politely. Then he slowly walked towards them. "Hello Lisa, how lovely to see you," he said as he turned to look at Oliver.

Feeling slightly stunned, Lisa swallowed and said, "Hello Christoph. This is my husband, Oliver. Oliver, this is Christoph."

The two men carefully surveyed each other for a moment before Oliver bent his head slightly to acknowledge the man who'd played such an important part in his wife's life. So, this was him. Not much to write home about, he thought.

Christoph also nodded hello. "Well, I'm afraid I can't stay," he said softly. "I have to collect my two boys from playgroup and then take Ariadne-Rose to town." After a slight pause, he continued, "Have a nice holiday, Lisa, Oliver. Goodbye," he said politely before walking briskly away.

Short. But not so sweet, thought Lisa. Then she realised that, apart from surprise, she'd felt nothing when she'd seen Christoph: no butterflies, no rapidly beating heart, no sadness. Absolutely nothing. It was over. Her story had its ending.

"I've got to dash, too," Rebecca said hurriedly. "Anyway, nice to see you. Bye for now and have a nice holiday. I probably won't see you again as we're going to Athens tomorrow." Turning to Oliver she added. "Nice to see meet you, Oliver." Then, after hugging Lisa tightly, she smiled broadly as she held her friend at arm's length. "Lovely to see you so happy, Lisa." Then, looking at Oliver, said. "Take good care of her Oliver! Bye both!"

"I will," promised Oliver. "Nice to meet you, too, Rebecca. Goodbye."

Lisa felt sad at having to say such a swift goodbye to Rebecca, and that Daphne had passed away, but she'd not been there for her at that time. She knew she'd always think of, and miss, her very kind, dear friend who'd cared for, and looked after, her so well. And who'd made the most wonderful cheese pies! Maybe she'd make her cheese pies in heaven, she thought with a smile.

Lisa and Oliver spent the last couple of days of their holiday swimming, eating, drinking, sleeping, and generally relaxing. They chose to eat their final dinner in the hotel's lavish restaurant overlooking Skala beach, and after enjoying a lovely meal, decided to take a leisurely stroll along the promenade for one last time. On reaching a deserted part of the beach, Lisa looked at Oliver, smiled and said, "Shall we?"

"Why not?" Laughed Oliver.

Loosely holding hands, they stepped together onto Skala's beautiful sand and shingle beach which Lisa had enjoyed so many times, just as the huge, dark orange harvest moon was beginning to slip down over the horizon, turning the sky a vibrant orange, red, yellow, pink and blue, and scattering sparkling orange and red diamonds across the dark Ionian Sea. Oliver gently let go of Lisa's hand and stepped back. Both knew what a truly memorable moment this was for her.

"Goodbye Skala," Lisa whispered as she gazed at the glowing sea and horizon; it felt like the setting sun was putting on a last stunning show just for her. "Goodbye, magical Kefalonia, my beloved Greek island with all your sadness and secrets, where fairy tales are told, love blossoms, and dreams can come true. Thank you for keeping me safe when I was in danger, and for looking after me when I was broken. But I'm whole now, my spirit's come home to me at last, so I don't need you anymore. I'll always miss you and keep you in my heart, but I won't be back so please look after all those I've loved and cared about, especially Christoph."

Finally feeling a sense of freedom and peace, she murmured her very last goodbye, and as the huge sun slowly disappeared in deep orange and red majesty below the horizon, she turned to Oliver and smiled, "Ready, darling?"

"Yes," laughed Oliver as he took both her hands in his.

"Okay, let's go, we've got a whole new life to live!"

Then, as they happily walked hand in hand back to their hotel, out of the corner of her eye Lisa glimpsed the small, dark figure of a young girl waving one hand as she silently mouthed, "goodbye."

But when she turned round to look properly, the girl had gone…

ACKNOWLEDGEMENTS

Firstly, huge thanks to everyone at Between the Lines Publishing for accepting and publishing my book, it means the absolute world to me.

Thanks also to my family who've always supported my literary efforts and have also put up with me popping off to Greece every now and then! I hope I've passed on to some of them the desire to travel and explore some of the world. They all know that Kefallonia is my spiritual home. If Google were a person, I'd also thank them for the research I've been able to undertake to enhance my understanding regarding the often-tragic history of Skala and the whole island of Kefallonia - most especially the atrocities during World War Two, and the devastating 1953 earthquake which destroyed so much and traumatised so many.

Thanks also to everyone I've known in Skala during my many visits, both as a tourist and as a traveller, without them I wouldn't have been able to write in such knowledgeable depth about those aspects of a Greek island resort which tourists never see, or may not even be aware of; I've been privileged to have seen the 'real' Skala. And to observe how it's changed over the years.

I have so many wonderful memories of this island - the majestic and enigmatic Mount Aenos, the people's warm and welcoming hospitality, the humour, the music and dancing, the deep blue, sparkling Ionian sea, the gorgeous turtles and silver fishes, the food and drink, the evocative scenery and beautiful flowers and olive groves - and of course the spectacular beaches! So much to love.

Finally, Greece still practices 'philoxenia' - the practice of welcoming strangers - and does so with kindness, generosity, humour, grace and respect, and long may it continue. So, Efharisto and Yamas Kefallonia!

Gillian lives in a pretty village close to where she was born in the heart of Kent. As well as being a family person she's very much a 'people-person' and enjoys observing human behaviour in all its fascinating diversity, especially at airports!

Gillian has travelled extensively, particularly to Greece which has a very special place in her heart. She also loves France where she once owned a remote, falling-down house, and conversation with her grumpy, apple cider-loving non-English speaking farmer neighbour, often proved a tad challenging!

Having started writing many years ago bits and pieces of poetry and prose ncluding paragraphs for Paragraph Planet, in 2022 Gillian wrote and illustrated a small booklet enititled 'Doris'. This was followed in 2023 by her first full length novel 'Secrets And Lies'.

With a glamorous career in social services and the like behind her, Gillian now enjoys spending her time writing and on her hobbies art and local history, as well as with her ever-expanding, large family and their various much-loved dogs.

www.ingramcontent.com/pod-product-compliance
Lightning Source LLC
Chambersburg PA
CBHW010740310726
48971CB00010B/2889